I0588584

# A SINGLE THREAD OF HOPE

## HANGING BY A THREAD DUET
### BOOK TWO

## GRACE MCGINTY

Copyright © 2024 by Madeline Young writing as Grace McGinty

All rights reserved.

No part of this book may be reproduced in any form or by any electronic or mechanical means, including information storage and retrieval systems, without written permission from the author, except for the use of brief quotations in a book review.

This is a work of fiction. Unless otherwise indicated, all the names, characters, businesses, events, locations and incidents in this book are either the product of the author's imagination or used in a fictitious manner. Any resemblance to actual persons, living or dead, or actual events is purely coincidental.

Cover Art by DAZED Designs.

Editing by Aubergine Editing.

# ALSO BY GRACE MCGINTY

**Hell's Redemption Series**: The Redeemable / The Unrepentant / The Fallen

**Damnation MC Duet**: Serendipity / Providence

**The Azar Nazemi Trilogy**: Smoke and Smolder / Burn and Blaze / Rage and Ruin

**Dark River Days Series**: Newly Undead In Dark River / Happily Undead In Dark River / Pleasantly Undead in Dark River

**Eden Academy Series**: The Lost and the Hunted (Prequel) / Heart of the Hounded (Prequel) / Rebels and Runaways (Book 1) / Sweethearts and Savages (Book 2)

**Shadow Bred Series**: Manix / Frenzy / Feral / Crave

**Black Mountain Mates:** Hunting Isla

**Stand Alone Novels and Novellas**: Bright Lights From A Hurricane / The Last Note / Inside The Maelstrom / Pay-Per-Heart / 8 Seconds to Fly / Make My Heart Race / The Daymakers

**Penalty Box Players:** Sticks and Stone / Break My Bones

**Omega Lottery:** Tryst In The Dark

**Hanging By A Thread Duet:** Tangled Threads Of Fate / A Single Thread of Hope

# A SINGLE THREAD OF HOPE

# CHAPTER I
## WREN

O

The man in front of me was naked. A moment ago, he'd been a dog.

If that didn't just sum up my life, nothing would.

"Wren? Are you okay?" Cy, the not-dog man asked, and I laughed. A man I'd tied to my very soul was dead at my feet. A monster who'd wanted to kill me and my babies had just fallen into the pits of Hell.

I think it was safe to say I wasn't okay.

"Of course she isn't, you simpleton," a woman's voice snapped. Her voice sounded… off. Like the tinkling of bells and the booming of a gong simultaneously. "She just got attacked by Ekhidna. Her blood pressure is probably through the roof, and you're standing there naked as the day you were created, freaking her out." A beautiful woman in a long black gown made of dead things appeared before me. Her hair was flame red, threaded with leaves, twigs, and spiderwebs, and as she moved, things bloomed beneath her feet.

A dark chuckle echoed from somewhere in the darkness, and the sound had the opposite effect to the woman's. It sounded like the crunch of bones beneath a boot, the howl of wolves on the wind. "She has you there, Cydon."

Cy gathered me up into his arms. His still-naked arms. *Fuck.* Pushing against his bare torso, I stumbled away from the group of people that had assembled in the courtyard. I would have tripped over the body of Demke if Cy didn't have a hand around my arm.

Demke.

I froze as I stared at him. His chest was still, his eyes closed and lips slack. A perfect corpse.

"Demke," I breathed, leaning down. His skin was cold, but I should do CPR. That's what you were supposed to do. Even if it was hopeless. My lessons at the Y had taught me that I was supposed to do it to the beat of "Stayin' Alive" by the BeeGees—I'd liked the irony of that at the time, but now I stumbled over the beat, panic making my chest constrict.

I didn't realize I was mumbling the lyrics out loud until the woman knelt opposite me, covering my hands with her own. The compassionate look on her face was at odds with the mouse-skull crown. At least, I hoped they were only mice skulls. "There is no need for that, sweet Vessel."

Ice spilled through my veins at her words. Cy didn't

seem worried, but the only people who'd called me Vessel so far had been creatures trying to kill me.

Like she could see my fear, she shifted away slightly. "You're safe with us, Wren." Her voice was soft and sweet, and I believed her. "You don't have to give him a heart massage, because he isn't really dead."

It was obvious that the pretty, scary lady was insane. My Demke was definitely dead.

The guy with the horror voice appeared behind her. He looked like a hard, slightly-evil Henry Cavill, with skin the color of death. Like someone who'd just been fished out of the Boston Harbor, all the color leached from his skin. "I know dead people, Vessel. In fact, some would say it's a hazard of my profession. And I'm very sure your God isn't dead." His voice made goosebumps instantly rise on my skin and panic skitter down my spine. Danger and death, that's what he sounded like. Like the embodiment of primordial fear come to life.

Almost subconsciously, I scrambled back on my hands and feet like a crab, which must have looked ridiculous. The pretty redhead with eyes that saw into my soul glared at the man disapprovingly. "Hades, you scared her more."

"Sorry, Sephy. I was only trying to make her feel better." His tone was bored, like he really didn't give a shit whether I was scared or not, but he clearly didn't like displeasing the woman before me.

*Wait, did she say Hades?*

"HOLY FUCK!" I grabbed Demke, pulling him

along, but obviously, we didn't make it far. I could barely shift him. "You can't have him. He's mine."

Hades, the freaking God of the Underworld, actually laughed at me. His eyes crinkled at the corners, and he had dimples. Gorgeous, but still terrifying. He looked down at the woman, Sephy, who I was beginning to realize might be Persephone.

"She's so cute. Can we keep her? Look at her, hissing and trying to protect him, as if I couldn't snatch the very soul from anyone in"—he tilted his head to the side—"a twenty-four-thousand mile radius. I'm pretty sure the old Minoan fuckers don't deserve her. We should keep her."

Persephone stood up, slapping him on the chest. "Stop it." She glared at Cy. "Are you going to do something? Appease her worry? Anything?" She put her hands on her hips, and Cy drooped his head down like a chastised puppy. "Wren, what my husband meant was that Demke is the God of Renewal, which means he dies at sunset on the day of the Solstice and is then reborn on the dawn. In a few hours, your grumpy little God will be back to being a broody, stubborn butthead."

Right now, I kind of agreed with the butthead bit. I stared at Cy. "And no one thought I should know that I might just stumble on Demke's *fucking dead body?*"

Cy looked at me, wide-eyed, before flicking his eyes to Hades. "Do you think it's too late to turn back into a dog?"

Hades chuckled. "Yep."

"Uh, I wasn't really aware that you didn't know... I

mean, I suspected when you were crying, but then there was Ekhidna, and the fight, and it kinda slipped my mind?"

I was so angry that I didn't even care that Cy was naked anymore. I wanted to wring his perfectly proportionate neck.

I blinked at him slowly, kicked Demke in the ribs with my bare feet—which definitely hurt me more than his unconscious, undead ass—and stomped back into the house. I was going to murder them all. I looked over at Hades as I left. "Keep the pits open, because I'm going to throw some damn Demigods right in!"

Shadowy demons were already being dragged into the black abyss, like sludge circling the drain. Man, Hades was really overpowered.

His laughter spread through the air like a sonic boom. "See, so entertaining. It's been so long since we had anyone interesting at home," he said to Persephone, almost sounding like a pouting child. I missed her response, though, as I left them in the courtyard, walking through Demke's bedroom straight into the chest of a pissed-looking Gryphon.

He opened his beak, but I held up a single finger. "Don't even *say* it, Griff! You and Teron are both on my shit list, and you're precariously close to catching hands." My voice broke. "Why didn't you *tell* me that Demke would die tonight? Before you yell at me, how about you consider how you'd feel if you saw my *goddamn dead body* out there under the moonlight!" I was definitely screeching now. "I had to find out from

Cy—who *isn't* a fucking dog—and the fucking God of the Underworld, who's hanging out back there near the fiery pits!"

Yep, if Griff had super hearing in this form, I'd probably just busted at least one of his eardrums.

*Mate...* His voice sounded hesitant, but I was already shaking my head.

"No. I could almost forgive you, because we haven't been able to speak like this before. But Teron definitely knew, and you had ample opportunity to warn me." I held up a hand to stop him from answering. "I'm going to find Nate, because he's the only one I can trust. Do not follow me. I don't want to see your feathery, furry ass. The danger is gone now, because Hades seems to be sucking them all down to the Underworld." Like it was an all-you-can-eat noodle night.

I pushed past Griff, though I wasn't dumb enough to think he'd leave me completely alone. He was wise enough to just hang back, and I'd take that.

There was very obvious evidence that there'd been a battle inside the house. Bits of gore lined the walls, with broken furniture and deep gouges across the floor. Bodies at different levels of decapitation. Surely it hadn't just been the Gryphon who'd caused this carnage?

I moved toward the doors that led to the main courtyard, and as soon as I slipped into the shadows that surrounded the building, a small group of dogs appeared. Definitely under the orders of Cy. I would never tell him this, but I found their presence reassuring. I'd seen what they'd done to Ekhidna; they were ferocious little warriors.

Some of them had even given their lives for me. For my babies. I saw the bodies of them cast around like discarded toys.

The shock of the night finally caught up with me, my anger draining away to shock. In the darkened courtyard of a forgotten palace, I broke down. Slipping to my knees, I was immediately surrounded by the wiggling bodies and darting kisses of a dozen dogs, each trying to make me feel better in a situation where there was no "better." There was just survival.

The dog from the other day—the one that had sat on my lap—put its tiny paws against my chest, kissing my chin. I cried even harder. "I'm happy you're safe," I murmured into her soft fur as she climbed into my arms. She didn't even have a name, but she would've laid down her life for mine. "I'm so sorry that some of you... died..." I choked out, crying into her fur.

She yipped, pushing her head beneath mine.

"She says it's an honor. They all knew the risks, and dying nobly in the defense of your little ones was better than dying hungry on the streets."

Looking up, I saw Cy, who'd found a pair of shorts somewhere. I continued stroking the dog's fur. "Does she have a name?"

"Kallini."

"I'll make sure no one is ever hungry again, Kallini. I promise."

Cy squatted down in front of me, his hand stroking

Kallini's head gently. "We know, Wren. They believe in you, even if you don't believe in yourself." He lifted my chin. "I believe in you too."

I shook my head at him, because I knew, deep down, that this wasn't the end. I knew that it was only going to get worse. More people would die in my name, and I didn't know if I could bear that weight on my soul. I squeezed Kallini to my chest, and Cy knelt down to wrap his arms around the two of us. "It'll all be okay. I know it."

He couldn't know that. This carnage told me that it wouldn't be all right. I wasn't made for battle.

"Wren!"

I looked up to see Nate running toward me, huge and shining, his ax hanging from his hand like an extension of his body. I let another choked sob out, placing Kallini down on the ground and holding my arms up to my lover, the man I trusted more than I trusted myself. "The guys?"

He looked over at Griff, who inclined his head respectfully. "They are all fine. We lost one of the Valkyries, however."

My heart shattered once more, and Nate lifted me into his arms, striding back into the compound as I cried. He was crusted in blood and other fluids I didn't want to think about. As he walked, he whispered sweet words to me in Gaelic. I didn't even try to decipher their meaning. I just buried my face in the comfort of his chest and let him carry me back to my room.

The doors had been barred, and apparently, that had

been enough of a deterrent, because my suite looked untouched. I walked over to the mural on the wall that depicted the Minoan Goddess. She didn't even have a name, or if she did, they'd never told me what it was. They just called her the Goddess, like she was everything that they'd ever needed, and they all had that same look of wistful sadness in their expression whenever they spoke of her.

Nate stood behind me silently as I traced my fingers over the dog that was running up the roots of the tree. Cy. I traced the bull that was on the ground at her feet. Milo? Demke was there, wreathed in vines and plants, looking solemn, a Gryphon standing beside him.

They were all there, beside the Goddess, along with other creatures. Snakes curled around her shoulders, the ones Demke had said died in the battle. Even a goat in the tree. Had he been just a goat? Or had he been like Cy? Had he died in the battle too?

"I'm repeating her mistakes, and I'll get the rest of her lovers killed." I ran my fingers over her face, the features blurred by time and Tryp's fading memories. "I'm sorry."

Nate stroked a hand down my hair. "Or you'll save them. Have faith, *mo stóirín*. It isn't hopeless yet."

*Yet.*

# CHAPTER 2
## DEMKE

The Goddess looked beautiful, the warmth of her light spreading through my bones, rejuvenating me once more. Her dark hair was like the softest curtain of silk. "My Demke, I miss you," she whispered to me, her lips not moving as she looked down at me lovingly.

"I miss you too, my Goddess," I breathed, turning my face to her palm. "It has been cold and barren without you."

She stroked my hair from my face. I tried to look past her, but there was nothing but light. "That's never what I wanted for you. I regret that I couldn't stay for you, for your brothers, but the sadness was too much for me to bear."

I shuddered at the echo of pain that tried to break through the happiness she was surrounding us both with. Shaking my head, I smiled softly at her. "I understood. Their loss was too much. I felt that ache too." There'd been so many more of us when the great battle happened. Brothers, lovers, friends. All dead at the hands of greedy new Gods.

Even as the bitterness built in my chest, it was swept away like debris in a warm breeze. "You were always so much stronger than I, Demke. So steadfast, so protective. You loved your subjects enough to stay, and I'll always be thankful for that strength."

Why did it sound like she was saying goodbye?

"The wheel is turning, my Goddess. You could return?" We could try again, be together again, but even as I thought it, something niggled at the back of my brain. A part of me rebelled at the idea. I couldn't remember why, though…

The sweet tinkling laugh I knew in my soul surrounded us. "Oh, Demke. My time has passed. But yours is just starting again. She is what you need going forward. She will give you a new life. A happy life, if you let yourself grasp the joy she hands out so freely."

*Who?*

"No, Goddess, I've only ever been devoted to you."

She was shaking her head, her smile sweet and sad. "You were the most devoted follower, the most steadfast lover, but our time is done. You must let yourself feel again." Gently, she gripped my chin until I was forced to look into the deep amber of her eyes. "Your soul isn't mine anymore, Demke. I know you're scared; I can see it casting shadows on your soul, but you need to be brave once more. She is your future. Be her strength, because she will need it."

I wanted to ask her again why she doubted my

devotion, but as I parted my lips, only one word slipped past. *"Wren."*

I WOKE TO CHAOS. There was a Hellmouth in my courtyard, small fires burning everywhere, a loud argument, and the God of the Underworld himself standing above me.

Hades raised an eyebrow. "You are in so much trouble, my friend," he said with a laugh, obviously amused by whatever was going on around us.

What the fuck was Hades doing here?

I sat up, and it took me only a split second to realize a battle had taken place while I'd been dead. I should have known they'd strike on the Solstice. I'd hoped we had more time, and none of my sources had even suggested they'd been launching an attack.

*Stupid. So fucking stupid.*

I took a quick head count. Milo was still in his shifted form, raging like the bull he was at that moment. He was shouting at Teron, who was holding his hands out, like he could appease the beast when he had his blood up like this.

Tryp had a huge gash across his chest that Erus was tending to, but they both seemed okay. Cy was there, talking to Persephone, but I couldn't see Wren anywhere.

There was no Néit either, and I frowned. Had she been taken?

"Wren!"

Everyone stopped to look at me, surprise quickly turning to annoyance. Even Erus and Tryp looked pissed. *What the hell happened?*

Hades was still chuckling. Surely he wouldn't be laughing if something had happened to her, right? "Where's Wren?" I demanded, mustering every ounce of authority I had.

Milo slowly turned his bull head toward me, and trepidation skittered down my spine. If Erus and Tryp looked pissed, then Milo looked livid.

Teron answered, "She's in her room."

"She's okay?"

Milo charged toward me, and I scrambled to my feet. He grabbed me by the lapels of my shirt, lifting me into the air. Not an easy feat; I wasn't a small man.

"She is, but no thanks to you." He shook me a little, and I almost laughed. There was a time that Milo had worshiped me, bowed at my very feet, and now he was throwing me around like a rag doll. "She found you in stasis, and she almost *died*," he roared. "She was almost murdered by fucking Ekhidna and Typhon, because you thought it was best to hide the fact you die once a year." He let go, and I dropped easily to my feet. "She almost died, because of your secrets. And now she refuses to speak to any of us."

He stomped away, and I watched him go. I'd mend fences with him later, but first, I needed to know exactly what had happened. Squeezing the bridge of my nose, I looked at Teron. "Tell me."

Teron recounted the call from Clio, which led to the

discovery that monsters had breached the island's wards. He explained why they'd put Néit in charge while I was indisposed, and about the Valkyries just arriving at the compound as if the wards didn't matter. I got more and more tense as they told me about the battle that included some of the oldest and most feared monsters in our history, Ekhidna and Typhon. If nothing else, this told me that the Moirai were serious about keeping their places.

And I'd been dead through it all.

Cy stepped toward me, and I held back the growl I wanted to throw in his direction. Despite the years of amicable cohabitation of the island, a part of me would always see him as the enemy. He was in his human form, which I knew was probably bad news in itself.

"I found her crying over your body, conversing with Ekhidna. Apparently, when the Moirai freed Typhon and Ekhidna, they promised to resurrect their children if they managed to kill Wren and the babies."

Hades whistled. "Those are some big promises."

Glaring at him, I couldn't help but snarl, "Why are you even here?"

His grin was sharp, and his eyes promised violence. "Watch yourself. I'm only tolerant of your belligerence because Sephy feels some kind of kinship with you, being both seasonal gods, or whatever." He curled his top lip, baring his teeth. "But if you don't check your tone, we'll see if the world really needs you at all."

Persephone appeared at his side, stroking a hand down his spine. "Teron called for help, and we answered. What you should be saying is 'thank you' because if we hadn't shown up when we did, you would've damned us all to another turn of the wheel under the Moirai. And I would not be happy." Her face turned to that of a skeleton, proof that she really was angry.

I bowed at the waist. "Apologies, Persephone, Hades. I appreciate the assistance, of course."

Teron shot me a warning look that told me to get my head out of my ass. "We are all thankful you answered our call of distress," he said softly. "Without you, Wren would be dead. She would have been consumed by Ekhidna." His words hammered home just how close we'd come. He looked back at Cy. "Please, continue."

"Ekhidna was lunging at Wren, and she was fighting her off with your sacred blade when the hounds and I turned up. Hades had impeccable timing, as always, and we managed to herd Ekhidna back into the Hell pit. We lost a few in the process." Cy's eyes were downcast, and I knew he felt the loss of his battle dogs as keenly as I'd feel the loss of one of my own.

Persephone rested a hand on his shoulder. "They'll run through the Elysian Fields with Cerberus."

That made him smile, and if he had his tail, he'd probably have wagged it. "Is he coming up?"

Hades rolled his eyes. "No, he has to stay and guard the Underworld. We were coming to a battle, not a puppy playdate."

Cy pouted, and as much as it pained me, I slapped

him softly on the shoulder. "I appreciate you protecting her when I couldn't."

He smirked. "I saw her first. She's mine to protect, as much as she is yours."

My eyes narrowed at his words, but now was not the time to get into that. Instead, I tried to process everything they'd told me, all the things that I seemed to have missed.

I turned to Hades and Persephone. "Please, come inside and rest for a little. I'll get us a drink."

Erus and Tryp eyed me warily, and rightly so—this was the first time I'd ever let any of the Greek Mythics inside our home. Even Cy wasn't allowed past the walls… normally.

"You too, Cy. Bring in the rest of the pack also; let them be safe and rest. If there are any injuries we need to look at, we're happy to offer assistance. Right, Teron?"

He nodded. "I've got it, Demke."

I ushered us all through my quarters, gritting my teeth at the very idea of having foreign Mythics in my space, and led us out into the kitchens. The place was a mess. The battle had made it all the way inside the walls, and I once again was slapped in the face by how lucky we'd been. And how woefully underprepared.

Erus poured the rakí for everyone, and Persephone downed hers like it didn't burn at all. "You're fucking this up, Demke."

I winced. She was never one to mince words. "It would appear so."

She shook her head at me, as if I was disappointing her again. "We can take her, keep her safe until the babies are born. Wren and I have a lot in common, with the whole mystical fruit thing," she said softly. I'd kind of forgotten about the pomegranate seeds and their effect on her life.

The visceral reaction I had at the thought of my Wren in Hades's domain was instant. She was life and light, and she wouldn't survive down there. I was already shaking my head. "Thank you for your offer, but she's safer here."

Hades lazily pointed at the broken furniture with his rakí glass. "Evidence would suggest otherwise."

I met his gaze. "I will make it so." I let him see the determination in my eyes, the vehemence to keep her safe. He would know the feeling; he'd burn down the whole world for Persephone. "We would be grateful for any assistance you could offer topside, however."

He raised his glass. "Consider it done. It is time for the reign of those old bitches to end, and I'll be more than happy to be the one snipping their strings."

He'd have to beat me to it. The Moirai were on borrowed time, and their own fates were coming for them now.

# CHAPTER 3
## WREN

O

**M**ate...

The sound of Griff's mournful voice in my head made me feel a little guilty that I was still giving them all the silent treatment, even if they deserved it. I was curled up in my damn *Gryphon nest*, yet they didn't think I'd be able to handle the fact that Demke died once a year?

Apparently, men could be stupid, no matter the millennium they were from.

Nate had been delivering me food and their apologies over the last few hours, as the cleanup began. I needed to come out and thank the people who'd gone to battle for me, though. The Valkyries. Hades and Persephone. The dog pack.

Now that I'd calmed down, and my adrenaline had evened out a little, I wondered if I was being a little bit dramatic. Then I'd remember Demke's slack face, and be mad all over again.

*I'm still upset, Griff,* I answered him, then sighed. *And angry.*

I could hear his grumble. *Men can be stupid in the nobility. Let me in so I can soothe you.*

Huffing, I opened the door. However, I was surprised to see it was Teron on the other side of the door. "That's cheating." I scowled, stomping back toward the nest.

He gave me a guilty expression. "I just wanted to check you and the babies out. That was… stressful."

I put my hands on my hips. "Which part, Teron? The bonding with a Gryphon, finding Demke dead, being faced with a monster that still makes me tremble with fear if I think about her, or meeting *the* Hades?!"

He winced. "All of the above? I apologize, Wren. We should have known that hiding this from you would end badly. I argued against it, but…"

Demke was their unofficial leader. Their God. If he hadn't wanted me to know, they wouldn't have struck out against his wishes.

"I didn't think you'd need the extra stress, and there hadn't been any indication of an attack. It's quite a confronting thing to see him dying. It isn't a sweet sort-of death," he explained desperately, and I softened a little.

Could I have watched Demke die and not freak out? Probably not. But I would've liked the option to decide for myself. *Assholes.*

I sat on the bed and let him check my vitals, because although I might be pissed at the guys, the health of the babies meant everything to me now. I would fight literal monsters in their name; I wouldn't let anything happen to them just because I was feeling miffed.

I stayed silent, only following Teron's quiet directions as he checked me out. Finally, he sat beside me on the bed, reaching out to brush his pinky finger along mine. "I haven't talked to you about the bond between you and the Gryphon."

I looked at him, and even now, I could see Griff's sharp intelligence reflected back in his gaze. "You're okay with it, right? I know it was kind of rushed, and you should have had an opinion—"

He gripped my hand and lifted it to his chest. "Wren, I'm definitely not unhappy with the bond between us. I hope that now the Gryphon has created a mate bond with you, our own bond will snap into place. It's difficult for the magic to take hold, considering I have two souls."

I leaned my head on his shoulder. "I didn't think about the fact that you and Griff being two separate entities must mean two souls to bind. I always did like a BOGO deal."

"BOGO?"

I shook my head. "Buy one, get one free. Honestly, it might be the title of my autobiography."

He kissed the top of my head, then rubbed my stomach softly. "It does seem to be a running theme. No regrets, though?"

I shook my head. Not about the babies, and not about bonding a literal mythical creature as a mate during a battle. My life was too tenuous to worry about regrets. "None." Shifting to the edge of the bed, I hauled myself up and looked down at Teron. "But I mean it when I say that I am a grown woman. I mightn't be six billion years old, but I can make my own choices. You aren't protecting me by keeping secrets; you're putting me at risk."

He nodded. "No more, Wren. I promise."

Man, he was so fucking beautiful, his golden eyes wide and honest, his long, straight nose and full lips just begging me to trace them with my fingertips. Now was not the time, though.

Holding out a hand, I led him from my suite. The house was in a state of repair, the broken furniture moved out, and everything put back to rights. It was almost as if the battle had never happened, except for the fact that the remaining Valkyries were drinking with Hades at the dining table. There were at least fifteen bottles spread between them, and they were loudly telling stories—about their fallen comrade, I realized.

"She never backed down. She once tried to mount Sleipnir and ride him out of the stables without Odin knowing, but... well, he's Odin." The Valkyries all cackled, like it was the funniest joke, but beneath their merriment was a sadness that I knew was my fault.

"She died a noble death," Hrist said wistfully, almost like she wished she was in her fallen friend's place.

Mist nodded. "To die protecting the future weavers

is a worthy end to an immortal life. She'll drink deeply in Valhalla."

Okay, so I hadn't been wrong; that *had* been envy in Hrist's tone.

Feeling eyes on my face, I looked down the table at Hades, who was eyeing me closely. I wondered if he could see into my soul, like some of the myths described.

He lifted his glass in my direction. "Speaking of the Mother of Fate. Feeling better?" Ice dripped from his words, like the haughty king he was. Without the softening effects of Persephone, his raw power felt far more ominous. Every word sounded like a threat, even though I knew that wasn't the case. My instincts told me to be wary of the God in front of me, because he was more powerful than I could imagine. Staying on his good side meant staying alive.

He waved a hand at me. "Don't look at me like a scared little rabbit. I've waited around all this time to see you give Demke an ass-kicking, so don't disappoint me by becoming a piece of fluff now." Teron put a steadying hand on my spine, his body somehow angled protectively around mine while still seeming relaxed.

I knew there was only one way to really deal with a big God like Hades. It was to go balls-to-the-wall outrageous. I wasn't made to fall to my knees for anyone.

Well, anyone except my guys.

"I'll get right on that. Where is the formerly immortal being?"

Hades lifted himself from his chair. "Ladies. Hopefully, I get to drink with you again in the Tar Pits."

Teron leaned down close to my ear. "The Tar Pits are where all the Underworlds meet. There's a bar there that isn't Pantheon specific. A meeting place, of sorts."

*Okay, that sounds wild.*

Mist stood and bowed, and the other Valkyries followed suit. Hades lifted his chin to them in respect. As one, all the Valkyries turned to me.

"If it is okay with you, we would like to ferry the body of our fallen sister to Valhalla, so she can feast with the heroes who have gone before us."

I was nodding before Mist had even finished speaking. "Please, absolutely. I… We couldn't have done this without you. I'm eternally grateful for your aid."

Hades snorted, but Mist just bowed once more. "It's our honor. We will come if you call."

With that, Hildr let out a piercing whistle, and in unison, they marched to the window, then jumped out one by one. Honestly, if I didn't know they had flying horses roaming around the courtyard, I would have freaked out.

Griff huffed. *Do you think they realize we have doors and stairs?*

Snarky bird-cat. I wished I could stroke his head. *You're more impressive by far,* I told him softly, and he let out a soft, happy rumble in my mind.

I couldn't help but smile. Being able to talk to Griff was so different to the exaggerated charades we'd had to do previously. He sounded wise and distinguished, with such a distinct personality. It was almost too easy to think of him and Teron as separate entities, to forget that I wouldn't ever see them both in a room together.

Teron led me from the dining room and out through the sunroom into the back courtyard. It wasn't so easy to hide the signs of carnage out here. At least the Hellmouth was still in Demke's separate courtyard. The pool was filled with debris, and I didn't want to think about what it was. Parts of the walls had collapsed, trees split and broken, as if a giant had stomped them.

I looked up at Teron. "The villagers?"

Stroking a calming hand down my back once more, he held me close. "Fine. Demke warned them, and when Néit raised the alarm, we sent out an alert for them to take shelter or leave. Hildr the Valkyrie guarded them in the town hall. But the monsters weren't interested in the humans."

No, they'd been here for one thing. My death.

Suddenly, Cy was in front of me, smiling widely. "Wren! You're out of your room." He hugged me close, spinning me around. At his feet was a crowd of dogs, yipping loudly, tails wagging. I squatted down and accepted all their love. I was quickly swarmed, much to Teron's clear annoyance, but they deserved the affection and appreciation just as much as the Valkyries.

"Thank you so much, my friends." I patted any fur I could find, and accepted kisses from an insane amount of dog-breath muzzles. I couldn't help but laugh as little teeth nipped at the ends of my fingers, asking for attention. "You're all so, so good. I'm going to order as many steaks as I can find; yes, I am."

When they got a little too rowdy at my words, Cy growled low. From his human mouth. *Jesus, that's weird.* The dogs immediately all backed off a little, giving me space. I glanced up at the man appreciatively, before turning my attention back to them.

"I'm going to learn every single one of your names, and if you don't have one, I'll give you one. Warriors deserve a name, and you're all heroes in my eyes."

There was more yipping, and then Cy pulled me back to my feet. "Thank you," he breathed.

*Fuck.* He was so damn beautiful. A broad face and high cheekbones, the hair curled tightly to his head glowed the same white as his fur as a dog. His golden skin and deep brown eyes seemed like they'd been kissed by bronze.

Why were these guys all so attractive? Was it an after-effect of being so long-lived?

I dragged my eyes from his pretty face. "I should be the one saying that. You saved my ass. Literally."

He was opening his mouth to say something else, but at that moment, I spotted Demke, and the fury that had been simmering in my veins surged back up. The pain of believing him dead at my feet bloomed once more, and I was marching toward him before I even thought about it. How dare he put me through that?

He was righting some olive trees with Persephone, whose hands were repairing the damage and making them bloom once more. It was a cool party trick.

Normally, I would've watched in awe. Right now, though, I had tunnel vision, and at the end of that red haze was one man.

He spotted me, and his eyes widened. I shuddered to think what I looked like right now—probably deranged.

"*You!*" I pointed at him.

He lifted both hands. "Wren, I'm sorry, I can—"

I didn't give him a chance. I didn't care if he was a God, a man, my bond, whatever. Lifting my hand, I punched him square in the throat. In all honesty, I'd been aiming for his nose, but I was short and had terrible hand-eye coordination.

"I thought you were *dead*. I cried over your corpse, you royal fucking asshole."

He wheezed, and I was glad he was immortal, because that looked like it hurt. My thumb ached, like I'd crunched it a little too hard.

Spinning away before he could give me a lame excuse, I nearly walked straight into a laughing Hades. "Fuck me, this was absolutely worth hanging around in this dingy fucking realm. You tell him, Wren!"

I was about to start crying again, so I did the only thing I could think of. I turned my back on them all, and went in search of Milo.

# CHAPTER 4
## MILO

I was losing patience with the humans, and I was snorting far more than appropriate with a human face. They were worried and scared; I got that, but I wanted to be at home with Wren, making sure she was okay, holding her close and ensuring that nothing could ever hurt her again.

Instead, I was here, moving rubble created by the monsters that had crawled out of the darkness, including fucking *Typhon*. I couldn't believe that they'd wanted Wren so bad that they'd released the Father of Monsters from his immortal prison. Talk about drastic measures. There was just as much of a chance that he'd turn on them, in revenge for his imprisonment, than do their bidding.

Ekhidna had also been there, and maybe that had been keeping him in line, because as soon as she'd disappeared into Hades's Hell pit, Typhon had roared and disappeared. My chuckle was dark, scaring some of the humans working beside me. I hoped he tracked down those witches and tore them to pieces.

Cy ran up to me in his dog form, dodging the hands of the townspeople. I always wondered what they'd say about their beloved village dog being able to turn into a man. Some knew, of course—the elders with long memories—but they'd never told the younger generation. It had been a long time since Cy had changed forms, so maybe the fact had just gotten lost to old age.

He yipped in my direction, flicking his head back toward the compound. His meaning was clear, even if he did bark it at me.

"She's out of her room?"

After the guys had told me what happened, I'd known I needed to leave or I'd wreck things: either Demke's face, or my relationship with Wren. I wouldn't be able to give her the space she demanded, because the very idea that she was angry at me was like barbs in my chest.

So I left to do something helpful, like clear the rubble from the roads and ensure the townspeople were okay. Anything so I wouldn't just pace outside her door until she emerged.

Cy nodded, and I wondered if the townspeople noticed. Probably not. Humans were great at ignoring the supernatural right in front of them.

I found Stavros, who was sitting on a small stone wall, looking annoyed that he couldn't help. He was walking with his stick more these days, and I knew our old confidant was rapidly spinning toward death. He was one in a long line of many. After all this time, I thought I'd hardened my heart to the inevitable demise of mortals, but apparently, Wren had ripped the scab off that wound too.

I clapped him gently on the arm. "I have to go, but I'll return after dark to finish the rest of the cleanup."

Stavros waved a hand. "It's fine, Milonos. You've done the work of ten men already this morning. We'll take care of the rest."

I inclined my head, trying to chase away the guilt. They didn't need to clean up after our immortal squabbles; their lives shouldn't be made harder by our presence. It was a topic on which Teron and I disagreed. He argued that our presence had created a protective circle around this small village, and perhaps the island as a whole. We enriched the town, not just financially but magically, and the olive crops around here were some of the most bountiful on the island. We provided protection and medical aid to the town's residents, and since many made it to well over a century in age, possibly longevity.

For hundreds of years, we'd been silent guardians. Now, it was a time of turmoil, and they would have to decide if the boons were worth it.

But that was a discussion Demke would have to have with the town leaders. My job was to find the woman I was bonded to, and make sure she didn't hate me for lying to her by omission. Cy trotted along beside me, and I was insanely surprised when he walked through the wall gate too.

Demke had never let *anyone* from the Greek Pantheon into the compound, not in the entire history of this stronghold. Not even Cy, who we'd lived in harmony with for a relatively long time. It had been the place we'd retreated to when we needed to lick our wounds after the great battle, and it was a strictly No Greek Mythic zone.

There were dogs stretched out all over the courtyard, some with all four legs in the air, exhausted and asleep, and some with various injuries, wrapped and tended, who were sleeping fitfully as they healed. They'd been great out there, though I was pretty sure one of Cy's abilities was to turn even the most genial pup into a battle hound.

If you looked at this pack right now, you'd never suspect it. One was actually dragging its ass across the packed dirt of the courtyard. I made a mental note that we should get dewormer in bulk. I knew my bond; I knew she'd want to take care of this insane hoard of animals.

As if my thoughts had summoned her from the chaos, she appeared. My breath stuttered in my chest. She was okay. I knew that; they'd all told me so. But it was different, seeing her with my own two eyes, doing a visual inspection of her entire self to make sure she wasn't hurt. I strode across the distance between us, my stride long enough that Cy had to trot to keep up.

When I made it to her, I dropped to my knees, wrapping my arms around her waist. It was awkward with the bulge of her stomach, my head stopping just under her breasts. We didn't say anything, but when she stroked her fingers through my hair, something relaxed inside me. The anger that had been coiled tightly inside my chest just let go beneath her soft touch.

"I'm sorry."

I felt her sigh leave her chest beneath my cheek. "I know."

She didn't say she forgave me, and I knew it wouldn't be that easy. We'd broken her trust, though I doubted Demke would see it that way. But I would work to regain it, and if I had to do it on my knees the entire time, I would.

I looked up to see her frowning down at me. "You're okay?" Her fingers traced over the raw cut on my cheek. I'd caught a stray Verserpent claw, but I was fine.

"Yes, love."

She nodded, but the frown didn't leave her face. "Good."

There were lines of exhaustion around her face, and worry once again flooded my veins. This had been too much, and I hated that there was nothing I could do to shelter her from it. Nothing more than I was already doing right now, I mean. Logic told me that it would be worse after the babies arrived, and I vowed that I'd be there to support her through it all.

I stood slowly so I didn't lose the closeness between us. "Let me take you to bed." She opened her mouth to protest, but I quickly covered it with a finger. "Not like that. I will tuck you in and come back to the cleaning effort." I wrapped my arms around her, and she rested her head against my heart with another heavy sigh. "You're tired; I can feel it. I can read it on your face. You need to sleep off this shitshow, and then I'll run you a warm bath." Kissing the top of her head, I breathed her in, reassuring the beast that lived in my soul that she was indeed okay. "We will protect you always. You don't have to worry about that."

She huffed an annoyed sound. "Like it's that easy."

Still, she didn't protest as I led her away from the crowded courtyard, back up to her rooms, which were thankfully untouched. I helped her undress, finding one of Néit's big t-shirts to help pull over her head. She was already fading into exhaustion.

Tucking her in, I kissed her head. "I'll make it that easy. No one is ever getting that close again," I whispered against her cheek, but her eyes were already fluttering closed.

Making sure her curtains were closed to block out the mid-afternoon light, I walked back out into the hall. Fortunately, Hades and Persephone had returned to the Underworld, after closing off the Hell pit in Demke's private courtyard. The King of the Underworld made my skin crawl, but not because he was creepy. Though the moon-like paleness of his skin was kinda spooky, and if he turned a certain direction, it was like you could see the bones beneath his flesh.

No, Hades weirded me out because he was so powerful. His power was like a physical force that whispered ominously around you, a promise of what he could do to you if you pissed him off. He was generally good-natured, for an overpowered Mythic, and I suspected that was only because the enemies of your enemy were your friends, or whatever the quote was. I didn't have to see his rage to know it was terrifying, however.

The Valkyries were also gone, and so the house had returned to mostly normal. If you didn't count all the dogs. Or the fact that Cy was inside the walls.

Demke walked out of his room, and I clenched my fists. I'd worshiped this man once, blindly following his rules and his edicts as if they were coming from the very mouth of the Goddess herself. I would've never thought I'd ever manhandle him and *shake* him.

We stared at each other, and I didn't know what to say. I wasn't sorry; I wanted to shake him still.

I hated the ill feelings between us, though. He had always been my lighthouse in the immortal world, and it was hard to navigate without him. If he decided to be pissed by the fact I'd basically flung him around like a rag doll, would he turn my brothers against me?

Even as I thought it, I knew that it wouldn't be that easy. Erus and Tryp were long past the worshipful stage, and we all had our own minds and hearts. If it came down to splitting the group, the Genii would come with me, I was sure of it.

Demke shook his head. "Stop looking so panicked, Milonos. I deserved that shaking and a lot more. You were correct—I put her in danger with my secrets. I won't make the same mistake again."

Relief whooshed out of me on a long breath. I hated

holding that anger inside me. I stepped forward and grabbed him up in my arms, hugging him tight. I didn't say anything else, just squeezed him for a few seconds until his free arm came up and patted me on the back.

"It will all be okay." He stepped away, and I did too, running my fingers roughly through my hair.

"I'm sorry for handling you so disrespectfully."

He nodded. "I'm sorry I earned such disrespect. We have more important things to focus on right now, however."

Like what we were going to do about the Mythics who were willing to do anything to kill the woman I'd fallen head over heels in love with.

# CHAPTER 5
## WREN

I woke up in my Gryphon nest, surrounded by sleeping dogs and one disgruntled Celtic God of War. I was nose-to-shoulder with Nate, who had his chin tucked on my head and a hand on my belly, which was huge between us. I was beginning to feel so large, I may as well have had my own orbital pull.

On Nate's pillow was a small dog, about the size of a chihuahua. It may have had some chihuahua in there, but it also had a whole bunch of other things, judging by the makeup of its face. Maybe a pug? Maybe a basset hound?

I reached behind me to find a large furry body there as well, though that didn't really narrow it down between bondmates and puppy dogs. But when the body rolled, and Cy's big blocky head appeared in my vision, it kind of answered my question.

"Are you the reason I'm sleeping in a puppy pile right now?" I asked him, though he couldn't answer me in his dog form, and I wasn't sure I was ready for a naked Cy in his human form in my bed just yet. My body clenched at the mere whisper of the idea of being the meat in a Nate/Cy sandwich. Honestly, my body really had betrayed me at this point—she was calling the shots, while I was trying to exorcize my grandmother's extremely Catholic disapproval from my mind. Nana would be rolling over in the family crypt.

Cy grumbled, licking my check, before turning in a couple of circles and flopping down at my back again. He snuggled in further, though I was about to rain on his parade, because I needed to pee.

I sat up to see a disgruntled Gryphon at the end of the bed. He was eyeing the dogs like he'd be happy to make them into a snack right about now, snapping if they came too close.

"Hey, Griff. You okay?"

*The mutts are messing up your nest.*

When I looked around, I realized he was right. There were dog bodies all over my room, of every size and shape imaginable. Geez, there must have been like fifty in here.

I gave him a sheepish smile. *Lucky I have a talented mate who'll make sure it's perfect again in no time. But you're right. I'll kick them out and set some ground rules with Cy about who can be in here and where they can sleep.*

I doubted Nate would be particularly thrilled by his current earwarmer either.

Griff huffed as a smallish dog, who couldn't be much more than a puppy, edged closer to him. The dog looked like he'd be huge eventually, but by the clumsiness of its gait, it hadn't quite grown into the size of its feet yet. It was brave, though. That much was obvious, as it curled up close to the Gryphon—who could literally eat it in one chomp—and went to sleep.

My monstrous mate looked down at it with disbelief, but didn't snap at it. I guess he'd also realized that it was little more than a baby. The big softie. I smiled at Griff, who huffed back.

*I doubt you'll get rid of Cydon. He is definitely tied to you as well. I can almost feel your bond through our own.*

I looked at the golden threads that spread through the room. The wispy lines made their way from all the dogs to Cy, and to me. There was a huge golden line, straight and true, between Griff and I, as well as between me and Nate. The one between Cy and me was surprising, though. It was different to the other threads that tied me to my bonds. It wasn't golden, but a deep bronze, like it had once been shiny and new, but was now weathered and strong. Patinaed.

What did that even mean?

I reached out and stroked my hand down the fur of Cy, whose tongue was sticking out the side of his mouth lazily. Whatever it was, he'd saved my ass, and I was grateful. I wanted to discover his story, because I was beyond thinking things were a coincidence. I was being moved around a board by beings who didn't respect the rules, and I either moved with it or lay down, checkmate.

Finally, my bladder decided that if I didn't move

right now, I was going to pee myself. I tried to wiggle out without waking anyone, but just ended up on my back like a beached whale. I nudged Cy. "Sorry, big guy, but I have to pee." He stretched, then nimbly leapt off the bed, like he hadn't just been snoring a moment ago. "Don't gloat," I grumbled. "Where's that pregnant mama dog? She'd understand."

I liked focusing on the dogs. Teron had suggested it was because I could control something with them, and I wondered if he'd been studying psychology with his obstetrics.

I looked down at Cy. "We can't all sleep together, unless you want to be a Gryphon snack," I told him. "But I'll find somewhere warm and safe for the pack."

Before my eyes, Cy shifted into a man once more. Naked. Again. I needed to invest in some pants repositories around the place, because talking to him while his dick was out was… hard. My eyes shot back to his face, and he looked way too pleased with himself.

"And me?"

Yeah, that was still to be decided. Instead of answering, I walked into the ensuite and closed the door.

When I made my way down to the living room, my suite had been emptied of occupants, and I was almost relieved to dress alone. Until it came to putting on my underwear, which was more difficult than it had any right to be. I was huffing and puffing and weighing up the merit of just freeballing it for the rest of my pregnancy by the time I managed to get somewhat dressed.

Moving toward the pool area, I was surprised to see dogs in the pool. *Man, Demke's going to lose it.* But when I saw the God himself sitting underneath the grape trellis, drinking wine, I was relieved. I was still mad at him, but it was hard to maintain, because my life was a fucking mess. I didn't want to hold onto petty grudges. We might not be about to fuck under the light of the full moon, but at least he wasn't looking at me like some temptress here to steal the souls of his brothers.

Tryp appeared beside me from the shadows, which was pretty impressive, considering how big he was. He had his arms around me and his cheek running over mine in an instant. He was mumbling, "Sorry", but I was enjoying the contact just as much as he was. Needed it just as much.

I gripped his fingers, turning him to face me. "Are you okay?" I asked softly, and he nodded, brushing his lips over mine.

"I'm fine, Dumpling. The other half of me just needs to mark the hell out of you as some kind of territorial warning."

Erus hadn't managed to beat that nickname out of him, but honestly, it was growing on me. I really did look like a little, overstuffed dumpling. I wasn't mad about it.

As if my thoughts had summoned his other half, I felt a warm body step up behind me, his hands skimming down my sides, before cupping under my belly and holding it up. The relief was instantaneous as he took the weight of my stomach.

"Oh my god," I breathed as my overused muscles got a reprieve. "You have no idea how good that feels." The babies were getting so big and heavy, and every ounce of my body hurt from hauling them around.

Erus kissed the shell of my ear. "Anytime you want one of us to help you, just say the word. I'd absolutely stand here all day."

*These guys...* I sniffed a little, giving my hormones a very stern talk about not bursting into tears at the smallest gesture, but my eyes misted over anyway. My body was a traitor. "Thank you," I choked out, and Tryp kissed the corners of my eyes and down my cheeks.

"Our honor. Now, let me feed you. Are you hungry? Thirsty? Want me to throw Demke in the pool and let the dogs try to drown him? They couldn't, but it might be fun to watch."

I smacked his shoulder before capturing his soft, pouty lips with mine. He tasted of Erus, sweet and firm, his breath minty like the peppermint leaves he sometimes chewed. I lifted my hands and threaded my fingers through his soft curls. As I gripped them hard, he moaned into my mouth.

*Oops. Better stop before this gets pornographic.*

I released him, and he whined softly, making Erus chuckle at my back. "Juice would be wonderful, thank you," I breathed, our lips still brushing together as I spoke.

He groaned and dragged himself away. Erus was

still holding my stomach, and bit the curve of my shoulder gently. "Such a sweet and seductive bondmate. I love watching you torturing him." He gently lowered my stomach, and the pressure on my body made me want to pout. "Come, how about you sit down and relax on the sun lounger? You're working hard."

There was a riotous bark-off as the dogs suddenly realized I'd arrived, running over until Cy—now clothed, thankfully—made a growling noise and shooed them away. He sat on the other side of the pool in swim shorts and waved cheekily. I gave him a finger wave and lay down in the sun; the short walk from the bedroom to the pool had been exhausting.

How had I thought I'd manage this while working? If I'd been back in Boston, I'd be manning the drive-thru at Java Llama, trying to lean out the service window. The idea of long shifts with Bob, my dick boss, made me physically shudder. Besides, if you took out the monsters and attacks and ominous prophecies and health problems, I was pretty damn happy here under the Greek sun, surrounded by men who'd brought me more orgasms than I'd ever had in my life.

Erus sat beside me on the warm tiles, his face pressed to my thigh in a way that wasn't sexual, but comforting. "Where's everyone else?" I asked.

"Teron, Milo and Néit have just left to go down to Heraklion to pick up building supplies for the town, and some more medical equipment. They also wanted to stockpile provisions in case of an old-fashioned siege.

Milo said, and I quote, he was 'going to buy a drum of dewormer for the fleabag brigade.'" He lifted his chin at a dog that was scratching an itch like it had personally affronted it. "He's also getting the steaks you promised," he said quietly, though not quiet enough, because at least fifteen dogs yipped at the word "steak." I laughed, stroking my fingers through his hair.

A body blocked out my sun, and I looked up at the shadowy silhouette of Demke. "Wren. I was hoping we could talk."

Erus huffed a disgruntled noise, and I stroked my hand down his shoulder, hating that I'd caused a rift between them. He gave Demke the stink-eye, but still stood and walked toward the pool, diving in, making all the dogs splash in after him. We were going to have to run the filter at twice the rate, otherwise it was going to get real funky real quick.

Demke sat at the end of my lounger, and I shifted my legs over so his big body had room. "I apologize, Wren. I didn't mean to cause you distress."

Distress. He called it distress. "I thought you were *dead*. It would have been hard on a perfectly calm night, but in the middle of a battle…" The pain of seeing him like that was quick to rush back. "You suck. You know that, right?"

He inclined his head. "I've been known to suck…"

Somehow, I didn't think we meant that in the same context. I really wanted to know more about that subject, but he was already moving on.

"I don't know why I didn't want to tell you. I tell

myself that I didn't want to add to your stress, even though it's something that happens every year, and I couldn't hide it from you forever." He shrugged. "We'd just achieved some kind of connection, and I didn't want to ruin it. But as history has a way of repeating itself, I ruined it anyway."

I sucked in a deep breath, the sadness of his words washing over me. *Dammit.* I wanted to be mad at him for longer, but right now, I needed to hug him. Opening my arms, I made a small *come here* motion with my hands. He didn't hesitate, wrapping his arms around my shoulders and pulling me close. He smelled like pine and salt and some kind of wild magic that I couldn't describe, but was insanely attracted to.

"You're forgiven, but no more secrets, okay? Secrets have never helped any relationship. They're just wounds that'll continue to fester until they explode like a pus-filled boil." I gagged a little at my own words.

He laughed, his chest vibrating above mine. "Graphic, but accurate. I promise, no more secrets, even by omission."

Leaning back, I looked up at him once more. "I mean it. You didn't just hurt me—you hurt them too." I indicated Tryp and Erus. "And hurting them is something I'm less inclined to forgive and forget."

He brushed his lips across mine. "And that's why fate chose you, Wren Mahone."

# CHAPTER 6
## TERON

Our truck was filled to the brim, nearly scraping the ground with what I thought we'd need to survive the next year. I'd even gone to the city to collect it myself, because it would be too big a task to push onto one of the villagers. I'd been surprised when both Néit and Milo had come along for the ride, however. They'd been reluctant to leave Wren's side up until this point, and when I'd suggested that, they'd both glared at me. But when I saw what they'd put in the back of the truck, I realized they were both doing errands for Wren in their own ways.

Néit had collected a large crate from the docks, paying off a bunch of shifty-looking men to bring it out of an unused warehouse. When I'd asked what it was, he'd said a gift from an old friend. When we made it back to the truck and loaded it, he'd popped the lid, and I'd gotten a peek at what was inside. It wasn't something I could have predicted.

Inside that crate were honest-to-goodness, God-blessed weapons. Finding one weapon was difficult. A crate full of them? I would have suggested it was impossible, if I hadn't seen it with my own eyes.

Milo had just whistled. "Who the hell is your friend?"

There was so much we didn't know about the mysterious Néit. He'd just grunted noncommittally as he closed it back up, and I wasn't going to ask too many more questions. If someone wanted to send him a gift hamper of blessed axes and swords, so be it.

Milo had us pull up to a vet next, and had come out with a box of pet medication. Flea treatments and dewormers. Bags and bags of dog food. He'd also bought a butcher out of dog bones and steaks, bringing out several large styrofoam boxes worth.

Combined with my pallets of canned human foods and dry goods, we looked like we were crazed preppers. In a way, we were. We were definitely stockpiling for what they would have called an apocalypse in the old days. Ragnarok. The End of Days. The Fall of Olympus. All of these had heralded the end of the world as humans knew it.

I would try to prevent that, this time. I was a healer. I didn't relish the idea that humans would die for the insane power grab of Mythics.

I watched the humans finish loading the truck, giving us a wide berth. They mightn't know why we seemed wrong; they just knew we were. It was a good thing. It might save their life if things went badly.

I walked up to the back dock worker and signed the docket. "Big party?" he asked, and I smiled at him politely.

"Something like that."

This guy would definitely report me to the authorities if he knew that the three big crates in the back were humidicribs. I told myself that we'd just donate it all back to the island anonymously at the end, and Wren wouldn't stress about the fact that each piece of medical equipment came with an eye-watering price tag.

With everything finally loaded, we jammed the three of us into the cab of the truck. It wasn't comfortable, and my Gryphon complained the whole time, but at least I got to drive. It must've looked a little like stuffing meat into a sausage skin from the outside.

I pulled back out onto the road, anxious to be back in Amourgeles. The mate bond in my chest pulled me back in the direction of her, and honestly, the Gryphon was a little pissed about being so far away. How could we protect her if I was walking around on two legs in my useless meat suit, buying chickpeas in a can? Direct quote from the Gryphon.

I could only appease him by explaining that this was the way we provided for our mate and offspring. That was the thing about the Gryphon; he didn't care that she was carrying someone else's children. Or, well, they weren't really someone else's, I guess. But to the Gryphon, they were his cubs. His children. He would protect them with his life, if need be. It was sweet and daunting all at once, because it left my more human sensibilities scrambling to catch up.

"Should we talk about where Typhon disappeared to?" I asked to break the silence.

The Father of Monsters deserved his title. He and Ekhidna had spawned some of the most fearsome monsters in the world's long history, including Cerberus, who guarded the Underworld. They were probably having quite the catchup down there, Ekhidna and Cerberus. Made me feel a little less bad that she'd had to die for the whims of the Fates.

Not that any of us truly died, unless we were removed from the weave altogether.

But Typhon was worse than all his offspring combined. Huge, with a hundred free-thinking serpents spreading from his shoulders that spat fire and acid, and mocked you as you died. One of the serpents had told my Gryphon that he was puny and smelled like offal as it attacked. I mean, that was slightly strange, even in the realm of monsters, but it had definitely stuck with him. He'd washed and preened at least six times since the battle.

"Is it too much to hope that he's just slunk back to the ocean and gone about his business?" Milo suggested, and Néit grunted his agreement.

I wished I could be that optimistic. "He isn't a friend of the Fates, either way. He may become an ally as we have a common enemy, or he might be pissed that we sent his wife to the Underworld. I think the best we can hope for is that he stays out of this battle altogether." See, I could be optimistic too.

"We need to have better plans. Attacks after the babies are born will not be so easily defended, and it would only take one—" Néit couldn't finish his sentence, shaking his head. I knew what he meant. They could only continue to be the Fates if there were three of them. "We need a better plan."

Milo shrugged. "I'm living with the hope that maybe they aren't the new Fates at all. Maybe they're going to be something else, or nothing at all."

I was optimistic, but that was downright delusional.

Milo continued. "There's one surefire way to find out, though. Her and Demke are on better terms, and at this point, she looks at him the way the hounds look at a juicy sausage."

I was already shaking my head. "No sex. It's too late in her pregnancy. I don't want anything bringing on labor early."

Both Néit and Milo looked at me as if I'd suggested they live a life devoid of happiness. "None *at all?*" Milo gasped.

Rolling my eyes, I took the turn-off that would lead to home. "No penetration, at least. You can undertake oral sex as much as you wish."

The sigh of relief that Milo emitted was kind of amusing. "Thank goodness. The idea of not bringing her pleasure for weeks, maybe months?" He was shaking his head, like that was the most preposterous thing we'd spoken of today.

Néit snorted a laugh, but didn't say anything. I got the feeling he wasn't a big talker, and given the amount of shit Tryp could say during a single mealtime, his tall, dark and silent vibe was refreshing.

We drove the rest of the way home in silence, lost in our own thoughts. We needed help—that was obvious—but we'd spent centuries purposefully not mixing with other Mythics. We were secular and unfriendly, and it was going to come back and bite us in the ass, I feared.

From what Néit had said, he was no more well liked in the Celtic community. We may truly be on our own, though we had the Valkyries' help, at least.

Pulling into Amourgeles, I waved at some of the townspeople as we passed. There was still evidence of the other night's battle, with gouged potholes littering the road, burned trees and outbuildings, rubble lying in piles. For the first time in a very long time, the villagers were looking at us with fear and trepidation. I worried that might quickly devolve to torches and pitchforks, especially if anything happened to Stavros.

Shaking my head, I pushed the thought away. I wasn't borrowing tomorrow's problems just yet. Pulling up to the rear gates in the wall, I honked. Erus appeared quickly, saluting me as he pushed open the heavy wooden doors, which had been there since before Christianity even took hold.

I honked again, and dogs skittered out of the way, making Milo laugh. He was clearly enjoying having the dogs around as much as Wren. They did liven the place up—there was never a dull moment when you had nearly a hundred dogs running around.

The basement of our building wasn't huge, but it was enough, with careful organization, to store all the food we'd bought. I'd thought about storing it in town, but if Amourgeles fell, then the Greeks would be able to starve us out of our compound. It was just one part of my plan to prepare for anything, though I hoped none of it was necessary.

Tryp appeared with the forklift he'd borrowed from the villagers, and I winced as he drove it around and around in circles, like a kid with a new bike. Milo rolled his eyes, but climbed from the truck, groaning with relief. Néit climbed out too, walking round to open the back.

Walking over to Erus, I watched Milo try and direct Tryp on how to pick up the pallets with his forklift. "How is she today?"

Not taking his eyes off the trainwreck in front of us, as Tryp clipped a tree and then the door of the truck, he replied, "She's good. She seems to have sorted her problems out with Demke, though I think he is walking on extremely thin ice."

I had a feeling we were all on thin ice, and my Gryphon huffed at how badly we'd all fucked this up. How badly *I'd* fucked up.

But I was going to make it up to her. I was going to be the best doctor, provider, confidant and—hopefully one day—lover that she'd ever had. I wasn't going to mess this up again.

*About time,* the Gryphon grumbled, and on that, we could agree.

# CHAPTER 7
## WREN

A large hand reached out to me, trying to swipe those acid-dripping claws through my torso, and I couldn't move. My feet were stuck, my whole body frozen as I just stood there and watched death lunge at me in slow motion. I screamed and screamed, but nothing happened; no sound came out.

"I'm really sorry about this." The face of Ekhidna switched to that of Demke, looking resigned. The hands became huge talons that had inky blackness pouring from them. "But I can't let them die, and they mean more to me than you." Demke's voice echoed around like thunder from far away, and I wanted to beg him to stop, to rethink what he was doing. "I can't love you."

I saw my parents crawling from the hole in the ground, their faces hazy, but their voices clear. "It was your fault we died. If we hadn't been trying to escape your bratty teenage behavior, we never would've gone on that godforsaken cruise," my dad thundered, before my mom's hand slipped on the rocks and she tumbled back into the portal to Hell.

"No!" I screamed, but it came out just as a strangled gasp.

*Wren.*

My dad looked at me like I was a fuck-up. "You'll ruin your children the same way you ruined us. Nothing follows you but death and destruction," he said, disappointment thick in the air between us.

I was shaking my head, trying to tell him I would be better, that I was sorry, but my lips wouldn't even part anymore. My dad let go and fell back into the pit, and I silently screamed once more.

*Wren, wake up.*

I stumbled to the ground, and Ekhidna was back, a giant knife in her hand. "We can make this all end now. Wouldn't you like to be happy? To be free from this pain?" she crooned.

*MATE! WAKE NOW!*

My eyes snapped open at the sound of Griff's shout in my brain, and he was there, nuzzling my face with his own feathered one. The coolness of the early morning air on my cheeks let me know I'd been crying in my sleep.

*It is okay now, my mate. It was just a dream,* Griff purred, and a sob I didn't realize had been trapped in my chest burst past my lips. Even as the specifics drifted away from my waking mind, the way it made me feel stuck with me like a dagger in the heart.

Wrapping my arms around the Gryphon's neck, I

held tight as he made the comforting thrum in his chest, his words in my mind soft and soothing. His huge head was across my chest, weighing me down in the here and now, and slowly, the thundering of my heart calmed to a dull ache.

Griff didn't move the whole time, his huge body half in the nest with me and the rest on his haunches on the floor. He must've been uncomfortable, but he didn't shift even an inch. I stroked my hand down to the point where his feathers turned to fur, and his chest vibrated with a happy noise.

"Thank you," I whispered.

*You're my mate. It is my job to keep you happy and safe. There's nowhere I won't protect you, even in your dreams.* He let out an aggravated sound that would have freaked me the hell out two weeks ago. *It irks me that you have to suffer through them at all.*

I huffed out a watery laugh. "Some places I have to take care of myself, Griff, and in my brain is one of them." I gently pushed at his head, which was massive, and he lifted it slowly, his shining gold eyes looking down at me. I wasn't sure I'd ever get used to the humanity in those eyes. I had a feeling that if he didn't think I was ready to leave the nest, he'd just plop his big head back down and keep me here until he was satisfied.

*You are correct,* he told me, making me laugh for real this time.

"You're kind of bossy—you know that, right?"

He rubbed his cheek on mine once more. *My flight is*

*full of unruly Godlings, and my cubs will be the chosen Fates. You need someone to keep everyone in line.*

I snorted at the Gryphon calling Demke a "Godling" but I wasn't going to argue. I might've forgiven him, but I was a little miffed still. With a sigh, I pushed myself into a sitting position. I was always so exhausted. Was it supposed to be like this?

The sun was high in the sky, and my bed was empty except for Griff, which told me that it was a lot later than usual. Every muscle in my torso ached with the weight of the babies, and I creaked my way to the bathroom to freshen up. I wondered if I could convince someone to just sit with me in the pool for a few hours, so I could get a little bit of relief.

Who was I kidding? I could ask for the skull of my enemy, and one of them would make me a piña colada in it.

"The Gryphon would very much enjoy that request."

I looked over my shoulder at Teron. It was a weird feeling, when they shifted between one and the other. I was always so happy to see them, but a piece of me was sad that I wouldn't see the other for an unknown amount of time.

*I'm always here, mate.* Griff's voice in my mind made me smile.

*Obviously, though my thoughts are meant to be private.*

Griff made a rude noise, and Teron rolled his eyes. "How are you feeling, Wren?"

I sighed, and when I was close enough, he wrapped

his arms around my shoulders. He held me to his chest, which was bare, and I soaked in his warmth. He tended to run hotter than the others, like the sands of his homelands were trapped just beneath the skin.

"The babies feel good. They're moving around as much as they can."

He kissed my temple, the familiar gesture making my heart thud pathetically. "I asked how *you* are feeling."

I slumped into his body. "Stressed. Tired. Sore."

"Understandable." He ushered me out of the room, down toward the pool. "Relax. I'll get one of the guys to bring you something to eat. I'll give you a checkup this afternoon, and maybe a hot oil massage."

I almost moaned at the thought of someone massaging my overly tight muscles.

True to his word, he led me to my canopied lounger and held me with soft hands as I shifted myself around to get comfortable. Although, comfortable was subjective at this point.

He squeezed my foot in his strong hands, and I groaned. Laughing, he kissed the top of it and moved away. "Unfortunately, I have a few tasks that need to be completed. Otherwise, climbing into that nest with you would be my only plan for the rest of the day."

*For the rest of my life,* Griff amended.

I waved him away. "Go. I'm just going to take another nap, probably." He nodded and left, and I was physically alone. Well, kind of. If you didn't count the babies. Or Griff in my head. Or the sleeping dogs around the pool.

I breathed in and out, letting my eyelids droop as I worked at making my whole body untense. Toes, feet, ankles… On and on I went, until my whole body felt like it lacked bones.

A foot suddenly poked out of my stomach, or maybe it was an elbow. I brushed a hand over it, and a bone-deep love flowed through my chest. I mightn't have been overjoyed about finding out I was pregnant, but I wouldn't change anything now. I'd come to terms with it, and the knowledge that I wouldn't be alone in the world anymore meant something.

Fuck, I was going to cry again.

"*Mo stóirín.*"

I looked up at Nate, who was blocking the sun. I licked my bottom lip, trying to swallow back the emotions, but I should have known better. Climbing in beside me, he pulled me onto his chest, and I snuggled my nose between his pecs. Honestly, I wanted to live in this spot forever.

He brushed his hand down my hair. "What's wrong?"

Shaking my head, I just frowned. "Bad dreams, but Griff chased them away." I playfully bit his chest just beside his nipple, and he growled softly at me. "It's all getting real, I guess. We should probably name them soon."

It had felt too scary to name them. Like it would

make me too attached if something happened. But who was I kidding? I was already attached.

Nate looked down at me. "We?"

Raising my head, I looked up into his face. "You don't want to?"

He lifted me up so he could kiss me, the harsh brush of his beard on my chin contrasting with the softness of his lips. I was obsessed with the sensation. I was obsessed with this man, period. He deepened the kiss, and I straddled his hips, wanting nothing more than to stay like this forever.

Nate pulled away first. "*Mo stóirín*, I'd be honored to name the babes with you." His voice was thick, his Irish lilt almost indecipherable. "It is a privilege I didn't think I'd ever have again. Thank you," he whispered against my lips.

He kissed me again, but they were lazy, gentle kisses, relaxing more than arousing. Eventually, he pulled off his shirt and lay down beside me, and we just lounged to the sound of the birds in the trees and our combined heartbeats.

My stomach growled softly, rousing me from my near trance-like state of chill. Nate chuckled softly, kissing the top of my head. "I'll get you something to eat—"

"Néit!"

The sound of Tryp's shout had Nate scrambling to the edge of the lounger. "What is it?" He sounded panicked, and my heart thumped.

"There's someone at the door for you!"

Nate looked over at me, a frown deep in his brow. Only one person knew where we were, and I trusted her completely. She'd saved our asses.

"Could it be?" I asked, and he shrugged.

"Stay here."

He was off then, but if he thought I was staying here, he'd lost it. I scooted off the lounger and waddled as fast as I could toward the front wall of the compound, slipping around the outside of the place instead of through the house. Sure, my belly barely fit through the gap between the corner of the building and the wall, but I still made it around to the door just as Nate bounded down the stairs, Milo at his back. I hid off to the side as he flung the heavy gate open.

On the other side was exactly who I'd thought it would be. "Néit, you big, burly fucker. You're a sight for sore eyes."

Hurrying over, I ignored the pissed look Nate gave me with feigned innocence.

Clio's face lit up. "Wren Mahone, you look as radiant as ever. Being thricely knocked-up and baking in this Goddess-forsaken heat suits you."

I laughed, because there was definitely a compliment in there somewhere. "It's good to see you, Clio."

She raised a brow, and it was then I noticed that Nate was so tense, his body was like stone. "Not as good as it is to see you right now. It makes it less likely that Néit will tear my head off," she said beneath her breath. "Remember, you big dummy, that you need all the help you can get."

Clio stepped away to reveal the woman behind her. She was beautiful, with hair so black, it seemed to absorb the sun, and eyes as dark as night. Her lips were red and full, though somehow, I didn't think it was lipstick. Gold streaks flared from her like fireworks, but even if I couldn't see her fate threads, I'd have known immediately that she was a Goddess.

"Wren Mahone, this is—"

Nate glared at Clio, shutting her up. "This is my Badb." He pronounced it like *bay-ve*. "My ex-wife."

*The fuck?*

The woman smiled, and in the expression, I could see a thousand deaths. "You may know me as the Morrigan."

Someone behind me whistled, and I heard Tryp whisper, "Holy *shit*."

That was an understatement.

# CHAPTER 8
## NATE

A face that I'd stared at for a thousand years, that had haunted me for a thousand more, looked back at me with one perfectly raised eyebrow. To some, that would sound romantic, but I meant haunted in a nightmare sense. We were a terrible match, bound only by blood and death, which was hardly a foundation for a good marriage.

They didn't call her the Queen of Nightmares for no reason.

"Hello, Néit."

She still sounded exactly the same, with the voice that made grown men piss themselves and pop an erection in equal measure, and the sarcasm that made me want to stab myself in the ear for at least seven centuries.

I turned to Clio. "The *fuck* were you thinking, Cliona?"

The *bean-sidhe* I'd formerly considered a friend gave

me a stubborn look. "I was thinking that if you're fighting monsters like Typhon, then you need some big guns. Someone who likes to fight and win. Someone whose battle cry can bring down a hundred men. Someone who gives a shit if you live or die."

I gave her an incredulous look. "And your mind went to my ex-wife?"

*Of all the foolhardy, stupid things to do…*

"She's a literal Goddess of winning damn battles, Néit. Pull your head out of your arse." Clio was getting riled too, but I was seconds from pulling my ax. Wren must have caught my tension, because she put a gentle hand on my arm, a gesture that wasn't missed by either of the women in front of me.

"I am also closely tied to the destinies of men, so who better to aid your lover than me?" Badb teased, and I narrowed my eyes at her. "Relax, Néit. I mean no harm to Wren Mahone or her children."

"My children," I snapped. "These children are mine, Badb, as if they were my own blood. I will slay you where you stand if you even *contemplate* harming them or their mother."

She tilted her head at me, so like the crow she sometimes embodied. "The God of War, finally softened, and by a mortal? I never thought I would see the day."

I curled my lip at her. "Exile will do that to a man. Gives you a different perspective on life."

"You are no man, Néit, son of Indui, King of North Lands."

I wanted to spit, I was so angry. Wounds I'd thought

were long healed broke open at the title. Thoughts of my father weren't pleasant. "You should leave. I neither need nor want your help, Badb."

Clio was muttering under her breath about my stubborn ass, but I knew she wouldn't push it.

Badb just shook her head. "Always so stubborn. It was what led to your demise, and apparently, you haven't learned too much in your exile. Are you willing to sacrifice this woman—who even I can see you love— for your pride? Again?" Old pain and shame surged through me.

"Again?" Wren whispered.

Badb turned to Wren. "I wasn't his only wife."

With those words, I pulled my ax. Milo stepped in front of Wren, pulling her behind him and shifting into his Minotaur form, ready to have my back, even though he had no idea what was going on right now. Appreciation of my new family—for that was what Wren had created—flowed through me.

Wren was as stubborn as I was, however. "Nate, I swear to fucking god, if you don't put that ax down, I'm going to jam it somewhere unpleasant. Move, Milo." The fucking traitor stepped away, though he hovered less than a breath from her. "Should I call you Morrigan? Or Badb?" she asked, addressing a literal Goddess of Death like it was nothing. The brave, stupid, love of my eternal life.

"Call me Morrigan. Badb died the same time Néit did." Her voice was almost vulnerable, and I glared at her. She'd always be Badb to me; the idea of calling her by her warrior title was insanity.

Wren nodded. "Do you intend to murder me or anyone in this house in their sleep—Nate included?"

Badb snorted a laugh. "If I wanted Néit dead, I could have done it a hundred times." She rolled her eyes at me, like *I* was being ridiculous. "Cliona is correct; I am uniquely qualified to keep you alive, and I once upon a time cared if this big oaf lived or died. I only have to see how he looks at you to know you hold his life in your hands. He has my battle loyalty still, despite the centuries between us." She smiled, and it was the same one that tended to lead soldiers between her thighs and then on to their death. Beguiling, in the worst way. "Not matrimonial loyalty, however. Many a man, woman, and monster have given me happiness since our marriage." She winked in my direction, as if I gave a fuck.

Now it was Wren's turn to eye this Goddess, like she could see inside her soul. And in a way, maybe she could. She could see the threads—could she tell if someone had good or ill intentions? She hadn't suggested she could, but it might be worth experimenting.

"And are you trying to, uh, win your ex-husband back? Because I'm not going to lie, I'm attached to him and I won't give him up without a fight." Wren stuck out her chin, and Cliona coughed to cover a laugh. It was like a lamb before a lion, but she was so fucking brave. I could see respect flicker through Badb's eyes, fleeting but there.

"No, Wren Mahone, I don't want him back. I am here because I wish to be on the right side of the wheel as it turns. I am here because it is time there were new Fates, and if the Greek Pantheon think they can fuck with the will of fate, then that affronts me personally." Yeah, I could see that. "But Cliona is also correct; I enjoy a good battle, and there hasn't been a decent God battle in a thousand years. I don't want to miss it."

Silence fell over the group, and I realized there were more of the guys at my back. They would protect Wren with their lives, as would I.

Finally, Wren shrugged. "Fair enough. Come in, we have lemonade."

Clio didn't manage to hold back her laugh this time. "I love this one, Néit." She stepped around me and followed Wren inside, but deliberately didn't show me her back. Clever, that little banshee. She was on my shit list for this stunt.

Badb hesitated. "I mean it, Néit. On Fea's eternal soul, I don't have any ill intentions."

Like a dagger to the heart, she made her point.

She sauntered past me, and I let her go. Because Badb might be a heinous bitch at times, but no one had loved Fea more than her, not even me.

I didn't even notice Erus hanging back until he stepped up beside me, laying a hand on my shoulder as we followed. I turned to the Demigod, who I barely knew, but who'd taken a place on the short list of people I would care about if they died.

"Are you all right?" he asked softly.

"Yeah," I muttered back. I could have done without this little family reunion.

Erus raised an eyebrow at me. "She seems... intense."

I laughed, because intense was an understatement. Badb took her position as the most fearsome creature on a battlefield very seriously. Her favor could win or lose wars. "Intense is putting it lightly."

I watched her with Wren, looking for any sign of treachery or ill intent, despite what Badb had sworn. I knew words were easy. But her posture was relaxed, and she didn't look like she was plotting. I remembered her plotting face well; it wasn't something you could easily forget.

*Fuck me.* This was a disaster. One thing I knew, though, was that neither Badb nor Clio were staying within the walls of the compound. I'd talk to Demke or Teron about alternative accommodations, but no way was my ex-wife sleeping down the hall from the woman I loved.

Wren and Milo led everyone out to the grape trellis, and I wasn't surprised to see Demke there, reclining like he didn't have a care in the world, not even the sudden appearance of another Mythic who rivaled him in power. I was also unsurprised to see the Gryphon lying beside him, almost like a pet. If a pet could pop your head from your neck in an instant.

It was a subtle show of force.

Cliona squealed as a whole bunch of the dogs yawned and stretched, some coming over warily to check out the newcomers. "Oh my goddess, puppies!" No one liked a squealing banshee, but she gushed as she fell to her knees and was ferociously licked by a bunch of dogs, who probably had terrible breath and more than a few parasites.

Wren chuckled, and as Cy sidled up to her in his dog form, she buried her fingers in his soft coat. She definitely forgot he was a man at times, and he took full advantage of that fact. But the adoring way he looked up at her had me holding my tongue and leaving my ax by my side.

While I'd been distracted by the spectacle the pack were making, Badb and Demke had been having a stare-off. Milo had an arm wrapped around Wren's waist, like he was ready to throw himself between her and dueling Gods at any moment. Wren was smart enough to recognize a volatile situation when she saw one, so she didn't seem to protest being shielded.

Finally, whatever pecking-order bullshit was over, and Badb inclined her head. "I am the Morrigan. I have come to pledge my allegiance to the Mother of Fate."

Wren's head snapped to me. *Mother of Fate?* she mouthed silently, and I shrugged.

Demke looked past Badb to me, and it was probably the first time in centuries that she'd been so easily dismissed. "Is her word good?"

*Well, fuck.* The Badb I'd known would have

murdered him where he stood for insinuating her word meant nothing. Despite the faint pulse of her jaw, she didn't seem angry at Demke's words. Everyone was looking at me now, and I knew that Demke was leaving it in my hands.

Did I trust Badb's word? She'd been known to lie, but I didn't think she was at this moment. Maybe that was naive of me, but still, I nodded.

Clio let out a sigh of relief, and I shot her a pissed expression. Dropping her gaze, she went back to stroking one of the dogs that had hair like a boar-bristle brush.

Erus appeared with glasses and a huge pitcher of iced lemonade. And a bottle of rakí. I didn't know where their supply was from, but the clear alcohol seemed to be more plentiful than water in this town. "Well, if that's sorted, please sit. Have a drink."

Clio came over to sit at the table, and soon enough, Badb sat beside her. I sat as far away as possible, while Milo led Wren to sit beside me. I wrapped an arm around her, an obvious show of where my loyalties lay —not with my ex-wife.

Throwing me slightly guilt-ridden looks, Clio smiled at Wren. "You're looking radiant. Huge, but radiant."

I rolled my eyes at my old friend. "You can't tell a pregnant woman that she looks huge, Cliona, for fuck's sake."

Wren, proving once again why I loved her, just laughed. "I think it's safe to call someone huge if they can't sit up in bed without the help of at least two mystical creatures." She shook her head. "I can't wait until they're here, but at the same time, I'm terrified of them being out in the world. It's like a sword of Damocles hanging over my head."

Out of the corner of my eye, I saw Milo run his fingers up and down her spine soothingly. I hadn't ever imagined that I could be happy sharing her, but I was beginning to realize that I was.

Nodding solemnly, Clio's face folded into one I knew well. Her business face. I might know her as my fun, lighthearted friend, but it didn't negate the fact she was the representative and key negotiator of our Pantheon in the States. "You aren't wrong. It's why I'm here. And it's why I brought Morrigan." She sucked in a deep breath. "There's a war brewing, and people are gathering armies. Some will stand behind the new Fates, and some will try to maintain the status quo. It's spread beyond the Greek Mythics now. You should expect more people like us to arrive soon. The time to hide is almost over."

Ice ran through my veins at her words. It might not be the cry of the *bean-sidhe*, but for our little group, it may as well be.

# CHAPTER 9
## CYDON

O

I looked at the large hound in front of me. Attie was a loyal, steadfast canine. He'd never had a home, had been born on the streets of Heraklion, and knew nothing but survival. Wiry and a dirty dishwater color, he wasn't a dog that would be rescued by well-meaning tourists. He was big, scary, and one hundred percent mutt, but he'd been the first to answer my call, and even now, he was the first to volunteer for missions.

*The street dogs say there's a weird energy on the island, but they don't know if it's the new Mystics still here, or intruders.*

Talking to the dogs was less coherent than communicating with humans—more single words, body language, images and sounds—but when you'd been doing it forever, it was like a second language. I let out a low growl in my chest to express my disgruntlement about strangers on our turf, and Attie yipped agreement.

*Keep an eye out. And be careful. Where Mythics might have ignored the pack before, after the latest attack, they'll be watching for you now. Keep low. Stay safe.*

Attie made a grumble of agreement. *I have enlisted the help of*—he made a hacking noise, like he was going to puke up rancid meat—*the cats. No one is watching for them, and they owe me one.*

Communicating with cats was different than communicating with dogs, and I couldn't say I'd been friendly with many of them over the years. But we could communicate, and if they were willing to help, I'd take it.

*Thank them for me. Tell them that if they need assistance, they have the gratitude of Cydon.* I looked at my old friend. *You do too. If you wish to get off the streets, the Mother of Fate will find you a home. Or regular meals, at least. This town will be safe for us all.*

Attie grumbled at the idea that he'd need assistance from humans. *I'll tell the street dogs. Some of the younger ones may wish for an easier life.* He conveyed the idea with a flash of an image—scraggly-looking puppies curled up on fluffy pillows beside full bowls.

I touched my cheek to his, a sign of affection from his alpha, and he huffed and trotted away back to town. I'd put the offer out there, and that was all I could do.

Tilting my face to the wind, I picked up the scent of Wren in the air. Even the thought of her made my heart thrum heavily in my chest. I wanted to go to her immediately, but I forced myself to finish my rounds of the village. Not all the dogs who'd fought in the battle had come inside the compound's gates. Some of my pack trusted me and would follow me into battle, but had a distrust of both Mythics and humans. They hid out in the unoccupied land around the village, making dens in dense bushes and rock crevices.

I particularly wanted to check on the pregnant female. She'd never been permitted to fight, but her mate had answered the call, and so she came too. Honestly, the extra food and shelter would be beneficial to the survival of their young, even if there was the risk of death during the fighting.

A street dog's life was always shadowed by the risk of death. Though this option came with an abundance of food and the illusion of safety, at least for a little while.

I yipped happily at the townsfolk I saw as I went past, stopping to greet at Stavros where he ate lunch at the *psistaria*. Stavros was a wily old bastard. Some part of him knew that I wasn't a normal dog. He'd always spoken to me like I was a human, just another old friend to share his worries with. It might've been because I had been an "old" dog back when he was a boy. I'd disappear down to Heraklion every ten or so years, and come back after a few more, so no one really could say for sure I was the same white dog who'd lived in the town for so long, but I knew a few of the older inhabitants wondered.

I always returned to this place. I never stayed away long, not in a thousand years. Because I knew this was the place I would be needed.

Stavros didn't doubt himself about anything, let alone this. He gave me a piece of cheese, which I ate from his fingers happily. "You seem to have more than a few friends roaming about the place, Cy." I tilted my head at him, the closest thing I could do to a shrug. I had my reasons, and he knew those reasons. "More than a few have made their way in front of the fires of locals." I gave him a toothy dog grin, and he shook his head. "The girl is okay up there with the Others?"

The townspeople always called them the Others. Not part of the town, but as fundamental to Amourgeles as the old stone roads they still drove on or the vista of the land they saw from their front doors. There was no Amourgeles without Demke and his Demigods.

But no one in town was ever quite game enough to call them Gods out loud.

I tilted my head at him again. What would he do if she wasn't okay? Stavros was a good human; he mightn't want to go against Demke and the others, but he would if he thought Wren was being mistreated. I sat and wagged my tail, my mouth opening so my tongue could loll out happily. Positive body language helped me communicate with the humans in this form too.

Finally, I nodded, in case he needed something more concrete than my attempts at dog body language. He gave a harrumph, then reached out to give me the remains of his lamb bone. I took it in my jaws and trotted away happily, out of town and down one of the dirt roads toward a small outcropping of trees and craggy rocks, where the less social members of the pack were staying. There was a weather-beaten stone building, with a roof that was one harsh storm away from collapsing, and I knew that's where the pregnant female was bunkered down to whelp her pups.

I accepted the greetings of the other dogs in the area, immediately feeling at peace in the pack. There was nothing like the sheer acceptance of street dogs. Sure, there were occasional squabbles amongst them to figure out who fit where in the hierarchy, but there really wasn't any of that alpha/beta stuff you heard about with wolves.

Street dogs were territorial over three things: food, mates, and dens. If everyone played nice on those three points, you were more likely to have a friend for life. And with plenty of food and no real need to fight for dens, it was relaxed outside of town in their temporary packlands.

No one even tried to take the food from my mouth.

When I walked into the rundown building, I saw the mother dog straight away. Turns out, she'd had her pups already. Walking over to her hovering mate, I dropped the bone at his feet.

*Congratulations. A fine litter.* From what I could see, there were at least nine puppies, which meant a lot of mouths to feed for the mother.

The male, Listís, gave a happy chuff of appreciation. He lifted the bone and took it over to the mother, sniffing at the squirming babies. They weren't more than lumps with legs at this point, but they were certainly cute. I padded over slowly, watching the parents for any sign they might get upset at my proximity to their young, but the mother, Tsíli, just wagged her tail at me tiredly.

I booped each of them with my nose, committing their scents to my memory. These were the first pups that had been born into the pack since I'd created it, and that made them special—at least to me.

*It would be safer within the walls,* I told the parents, and they looked at each other. *There is no pressure, but the Mother of Fate will make sure you're safe and they're protected, just like her own young.*

I was making promises on Wren's behalf, but I felt like I knew her enough to know this was what she'd want. She wouldn't want them to be out here, at risk of becoming food for a monster creeping through the darkness, trying to breach the walls of the compound.

Tsíli laid her head down, obviously still tired. Listís stared at his young, all different shades of gray and red and white, making it impossible to tell what breed they might have originated from.

*We'll do what's best for the pups,* he said. *Take us to your mistress.*

I laughed at the idea that Wren was my mistress, but didn't protest. Shifting into a man, I went to the basket in the corner of the building. I kept some old clothes here, in case any situation called for me to be a man and not a dog. It looked like today was that day.

A plain blue t-shirt and a pair of well-worn jeans with one too many holes in them were pulled out of the basket. Thankfully, Tsíli hadn't decided to have her babies on them. There was also a hooded sweatshirt in case I needed it in winter, but for today, it would do as some soft bedding to transport the young.

I looked down at Listís, who was now eyeing me warily. *It's true that you turn human. I always thought it was a rumor, despite the call. You really are a God.*

I grinned at him, wishing he could see that I was the same entity, on two legs or four. *I'm not a man. I'm not a dog. But I am pack, first and foremost.* Mostly true. I was Wren's first and foremost, but she was also pack. She just didn't know it yet.

I put the basket down beside Tsíli, then stepped out so they could put the pups in one by one without having to keep one eye on me too. While I might be pack, a parent's protective instincts overrode such things as hierarchy.

The day was getting hot, but I knew that soon enough, the nights would cool considerably and winter would come. I smiled at the dogs outside, who were also more wary of me in this form, wagging their tails in greeting but staying a healthy distance from me.

Just over the rise was the house I'd used for myself over the last few centuries. It was basic, just a place to lay my head until destiny finally presented what it had planned for me.

A flash of golden hair in that direction had me stiffening, my whole body going ramrod straight. *It couldn't be... could it?*

Leaning into the shack, I found Listís in the darkened corner. "I'll be right back." Moving back across the small clearing, I searched out one of my most trusted hounds, guarding the edges of the shaded packlands. Much like Attie, Sola was a street dog who had no interest in becoming someone's pet. "Be on alert, but don't alarm the others just yet," I said softly, then jogged as casually as I could up the incline toward my home.

*What the hell's going on?*

Apollo stood beside the small wooden door of my home, though he didn't turn to acknowledge I was there. "You know, this is the first time I've set foot on Crete since the fall of the Minoans."

I tried not to growl. "There's a good reason for that."

"This island was as much mine once as it was theirs," he sniffed.

I shook my head. "Then you chose the wrong side. Why are you here?" I knew from experience that if I didn't get him to the point, he'd talk in circles for hours.

"Can't a father come check on his son after he's been locked out of his house for centuries?"

My spine stiffened at his words. "No."

Apollo sighed, putting his hands on his hips. He was a good-looking man, which was why he had more progeny. He was hard to resist, according to my mother. "Fine. Your brother had a prophecy."

Delphos. Founder of Delphi and all those annoying Oracles. Apollo was known as a prophetic God, which meant many of his offspring had inherited the power of prophecy. Except me. I turned into a dog.

I lowered my head. I wanted to throw him out, make him leave, but I knew that if I didn't hear it, I would forever wonder.

Lifting my head, I glared at the man who sired me. "Tell me."

# CHAPTER 10
## WREN

Lying against Nate's chest in front of the television, I could almost fool myself that nothing had changed today. Nate's arm was banded tightly under my breasts, like he was worried I'd run from him, now that I knew he wasn't a virgin when I'd met him. I wasn't that delusional.

Sure, Nate's ex-wife was beautiful. Scary as fuck, but gorgeous in a way I couldn't even imagine, let alone envy. She held herself like she knew she was the baddest person in the room, and while Nate might protest, I wasn't sure any of the guys could take her one-on-one. Her power felt more like Demke's than Nate's. The Godliness of her made my eyes sting.

We'd all suffered through the world's most awkward sitdown meeting, with Nate glaring at both Morrigan and Clio in equal measure, as they delivered bad news after bad news. Apparently, I'd split the world, which seemed to delight Morrigan endlessly, which in turn was terrifying. The infighting was already becoming bloody, like everyone had just been waiting for an excuse to turn on each other.

Clio had told us that Boston became the epicenter for a time, as monsters tracked me to my hometown. They'd even begun circling Java Llama, scaring the shit out of my former boss. The idea of Bob pissing his pants in front of his beat-down Nova made me sadistically happy.

Nate had asked about Mrs. Byrne's house—which was our house now, I guess—and my stomach had soured at the thought of the place being destroyed.

Fortunately, Clio had given us one little piece of good news on that front. "Someone bolstered the wards. I'm not sure anyone but Wren and the Dalai Lama could get in now."

"Do you know who did it?"

Shaking her head, she'd told us she hadn't recognized the signature of the wards' magic, but knew they weren't Celtic in origin.

I didn't know if that was reassuring, or even more terrifying. Who would do that? It seemed almost... personal.

Had I been around more Mythics all these years and never known?

I rolled my head to look up at Nate. "Mrs. B wasn't a Mythic, was she?" If she had been, surely she wouldn't have died.

Nate nuzzled his cheek against the top of my head. "No. She was human. The best of them, at that."

I frowned. "Did she know about you, and all this?" I tried to imagine devoutly Catholic Mrs. B, who'd gone to church twice a week and lit candles, holding onto that faith, knowing Gods like Nate and Demke existed.

Nate chuckled. "Oh yeah, she knew all right. Didn't stop her from ordering me around like she was my elder, as if I didn't have shirts older than she was. It was part of her charm. She treated me not as someone to be worshiped, but just as someone who mattered, who needed to be kept anchored to the world." He sighed. "I'll miss her."

A tear rolled down my cheek, dripping down to land on his bicep. "Me too." I sighed, snuggling closer to his chest, even though the heat made everything sweaty and sticky. "If we were having a girl, I would've called her Zelda."

He huffed a little laugh. "Next time?"

The noise I made could've been mistaken for a laugh, if you ignored the slightly hysterical undertones. "I think we'll be a little busy for a while, don't you think?"

He growled, rolling me easily so I was straddling his hips. He was clad only in thin swim shorts, and they provided very little barrier to the bulge beneath. "Maybe a little busy, but I'm still going to imagine pumping you so full of my release that you can't help but get big and round with my baby every time we make love. Practice makes perfect."

I groaned. Teron had suggested no sex until the babies were born, but man, that felt like an eternity when Nate's hard cock was *right there*, nudging my clit. I moaned a little as I wriggled my hips, trying to get some relief.

"Are we too old to dry hump?" I whispered conspiratorially, catching his lips with my own. His hands landed on my hips, dragging me against him as he fucked my mouth with his tongue. When he finally pulled away, I was gasping for air, my whole body on fire.

He grinned at me, a smug smirk that was full of male pride. "You're never too old to grind on my cock, *mo stóirín*."

He thrust up against me, and I moaned against his lips. It wasn't quite what I wanted, but it was enough. Grinding on him, I threw my head back as his hands wandered higher, cupping my full breasts.

Until someone cleared their throat.

The low rumble of annoyance in Nate's throat might have been more terrifying if I didn't know him so well. Looking over my shoulder, I took in Cy's grinning face.

"If I were you, I'd run," I teased, but Cy just grinned wider.

Beside him were two dogs—one big and bulky, and if I wasn't wrong, the very pregnant mama dog who now looked a little less pregnant. I blinked in surprise, then noticed the basket in Cy's arms.

"You had your pups," I squealed, climbing off an irritated Nate's lap. Before, I might've run over and looked in the basket, but I was beginning to realize that dogs were a lot more empathetic than humans gave them credit for. Stopping a few feet away, I looked at the dogs on guard at Cy's feet. "Congratulations on your litter. I'm sure it's a relief not to be pregnant anymore." I stroked my own rounded stomach, unsure if they could understand me, but I trusted that Cy would translate later for me if they couldn't. I bowed my head in their direction, trying to remember what the dog whisperer on TV had said about body language and eye contact. "Thank you for coming to my aid."

I'd been thanking each of the dogs as I came across them. They'd had the most significant losses, and it seemed only right to show my appreciation to the pack.

The mama dog gave a small butt wiggle, and I took that to mean she didn't find me a threat. Looking at her soft brown eyes, I smiled. "May I see your babies?"

I looked between her and Cy, who I was pretty sure was communicating with them somehow. He gently lowered the basket to the ground before helping me sit down. Not going to lie, with a belly this big, it wasn't an easy feat. Though as the tiny bodies wiggled around in the mish-mash of clothes, it was worth it.

"They're just beautiful," I whispered to the mama dog. The pups squeaked for their mother, and she nuzzled them with her nose. I wanted to reach out and pet them, but knew that would be overstepping. I wasn't sure how I knew, but I did.

Looking up at Cy, I tilted my head toward the adult dogs. "What are their names?"

"Tsíli and Listís. They're mates. They haven't named the pups; they'll grow into their own names, eventually." He smiled down at them. "Listís is an excellent warrior." Tsíli gave him a sharp-eyed expression, making Cy chuckle. "Tsíli wants you to know that she is also an excellent fighter, when she is not mothering a litter of puppies."

"Mothers are the most ferocious of fighters," I told her admiringly. "Cy will get you settled somewhere safe and quiet."

Cy nodded, and the amusement slid from his face. "We need to speak once I get this family settled." He looked between me and Nate, and I could tell it was serious by the downturned curve of his lips. Cy was usually happy, a golden retriever of a man.

I sighed. Small happinesses. I had to hold onto these fleeting joyful moments, or I might have a complete breakdown and run screaming naked through the streets of Amourgeles. Nodding, I wandered back toward Nate and lay down beside him. "It's always serious news. Maybe I should move to a tiny, uninhabited island in the middle of the ocean."

Nate raised an eyebrow at me, but didn't disagree. "It's okay to be angry, *mo stóirín*. You didn't ask for any of this. Though, selfishly, I'm glad you needed me in some small way. Otherwise, I would have spent decades just watching you from afar and never making a move."

My lips curled. When Nate had been my neighbor, I'd spent my fair share of time looking at him with goo-goo eyes from across the hall. If it hadn't been for the babies and how overwhelmed I'd been, I probably would've run the other way every time he spoke to me, just as I had for the last five years.

Rubbing my stomach, I leaned up and kissed his chin. "Selfishly, I'm happy too." One of the babies head-butted me in what felt like a lung, and I coughed. "What about Byrne as a name?" I laid my head on Nate's chest, and he rubbed my stomach, like he was trying to herd the babies downwards. There really wasn't that much room in there.

"I like it. Though Byrne means 'from Bran' after the king from the area where the name originated. He was a decent king for the time. Bran's a good solid name, not quite as harsh as Byrne."

*Bran.* I tasted the name, and it felt right. "Did we just name our baby?"

He laughed, leaning forward to give me a scorching brand of a kiss. "I think we did. One down, two to go."

Cy reappeared, and with him came Demke. The enigmatic Minoan God looked at my position against Nate's chest, and for a moment, I thought I saw a flash of envy on his face, but it was gone just as quickly.

I'd figure that out later. One crisis at a time.

Flopping onto the floor beside me, Cy looked longingly at the end of the couch. Sometimes, he slept behind my knees in his dog form. A totally normal place for a dog to sleep, but if I actually thought about the fact he was a man nuzzled beneath my ass cheeks with his nose pressed into my thighs, I freaked out a little.

He held my gaze, but I got the feeling that his attention was on Demke. "Apollo is on the island."

Demke's hiss told me that was a bad thing, but I didn't need to be a theologian to know that Apollo was part of the Greek Pantheon. "What does he want?"

"There's been a prophecy."

The world went quiet. Nate's chest went rigid beneath me. It was like time stopped, like history was holding its breath.

Demke turned ashy beneath his normal golden tan. Fear flashed across his face, his eyes recounting a moment far away in a time, long before the world as I knew it existed. He was caught in a memory of a different woman, a different prophecy.

I reached out, gripping his hand, anchoring him to this moment with me. He looked down at our fingers, recognition slowly leeching back into his face along with the color of his cheeks. Swallowing hard, he nodded at Cy. "Tell us."

Not taking his eyes from mine, Cy blew out a long breath. "With the death of the mother, the new weavers will be born into the tapestry, and a new age will begin."

Icy dread filled my veins. *Well, that doesn't sound good.*

# CHAPTER II
## TRYP

The prophecy from Apollo had been like pouring hot oil into an ant nest. Everyone was panicking, and we were almost divided about how to react. None of us wanted to lose Wren. It would also mean all of us would go with her, our lives intrinsically bound to hers now. Then who would care for the babies?

I almost wished that Demke had held out a little longer before bonding with Wren. He might be apathetic at times, but there would be no way he'd leave the babies to fend for themselves if anything happened to the rest of us.

Wren, on the other hand, seemed to be pointedly ignoring the prophecy. She didn't want to talk about it, plan around it, or hear about it. She'd decided to be in complete denial, and honestly, I was right there with her. Prophecies weren't set in stone; sometimes it only took one small deviation for it to not come to fruition. Worrying about it every day wasn't going to help, and it would probably just be fulfilled sooner, especially as stress was bad for both her and the babies.

Teron, however, was beside himself with worry. He'd been awake for days, consuming every piece of literature he could find, sourcing medicine and equipment we probably wouldn't even need. He was basically setting up a specialist obstetrics hospital in our formal living room. Well, he was when he could wrestle control back from the Gryphon.

The very thought of his mate dying had turned the normally reasonable beast into an absolute nightmare. He'd built the walls of Wren's bed nest so high, she was going to need a stepladder to climb into bed soon.

"How much can we trust Apollo's word, anyway?" Néit asked. He made a good point, but I wasn't so sure that Apollo was lying. He'd gained absolutely nothing from handing us this prophecy.

They were considered almost sacred among Mythics. Somewhere along the line, a myth had been perpetuated that if you didn't give a receiver their intended prophecy, ill fortune would befall you ten times over. We were all a superstitious bunch, so if someone had told Apollo the prophecy, he might've felt obligated to share.

But I wasn't about to take it at face value, even if he was Cy's father. Even if he'd once been as happy here on Crete with the Goddess as we'd been.

Delphos had always been rather impartial as well. I doubted he would suffer too much from the change of the Fates. He hated people. Rumor had it that he'd been absolutely elated when people stopped doing pilgrimages to the temples of Delphi. He just wanted to live in his little cave and have his prophecies and get on with his life. He would still have prophecies under the next Fates, and the ones after them. He wouldn't be losing power with the shift.

The only people who stood to lose real power were the Moirai, and if Clio and Morrigan were to be believed, they were good at convincing others that they too would lose power if there were new Fates, especially because the triplets wouldn't be obviously aligned with any Pantheon.

Morrigan obviously believed that they would fall under the Celtic Pantheon, since Wren had been maneuvered into Néit's path. There weren't enough of us Minoans left to rise through the ranks of power. Unless Demke rose to some monolithic level of power, we were no threat to the status quo, yet she'd been very obviously placed in our path too.

Would these be the first impartial Fates? Would we all die, and the different Pantheons come to fight over possession of them, to raise them and use them for their own gains?

Worry was beginning to burn a hole in my gut, but Wren was looking to me to be the calm, easygoing one right now. Teron had her in his examination room once again, and then I intended to eat her out until she was so relaxed, she'd be as floppy as overcooked noodles.

I had to do my part, and realistically, I was never going to be useful in the war room with Néit and

Demke, or Morrigan. I couldn't look after her health like Teron, nor protect the borders like Cy. I couldn't construct her a fortress masquerading as a nursery like Milo. In fact, he was constructing nursery-style bolt-holes all over the compound, with Erus helping him.

What I *could* do was make her orgasm on my tongue several times a day, ensuring she was happy and content. A task I would do with a smile on my face.

I skipped into the examination room, and when Wren looked up at me, giving me a tight smile, I knew I wasn't a moment too soon. Teron was checking on the babies yet again with the ultrasound machine. If he kept this up, by the time the triplets were born, they'd have enough radio waves in them that they'd come out picking up the BBC.

Just like a week ago, they looked like tiny little aliens, all smooshed together with hardly any room. Teron was making satisfied noises as he entered numbers on his tablet.

I walked over and leaned down, kissing her softly. "Beautiful girl, you take my breath away."

She did. She was glorious, the epitome of life and nurturing. I'd already started painting her every time I picked up my brush, and I had no intention of stopping until I'd recreated her in every position, every light, and every season, even if it took my entire immortal life.

She snorted. "You can't say that when my belly button sticks out so far, it may as well be a nose."

I leaned down, kissing the aforementioned button. She gripped my hair lightly, making me moan softly.

Everything was stretched tight like a drum, and along with massaging her feet, I made a note to rub some lotion into her stomach as well.

Teron made a tsking noise. "No sex." He sounded no nonsense, but his eyes said something entirely different. They were full of longing, of desire for the woman in front of us. Maybe he needed a little push, a little demonstration to show him what he was missing, being so noble and professional.

Smirking at him, I shifted down the other end of the chaise lounge he was using as an examination table. "You say that like there aren't a million other options." I kissed her shapely calf muscle and felt her eyes on me, but she didn't move to stop me. In fact, when I reached her knees, she let them fall apart, giving me a perfect view of her delicious body. I had to sit up like a meerkat looking over a molehill to see her face over her stomach, but when I met her eyes, they stole my oxygen. She was staring at me with so much desire, it threatened to burn me alive.

It spurred me on, sending pleasure down my body as I climbed higher. I dragged her shorts and underwear down her legs and tossed them over my shoulder, then got back to work as I sucked and licked at her thighs. Already, I could see her folds glistening, ready for me.

"Have you ever seen a more beautiful pussy, Teron?" I asked my brother, who was watching us with heat in his eyes, his tablet sitting forgotten in his hands. "So wet and ready to melt on my tongue." To punctuate my words, I licked up her slit in one long stroke, and she groaned, writhing around, trying to get closer. I flicked her clit with the tip of my tongue, making her gasp.

"So perfect," Teron grunted, and I could see the hard bulge of his dick in my peripheral vision.

I feasted, reaching up one hand to stroke at her breasts, pinching a nipple and making her buck hard against my body. She was so beautifully receptive, and I would happily do this every day for the rest of my immortal life, because this would never get old. Oh sure, maybe she could ride my face. Or maybe she could suck one of the others' cocks while we did it. The possibilities were endless. But I was addicted to the taste of this woman.

*Send me to the Underworld with a messy mouth and her cries of pleasure in my ears.*

I mean, the no-penetration thing made it difficult, especially when I wanted nothing more than to plunge my tongue deep inside her and lick her juices from the source, but I resisted. Instead, I worked her clit like it was my own personal pleasure button.

She was hissing like a wildcat all too soon, and as she came all over my face, I let my sigh of happiness cool against her folds. I wasn't done, though, not yet. I looked at Teron, who looked like he was in pain, his eyes almost glowing from watching his mate come. He was massaging his cock on the outside of his pants, and I knew it must be doing something for Wren, because her pretty core was fluttering hungrily.

"Do you want to watch our doctor fuck his hand, wishing he was me right now, Little Dumpling?"

She sucked in a breath, and when she released it, it manifested as one delicious word. "Yes."

I looked over tauntingly at Teron, daring him to play. He was many things—cool and calm, but also competitive as hell. There was no way he'd turn down the challenge in my eyes.

His hand went to the button of his pants, flicking it open easily. It had been a long time since I'd seen Teron naked. He didn't play the way Erus and I did, and it had been an age since we'd all participated in group sex. Nearly a thousand years, if not more.

However, one thing hadn't changed. He was a beautiful man, all deep golden skin and rippling muscles. I knew exactly why my Wren was looking at him hungrily.

He pulled his dick from his pants, and she moaned softly, which I took as my cue to get back to work. I mean, they say if you did what you love, you'd never work a day in your life, and I intended to become Chief Head of … well, Head. Chairman of Cunnilingus.

Sucking her clit between my lips, her thighs straining against my head, I reached out one hand to grip her ankle, holding her still as I dragged my mouth away. "Tell him what you want, Wren." Then I left them to it as I went back to swirling my tongue, tracing the words to *The Iliad* on her clit.

"I want you to stroke yourself," she gasped, and when he did, I swear her clit pulsed.

*Good.*

He had an intense look on his face, and I wondered if the Gryphon was also participating in our little voyeurism session, because she went from wet to gushing way too fast. I lapped and sucked, chasing her orgasms until Teron's groan told me he was finishing. Wren reached down and gripped my hair tightly to tug me away.

I moaned, but I wouldn't touch my dick. Not yet. I wanted Erus to taste her on me and then fuck me senseless.

"Enough," she gasped out, and I smiled smugly against her.

*Oh yeah. Guess who's gonna get a Christmas bonus for a job well done this year?*

# CHAPTER 12
## ERUS

Given the Morrigan and the leader of the *bean-sidhe* were in town, I shouldn't have been surprised by the knock at the front door, and was even less surprised to see the Valkyries had returned. I was slightly concerned by the amount of luggage they seemed to have brought with them, though.

"Erastus! We've returned to continue our sacred duty."

Without their armor, and with their wings on display, they looked like tourists on the island for a girls' trip. It was disconcerting, given that I'd seen Hildr with monster insides splattered across her body and a smile on her face.

Stepping aside, I ushered them in, though I didn't even attempt to take their bags. I liked my hands attached to my arms. "Your sacred duty?"

"Protection of the new Fates, and the Mother of

Fate," Hrist informed me like I was stupid. "We also brought gifts and mead. Where are your barracks?"

We did not have barracks. We didn't even have enough bedrooms in this place, despite the size. "Uh, come on into the kitchen, and we'll figure something out."

Maybe we could eventually appropriate one of the outbuildings as a bunkhouse, but none of them were at that stage yet. Plus, we didn't have enough beds, food, or linen.

They seemed to have dipped into their mead already as they chirped loudly with each other, roaming the house like they owned it. It was still standing because of their help, though, so that gave them a little bit of ownership in my book. They were smiling and laughing, so at odds with the serious warriors we'd met last time.

Wren was drawn from her room by the sound, meeting us in the hall. Noticing her, as one, they dropped to a single knee. It was hilarious, considering they were all in sundresses and cross-body bags. "Mother of Fate."

Giving them an amused smile, she shook her head. "Not you guys too? Just call me Wren, please. I'm not sure I'm ready to have such a serious name."

Hrist shrugged. "Ready or not, the annals of history have named you this. Better to just roll with it. Plus, being named is a serious honor in our Pantheon, and most others. You would be a fool to reject it and the influence it gives you over others."

Wren gave a short nod. "I understand. But how about here, among us, you call me Wren? I'd like to have a break from being 'The Chosen One' inside these four walls."

Hildr bowed her head solemnly. "Understood." Then she bounced to her feet. "We bought gifts for the new Fates from home." Her voice was muffled as she looked inside a giant box on wheels. "But most importantly, we brought you these, from Odin and Frigg, as well as Freya, and her twin Freyr." Swooping her hands into the box, she pulled out a gray tabby kitten, a piglet that looked almost golden, and a raven chick. Well, not a chick; it had all its flight feathers, but it still looked young.

Wren stared at the baby animals, shock making her lips fall open. She didn't know what these were, but I did. Obviously, Hrist understood that the Norse histories would be foreign to Wren as well, because she explained. "It is the whelping season in Asgard, and these are the offspring of some of our greatest animal companions." She pointed to the raven. "One of the most recent chicks from Huginn's sired clutch. His name is Trig. He will help the Fates decide what is truth and what is deception as they grow."

She pointed to the kitten. "This is Von, the kitten of Freya's favored battle cats. He will be a fierce warrior and will protect them for as long as they have him by their sides." Lastly, she pointed at the piglet, who shone golden under the overhead lights. "A piglet sired by Gullinbursti, the boar mount ridden by Freyr. He will be protective, and his golden mane will show them their way, even in the darkest of times. His name is Galt."

She cleared her throat, her eyes catching Wren's, her face as serious as it was in battle. "You have been honored by these tributes. These are the offspring of some of our greatest steeds and warrior companions. They've never been given as gifts outside of our own kind before."

The solemnity of the gifts wasn't lost on Wren. "I am deeply thankful. How do I express my thanks to Odin and Frigg, and Freya and Freyr?"

Hildr smiled. "I'll help you with the appropriate prayers of thanks later. We also brought mead!"

The moment over, the Valkyries left their suitcases in the long hall as they all moved toward the back court-yard. Wren leaned down, holding out a hand to the small animals still sitting on the ground where they'd been deposited. They looked slightly freaked out.

"Hello, little ones. I bet this is scary, isn't it?" She left her fingers slightly curled in front of them, so they could sniff. Trig, the raven, hopped up onto her wrist like he was trained to do it, walking slowly up to her shoulder before snuggling into her hair. She laughed softly, as both the boar piglet and kitten sniffed at her fingers. "I will care for you until my babies are old enough to care for you themselves. I'm sure you're hungry. How about I grab you some food, then we'll find a place for you to live? Maybe introduce you to the puppies?"

She stood, the raven clutching tightly to her shoulder, and the kitten and piglet following behind her. As she walked away, a different memory, a different age, overlaid the present. A different woman, always surrounded by animals, always with something perched on her shoulder or weaving around her feet. A time long ago, when I'd also been happy.

Wren looked over her shoulder, her eyes wide and joyful. She let out a silent squeal of happiness that the tiny animals were following her. My heart wanted to burst. It might be a similar scene, but I was a different man. I'd been happy back then, but not like this. Not like I was with Wren.

She completed a part of me that I hadn't even known was empty. I loved her so much that it felt like a part of my heart, of my soul, had been closed off, just waiting for her to burst in and make it her own.


THE HOUSE WAS alive in a way that I never could have predicted. If an Oracle had come to us last year and said that in twelve months' time, you'd have a pregnant bond, a house filled with Gods and Demigods from other Pantheons, and so many animals that you had to watch where you stepped, I would have laughed in their face. I would have told them that no one could cross our wards. That I had lost my heart to a dead Goddess so long before, and it was shriveled and useless now. That we were too set in our ways for such trivial things as the fleeting lives of pets.

Yet here we were, once again, in the courtyard, because no room inside the house could hold us all. The Valkyries had cracked the mead and were actually fangirling over the Morrigan, much to the amusement of Néit.

Wren sat securely in Milo's arms, looking tiny against his huge form. She was thirty-two weeks today, according to Teron, and we were all watching her like a time bomb that was ready to go off. We were keeping her due date a secret from everyone else, but honestly, it wasn't much of a secret if you got a good look at her. She really did look ready to pop, though the new kitten seemed to enjoy the warm sleeping spot the shelf of her belly made.

If Wren's army got any bigger, we were going to struggle to feed them all. We'd resorted to cooking outdoors on the spit to accommodate all the hungry mouths, and while we were originally going to do a *kontosouvli*, the presence of Galt had kind of soured the idea of pork products. The little piglet was super cute. He was running around chasing some of the dogs, who were entertaining him as if he was just a really unfortunate-looking puppy.

Tryp came up beside me, kissing the top of my shoulder in a gesture he'd done so many times, it was a wonder his lips weren't permanently grooved into my skin. I leaned my cheek against the top of his head, rubbing my scent on his hair and temple. We hadn't had as much time to be consumed by each other, and I found that I missed the other half of my soul. It was an unusual sensation.

"Sleep in my bed tonight?" I asked lightly, and he grinned at me, that wicked expression I knew better than my own reflection.

He kissed my lips softly. "Every night, if you'd like. You just have to ask."

"Just don't want you to forget how much I love you, with all this madness."

He wrapped his arms around my waist, pulling me tight against his bare chest. "I have known your love for centuries, Erus. It's encoded in my very makeup. I could never forget." He kissed my shoulder once more. "We have more people to love, that's all. It doesn't diminish our feelings for each other—only makes them more vibrant."

Tryp made out like he was a dick-swinging playboy from time to time, but he was probably the most in touch with his emotions. Definitely more than me, and a mile more than Demke or Teron.

A dog came over—I didn't know their names, the way Cy and Wren did—and sat at our feet. Checking the lamb, I sliced off a little piece of the skin and dropped it beside him. "Wait for it to cool," I warned him. His tongue lolled out of his mouth as he smiled a toothy canine smile.

I looked back over at Wren, because it was nearly impossible to keep my eyes away when she was in the room. She was running a hand over the underside of her stomach. "She's been doing that a lot," Tryp murmured, and I realized we were both looking at her.

"Rubbing her stomach? Yeah, I noticed. You think it's just the babies moving around? Or muscle strain? Or…" I trailed off, because the other option involved contractions, and I wasn't ready for that. The idea of losing her terrified me.

The prophecy delivered by Apollo had been pretty succinct: that she had to die for the babies to live. It might be just one possible outcome, or it might have been Apollo talking shit, but the possibility that it was true was like acid in my veins.

She looked happy enough, though, laughing with the *bean-sidhe* Clio, and petting the kitten who'd migrated from her stomach to her chest. It was probably just growing pains. She'd been complaining of her hips hurting earlier.

A howl went up, and the dog at my feet skittered away, the piece of juicy, hot lamb forgotten. Half the dogs cleared out of the courtyard; the other half raced toward Wren. I searched out Cy, who had his head tilted to a large dog, listening intently.

He looked over at us, his expression panicked. "The Moirai are here." With that, he transformed into a white dog and disappeared.

The Fates were here? How had they made it so close?

Demke was immediately on his feet. "You know what to do. Everyone in position. Milo, take her somewhere safe."

Shifting her into his arms, Milo climbed to his feet, but Wren slapped his chest. "Wait! Just fucking wait. Cy! Get back here." She wiggled in Milo's arms until he was forced to put her down. "Cy!"

Cy reappeared from around the corner, switching back into his human form, sans clothes. He pecked a quick kiss on Wren's cheek, and I wanted to growl. "Sorry. I had to check it out."

Rolling her eyes, she gripped his chin, forcing him to stop his marking and look at her. "Did the pack say if anyone else is with them? Another army? Titans?"

Shaking his head, Cy spoke to the huge mutt beside him. "Attie says there isn't anyone further out either."

Demke looked disapprovingly at both Cy and the dog. "Excuse me if I don't trust your intel. How did they get so damn close, unless the pack missed something? You're meant to be the sentries."

Attie, the mutt, growled low, and Cy's lips pulled back from his teeth in his own human version of a snarl. "They portaled in. My hounds threw up an alarm as soon as they were spotted, which is a lot more than your wards did."

"Hey!" I protested, but he was right. The wards still hadn't gone off, which meant that someone had disabled them without me knowing.

I wasn't a wardsmith. I wasn't even good at it. I'd been able to maintain the very basics for a few centuries, simply because there hadn't ever been anyone who seriously wanted to make it across them.

Until now.

Wren raised a hand. "We can bicker like a bunch of old people later. If it's just the Fates, I want to talk to them. I have a few fucking questions that need answers."

We all protested at once, but the stubborn tilt to her chin told me that we could protest all we liked. Unless we wanted to pick her up and physically move her against her will, this was happening.

"I have a matching set of Celtic War deities, some of the fiercest warriors of any Mythics, and an entire pack of dogs. If we can't hold back the Fates for one conversation, then we're in much more trouble than we thought." She looked between Demke and Néit, who was once again holding his big ax.

*Where did he even pull that from?*

She sucked in a deep breath. "Please. I trust you to keep me safe."

The ward made the ominous *knock, knock, knock* reverberate around the entire compound. We all deferred to Néit. If anyone had their entire heart and soul wrapped up in Wren, it was him. He was the strategic one. The God of War.

He let out a shuddering sigh. "Okay. But you stay behind us, and you run if we tell you to run. Got it?"

She nodded solemnly. "Let's go meet these bitches."

# CHAPTER 13
## WREN

I might've wanted answers, but no one had prepared me for the rage I felt, looking at the three women in front of me. They were vastly different, but so obviously related. I wondered if they'd started as triplets, but then aged differently. Or if their different roles had just become etched on their faces. Either way, I recognized the one on the right, though she looked decades younger than the last time I'd seen her.

*"You!"*

I mean, we'd all but decided that my babies were the result of that fucking apple, but standing in front of me was irrefutable proof. The fruit cart lady was there, grinning at me with a face that was barely fifty in age, her smarmy expression making me want to launch through the door and scratch out her eyes.

"Come now, child. It has ended well enough for you, has it not?"

*This bitch has to be screwing with me right now.*

"By ended well, did you mean that I was forcibly impregnated by a piece of fruit"—apologies to Mrs. Selene from Health class, who I'd argued with in my teenage righteousness that I shouldn't *have* to put a condom on a banana, since it wasn't like I could get pregnant by fruit—"and then spent months running from monsters you kept sending my way?" Sucking in a feral breath, I hissed, "You *killed* the closest thing I had to family."

The elder Fate waved a hand. "It was her time anyway."

Nate growled beside me, his body vibrating with the same rage I felt. "What the fuck do you want? Leave before I rend your heads from your bodies and dance in your fucking lifeblood."

The one who looked the youngest—barely older than me—gasped at the brutality of the words, but the middle one hushed her. "Wren Mahone, I am Lachesis of the Moirai. You've met my sister, Atropos." The older one smirked at me. "And my other sister, Clotho."

"It's not nice to meet you. I loathe you, in fact," I grumbled, and Tryp chuckled behind me.

Lachesis rolled her eyes, as if I was being a drama queen. An annoyance. "Regardless, we have come seeking a truce. Despite our best efforts, you are annoyingly resilient, and now you have garnered more support than I would have liked from some powerful deities in our own Pantheon, and others."

She was talking about Hades and Persephone, I knew. I sent up—or down, I guess—a silent thanks that he'd rolled the dice and come out on my side of this conflict.

Demke snorted. "No one is dealing with you. Your words are as twisted and poisonous as a tick on a great beast. You need to disappear. Leave my island and accept your own fate. You will get no quarter here."

Clotho fluttered her lashes at Demke, and I gripped his hand, pulling him closer to me and glaring at her. She just smiled prettily at me, though it was a shark's smile.

Atropos sneered at him. "Your island? You mean your *prison*, relic. You are getting wiped this turn around, and everyone knows it. There aren't enough people even in this backwater little village to keep your memory alive."

I stiffened, and Demke's fingers flexed in mine soothingly. Was it true? Would they be wiped away, even with all this effort?

*That can't be true. I won't let it be true.*

Demke shrugged. "Then I go with the satisfaction that you'll be coming with me, Atropos."

The smirk fell from her face as her barb didn't reach its mark. Instead, she turned back to me. "Another downfall at the hands of *love*." She spat the word like it was arsenic. "You Minoans are nothing if not predictable, even if I didn't know your future." She shook her head at me, as if I was less than dog shit on her shoe. "Why you? Such a disappointment, when we have been holding this world together for centuries. The universe chose *you*?"

Clotho giggled. "We did try everything to keep you from this fate. Tried to turn you so many times from this path, gently at first, but you are unfortunately stubborn. That shitty boyfriend your senior year? He was meant to get you pregnant, but as always, you were too *good* to do anything that would jeopardize your future." She rolled her eyes. "We tugged at all the strings around you, yet you stayed stubbornly on course. Even when we cut your parents' threads, you didn't do what a normal teenage girl would do and go off the rails, maybe get a drug addiction or drive off a cliff. No, you had to get a job and then fall into the hands of the damn Celtic Mythics."

"My parents?"

Lachesis sighed. "This thread really is wasted on you. You are no great mind, no great warrior. You are all too *ordinary*, Wren Mahone. Yes, your parents. They were meant to live long, happy lives, but your stubborn goodness meant they had to die young. Honestly, a weird parasite on a cruise? What part of that sounds natural? We couldn't directly cut your strings, but we control the fates of all others. All the humans you know? They could all die with a snap of my sister's fingers, and it would be your fault."

I was shaking so hard, I could feel it vibrate in my bones. They'd killed my parents. They'd killed my parents to stop some random destiny that may or may not happen. They'd made me an orphan to keep their power.

"*Why?* Why go to all that effort, just to feed me an

apple and do all this yourself?" I could barely remember my parents' faces, and they'd murdered them for *nothing*. "I don't understand…" I breathed.

A hand landed on my back, but I didn't turn to see which one of my bonds was anchoring me.

"We were loading the dice," Clotho responded, and Atropos hissed at her, but the younger-looking woman shrugged. "What does it matter now? It will end how it's supposed to, right? You were meant to meet your soulmate at your shitty job, and you'd get pregnant quickly, and then *they*"—she waved a disgusted hand at my stomach—"would be even stronger. He had some ancient Mayan bloodline, but no one wants the Mayans back in power. So he had an unfortunate accident on the freeway, and we did what we had to do to load the board in our favor.

"We can't kill the new Fates ourselves, but we could make sure they were snuffed out while still defenseless. Best way to do that was in your womb, while you were too stupid to know what was going on." She gave Nate a kittenish grin. "But we didn't prepare for the Celtic God. He was an annoying blindspot for us," she cooed. Her eyes slid back to me, and all coquettishness disappeared. "You know the rest."

She made it all sound so reasonable. Like my death, and the death of my unborn babies, was just another day at the office.

"Are we to believe you've had a change of heart?" Nate spat the words at them like bullets.

Atropos rolled her eyes. "No. But we see the future.

We see where this ends without a truce, and some of the endings are not ones we wish to risk." She shivered almost subconsciously. "We see all, God of War. All the prophecies. All the outcomes."

I didn't see the golden knife until it slipped from the sleeve of her long dress and was flying through the air.

"Nate!"

But the knife was flying toward me, not toward Nate. I watched in frozen horror as it flipped end over end toward my chest.

Clio screamed. Everything was slow motion, almost supernaturally so. The old myth of your life flashing before your eyes was kinda bullshit, but that dream where you couldn't run, no matter how hard you tried? This felt a little like that.

But everyone, including the Fates, was so focused on that golden knife, we missed the monster. In those indeterminable moments before death, I saw a horrifying specter rise up behind the Moirai.

I saw Typhon grip Lachesis by the head.

Saw him lift her into the air.

Saw him drop her into his wide-open maw and eat her.

*Good.* If I was going to die, so would one of those bitches. With my death, the babies would live. That's what Apollo's prophecy had said. This was meant to be.

Like the snap of a rubber band, time reverted back to normal.

Because I wasn't dead. Morrigan stood in front of me, the knife embedded in her hand where it was thrust in front of my chest. The golden knife turned black as her blood dripped down it.

The remaining Moirai stared at the empty spot beside them, where their sister had once stood, turning around to see a huge monster with coiled snakes for legs and a visage so horrendous, it turned my blood to ice. Typhon looked furious, even as he chewed on the bones of Lachesis with an audible crunch.

I was going to vomit.

The screams of the remaining Moirai joined Clio's banshee wail, a truly horrifying sound. Atropos gripped the arm of her remaining sister, Clotho, and disappeared in a blink.

Then it was just us, and the monster.

"Typhon," Demke whispered, fear in his tone.

*Oh, shit...* He was going to be mad that I'd kind of killed his wife, right?

Something dripped on my feet and cooled, and I realized Morrigan's hand was still in front of my chest, her blood pooling on my feet. She'd saved my life. I looked up at her, my eyes feeling like they were about to bulge out of my head.

The Valkyries gave a yell, ready to launch themselves at a beast that had just *eaten* one of the Fates. But Morrigan held up her hand. Yeah, the one with the knife in it.

"Hold!" She stepped from the invisible barrier of the ward, toward the snake monster-man. "Does this satisfy you?" she asked softly, and Typhon, who was literally the size of a four-story building, dipped his chin.

"Yes."

"I will negotiate on your behalf with the God of the Underworld. You've been lied to. You have vindicated your wife until you can join her." Her tone was lulling —part promise, part spell.

An earthquake rocked the area around us, and Milo appeared behind me, draping his body over mine as loose stones from the walls rained down. When a chasm appeared before Morrigan, I worried that she would fall into it, but her face didn't change. She didn't back away. She stood there, feet spread, still with an impaled hand in front of her. She watched nonchalantly as Typhon disappeared into the cracked earth, then turned back to us, a grin on her face.

"Well, that was satisfying, wouldn't you say?"

"Milo?" I breathed, the giant man's arms still around me protectively. "You're going to need to catch me."

Then I passed the hell out.

# CHAPTER 14
## WREN

"Milonos, you must put her *down*." Teron's voice sounded firm and kind of peeved in the darkness.

"No." The sound of the word vibrated against my cheek, and I smiled.

A huff, and a growl, echoed in the room. "I need to check her and the babies. Please lay her down over there, and I promise, you can continue to hold her hand."

A rumble deep inside the chest I was pressed against told me it was probably time to swim my way out of this in-between consciousness before there was a fight. I was clutched tightly in Milo's arms, and there was so much of me, it wasn't particularly comfortable. But it was warm and safe, and I loved him more than anything at that moment.

Patting his chest to get his attention, I wasn't surprised he went from noticing I was awake to kissing the ever-loving hell out of me, all in the time it took me to gasp out a breath. Into that kiss, he poured all his worry, fear, love, everything.

"If you don't let her up for oxygen, she's going to pass out again," Demke said dryly, and I pulled back.

Everyone was here. All my guys. And Cy, still in his canine form. We were in Teron's medical suite, and the man in question was pacing the floor, looking like he was barely moments from ripping me from Milo's arms.

Reaching up to cup my Minotaur's cheek, I smiled reassuringly at him. "I'm okay. You can put me down."

He rubbed his cheek hard against my palm. "You almost died."

*Well, that's true. But it wasn't even the first time this year.* "I didn't die. I'm okay."

"No."

I raised an eyebrow at him. "No?"

"I don't want to put you down. Please don't make me." His words quivered, and I melted faster than an ice cube at a frat party.

Looking past him to Teron, I shrugged. "I tried. We'll work around it. Come on, big guy. We'll go sit down so Teron can check me out. You can be my chair."

I spotted Nate in the corner, his face pulled down in a frown. "Is Morrigan okay?"

He nodded. "Healed as soon as the knife was removed. It was an enchanted blade, but she's not human like you."

The words *human like you* echoed around the room like a death knell. If Clio had been in the room, maybe she would have given a soft banshee wail. It was an irrefutable fact that had been sitting there between us, ever since Apollo had delivered that stupid prophecy.

I choked down the emotion that stole my voice, giving a nod. "Good. I'm glad."

Taking his job as chair very seriously, Milo rearranged me on his lap and leaned back slightly to give Teron room to work. Teron cupped my cheek and ran his thumb across my bottom lip. His face was stern, but beneath that, I could see the worry. "You have to stop losing consciousness. It upsets everyone."

*It upsets me*, Griff huffed in my brain. I could tell there was more to it, though, beneath the gentle reproval of his tone.

*Well, my heart is beating for four right now, so I make no promises.* My tone, even inside my head, was teasing, but the only thing he was sending back was fear and self-loathing. *What's wrong?*

Despite the fact Teron was moving away, Griff's voice in my head stayed steady and strong. That was never going to not be weird.

*I can't protect you. I'm a terrible mate.* It was nearly a wail, and I saw Teron wince. I was going to have to get him to shift at some point today so I could snuggle with the big Gryphon.

*You're the best mate. I wouldn't want any other. It's definitely not your fault that I come with a lot of drama in the form of monsters and angry Gods.*

Huffing, he fell into a sullen silence, and I just wanted to tell him it was all going to be okay. I wanted to tell all of them that, wipe those traumatized expressions from their faces. But it would be an empty promise.

"We should talk about what happens if…" If I died. If my bond to them took them all with me. Who'd care for the babies?

Tryp and Erus looked solemn, and Nate was shaking his head. "Nothing is happening to you, *mo stóirín.*"

I tilted my head. "Of course not, but if it does?" I looked at Demke, whose jaw was tense. Arguably, he was the least attached to me, despite the long, thick golden thread that bound us together. Would he survive my death?

Demke's nostrils flared as he came to the same conclusion. "After the birth of the babies, we don't know what our fate will be. Maybe the threads will stay with you, or maybe they'll move to bond us to the infants for their protection. Everything is unknown. This isn't a situation that has occurred within living memory."

I understood that. I also understood that the Moirai had stood as the weavers of fate for so long that it was easy for them to gather an army to defeat us.

Well, two of the three. "You think I can get Typhon to eat the other two as well?"

Nate snorted. "Badb—I mean, Morrigan—apparently promised him entrance to the Underworld to be with Ekhidna. I don't know who is going to tell Hades that."

"Dibs not it!" Tryp shouted, and I couldn't help the laugh that burst out.

"What he said." As Teron took my blood pressure, grinding his teeth because it was high, my smile slid from my face. "I'm serious. We need a worst-case scenario."

Teron sat back, his stethoscope on my stomach. "We understand, Wren. We do. But this decision could literally change the Mythic political landscape for millenia. That's without the more personal decision of who we'd actually trust to care for the triplets."

"Clio?" I asked Nate, but he looked like he wanted to start tearing the room down with his bare hands rather than have a sensible conversation about guardians.

He lifted his chin. "She would help them navigate the politics, but she isn't a nurturer. I'm also not sure she's powerful enough to fight anyone who would come for the babes to consolidate their own power. Not without the backing of Morrigan, and possibly the Valkyries."

I mean, Morrigan had saved my life. "Would she…" I couldn't believe I was asking if Nate's ex-wife would look after our children if we died.

"Yes. She would. But again, I don't know if she would be enough." He looked around the room, like she was about to pop out of the walls and defend her reputation with a knife fight.

Erus leaned back against the wall he was propping up. "There's one logical person. Powerful enough to keep anyone who thinks to take the power for themselves at bay. Already invested in the outcome."

"Cy?" I asked, and Demke snorted.

"He wishes." The dog-man in question just smirked a doggy grin at me. If a dog could flip the bird, I was pretty sure he would.

Erus chuckled. "No. Not Cy. He is more bound to you than most of us. If you die, there's no way he isn't following you."

I frowned, and looked at Cy. Really looked at him with my other sight. The one that I'd been avoiding, to save myself from the pain, now that I'd kind of learned to control it. The connection between us was darker, more tarnished. Dulled from weathering or time.

I tilted my head at him, and he just echoed the movement. "What does that mean?" I asked him, but he didn't turn into a man. He just gave me a long look that wasn't even remotely canine. It was knowing, and next time he was walking around on two legs, we were going to have a long fucking talk.

Saving him from my inquisition, Erus spoke up again. "No, the logical answer is Hades, along with Persephone. No one is fucking with them or their... friends."

There was a hesitation there that I wanted to investigate too, but Teron stood up. "Everyone needs to leave so I can give her an exam."

Tryp pouted. "You're playing doctor without me?" He ducked out of the way as Erus swung a palm at the back of his head.

One of the babies was sitting right on my bladder, so if Teron didn't move this shit along, we'd be acting out a whole different kink that was a lot messier.

Demke shooed everyone out, though Nate lingered. "Go and check on everyone. We don't want Teron to get performance anxiety as he's fishing around in my coochie. I'll be out in a minute," I said softly, and he left with one more tortured look. "I really fucked up his life, you know." I wasn't talking to either Milo or Teron specifically, but Milo's hands tightened around my ribs.

"No, you haven't."

I nodded. "Yes, I did. He had a good life before me. Friends. A job working with horses and kids. I came in and dragged him halfway across the world, putting his life in danger more times than I can count. And on top of that, there's all this." I vaguely waved at the two of them.

Teron knelt between my knees to examine me. I had to shift my mindset between Teron the doctor and Teron the man, who'd had his dick in his hand, jerking off to my moans a few days ago. *So weird.*

"No, Wren. He was merely existing before you. He was living each day in an indeterminable existence of loneliness. I can only speak for myself when I say I would take all the fear, all the danger, to spend just a day with you," Teron said vehemently.

That would've been so sweet, if he didn't have his head so close to my vagina in a non-fun way. I chewed my lip and resisted the urge to cry. "Same. Love you."

He looked up at me, and there was a world of feelings and desire in his eyes, right along with the flash of gold that told me Griff was close to the surface. "You've brightened my world." He frowned. "Have you been having any cramps? Back pain?"

I raised an eyebrow at him. "I'm carrying triplets. My whole body is in pain."

He hummed. "I don't want you to freak out, Wren, but I think your body is preparing for labor."

Lifting my head up, I stared down at him. "Like preparing for, when?"

Shrugging, he pulled my skirt back down. "Days? Weeks?" He cleared his throat. "Hours? Probably not that soon, but we need to prepare for the inevitability that you'll give birth in the very near future. Your blood pressure is also quite high, so I'm putting you on bed rest."

The pounding in my ears was my heartbeat. Milo was making a soothing noise in his chest, but it didn't help. Not at that moment.

Teron threw his gloves in the trash and came over, gripping my chin. "We'll get through this, Wren. You will live a long life, watch your babies grow, guide them and love them. I swear this to you." His yellow eyes were molten. "Do you trust me?"

I let out a shuddering, panicked breath. "Yes."

"Trust me that I'll get us all through this." He stroked a fond hand over the large globe of my stomach. "I won't fail you."

I believed him. I had to, because the alternative was too much to bear.

# CHAPTER 15
## DEMKE

O

I didn't think I'd have to call on Hades so soon after seeing him last. Honestly, we could go another thousand years, and it would probably be too soon. Our relationship with Hades was much like our relationship with Cydon all those years; we were cordial, but mostly because the enemy of our enemy was our friend. Cy had proven his loyalty over the years, but I knew that Hades was only loyal to Persephone and his Underworld friends. Everything else depended on how he felt when he woke up in the morning.

He did hate the Fates, though, even though they supposedly dwelled in the Underworld with him. Or maybe *because* they dwelled there with him. He hated ninety-nine percent of the other Greek Mythics too. He hated basically everyone and everything, except Persephone, and just tolerated a few others.

As a God of Renewal, I'd been in the Underworld before he was King. Every year, I'd gone down there, when it was just a rough, fuzzy pit of darkness. As more religions were created, the more the Underworld had evolved into the Necropolis it was now. Hades had a lot to do with that.

So yeah, I was on good terms with him and his trusted advisors, but I wouldn't call him a friend. It irked me to call him now and ask him the most important question I'd ever uttered.

First, though, we'd ply him with food and wine. There were few pleasures that could stand the test of time, but a perfectly made feast with *kalitsounia, hirina apakia,* and *gamopilafo* was one of them.

I'd sent a message to the Underworld, and the request had been accepted, so I'd been cooking for two days, with Erus and Tryp's assistance. Sometimes, Milo would carry Wren down from the bedroom and sit her on the island counter, just so she could watch.

She tasted sauces and kissed Erus and Tryp easily, while a jealousy I hadn't ever felt before burrowed in my chest. Instead of letting it fester, I fed her as much as I could. I didn't let the worry I felt about the birth of her babies, or the Moirai, or the possibility of her death show on my face. I was her steadfast anchor, and her appreciation showed in small ways. A lingering touch, a soft smile.

However, I'd never wanted to be inside anyone the way I wanted to be inside Wren Mahone right now. She was dressed in a soft kaftan that billowed around her, though it stretched tight over her stomach. She looked like a goddess, but she was also terrifyingly mortal.

Now, as we waited for our dinner guests, Néit had her on his lap, his face buried in her nape as he breathed her in. I was nervous, but knew better than to let that show on my face.

Wren rubbed her stomach, and I thought about calling Teron into the room. "Are you okay?" I murmured, giving into the impulse to run my hand down her arm.

She nodded. "Cramps. They've been coming off and on all day. Teron said they're Braxton Hicks."

Nodding, I resisted the urge to reach out and cup her stomach. I trusted Teron's medical opinion, and all I could do with my magic was vaguely tell her how close she was to giving birth, whether the babies were Mythics, and aid in the rejuvenation of her womb later.

None of that was helpful right at this moment.

The sound of a door knock reverberated around the room, and Erus bounced off the couch to open it like a spinning top wound too tight. We were all tense, I guess.

"At least they used the front door this time," Tryp grumbled softly. "No one wants a portal to the Underworld in their living room."

No one said much more as Erus led Hades and Persephone into the room. I was a little surprised to see a third member of their little Hell harem. Asclepius was a healing Demigod with such purity of heart and deftness of skill, Olympus couldn't abide him to live and show them up as the petty, narcissistic assholes they were. Zeus had killed him, and rumor had it that Hades had snatched him before he could be completely obliterated. I wasn't even sure Hades could stand between destiny and death like that, but I was not about to ask.

Cy perked up. Dressed in jeans and a shirt, he looked like he should be a cliff-diving college kid, not a Demigod who was the illegitimate son of one of the most powerful Mythics of all time. Or, I should say, *one* of the sons.

Apollo was a fucking manwhore, and he had more than a few progeny. But unlike Zeus, Apollo seemed to at least tolerate them all, if not love them all. It was said that Apollo had asked Hades to save Asclepius, who was one of his offspring, and now owed the God of the Underworld a great debt for the action, but again, that was hearsay.

"Brother! It is good to see you so well." Arms wide, Asclepius walked over to Cy and hugged him tight to his chest. Asclepius was the real golden retriever of the two. Sweet, kind, and completely unsuited to the Underworld, I knew he survived down there purely because he radiated such goodness.

Cy patted his back before stepping away. "It is good to see you too, Clee. Let me introduce you to Wren." He led him over to where Wren still sat with Néit. "Wren, this is my half-brother, Asclepius."

Asclepius held out a hand to Wren, his eyes taking her in with a practiced manner of a man whose gift was healing. "Please, call me Clee. You are Cy's little bird, I see."

Cy gave a quick, sharp nod—perhaps too quick—

before diverting Asclepius to Néit. "And this is Néit, Celtic God of War, current protector of the Mother of Fate."

When I saw Wren narrow her eyes at Cy, I knew she hadn't missed his unusual response either. I would question him later, when we were alone.

Waving a hand at Hades and Persephone, Erus indicated the sitting room. "Come in. Have a seat. Would you like a drink?"

Persephone gave a tinkling laugh. "Absolutely. I never turn down a good Creten wine." She dropped her voice, leaning a little closer to me. "Apologies for the extra guest. We thought he might take a look at Wren, make sure everything's going well."

So they had brought him for his medical knowledge. I'd wondered, because he never usually made appearances topside. Not worth the wrath of Zeus, who was apparently still a little pissed about the situation a couple of thousand years later.

With this knowledge, something in me loosened. It was like the universe telling us we'd chosen right. "Thank you. It's appreciated. Teron says that it's soon, and my magic is going haywire. If our meeting wasn't so important, we would have postponed it for a later date." I included Hades in my thanks, because while it was probably Persephone who had pushed the idea, no one got in or out of the Underworld without his approval.

Shrugging, Hades picked at his nails. "Clee doesn't get out enough, or get to use his healing abilities, since most inhabitants of our home are already well beyond even his skills. He likes to see Cydon as well. When Cydon's down below, Cerberus monopolizes his time."

Yes, Asclepius was one of the few people who Hades cared about. Possibly even loved. I knew that in the Underworld, Persephone had created a little harem of men, though I'd always assumed she was the nexus that held them all together. But Hades's words, coupled with the look in his eyes, told me that maybe they all loved each other.

Given our situation, I wasn't one to comment. "I'm glad it works for us all then."

The Valkyries had gone to the house that Morrigan and Cliona had rented, and were having something called a mani-pedi-murder night. I hadn't asked questions.

Erus reappeared with drinks. Persephone drifted toward Wren, stopping next to Asclepius, her hand resting gently on his spine. "I appreciate you coming on such short notice," I said to Hades softly, who had flopped back into an armchair, like the weight of being topside was almost too much to bear.

"Any reason to get out of the house, you know?" He said it flippantly, but I knew he wasn't as casual as he seemed. There were depths and treacheries to the Lord of the Underworld that made him a powerhouse, and also the perfect person for our life-altering request, just as Erus had said. Hades raised an eyebrow at me. "Plus, I must admit, I'm a little intrigued why a God who has studiously avoided me for a handful of centuries now wants me to make house calls."

Curiosity would kill us all, eventually.

"Let's eat first."

Nodding, he lifted his glass. "*Yamas.*"


COOKING traditional food made me feel like I was still in touch with my past. It was something that I'd fallen into after the Goddess had faded, something to keep me grounded in the world when I had nothing left but sadness and a desire to follow her.

And anger. I never talked about the anger, but I'd felt a rage that had burned hot enough to level cities at her betrayal of me, of my brothers, of the village that had devoutly followed her for so long, of the memories of those who fell in the fight for her. She had faded with little concern for those of us that were left behind, and I'd felt so betrayed.

So I'd cooked. It had kept my brothers fed in their own grief, and had been a way to connect with the village that also felt betrayed. I'd learned from the villagers, who'd continuously offered to cook for us, but understood when I wanted to do it for myself.

After all these years, it was the one thing that kept me sane. And now, as I looked down the long, rough-hewn table covered in food that I'd worked over diligently for the last two days, I felt pride. Wren was squished between Erus and Tryp, across from Persephone and Teron, and she was laughing and smiling. It was a brief moment of normalcy for her, which made me proud too.

Plates were heavily laden, and Asclepius was making happy humming noises around thick chunks of smoked meat. I looked over at Wren, who nodded.

She needed to ask the question. They were her children, first and foremost. As much as I wanted to navigate this for her, she had to do it herself. Clearing her throat, she got everyone's attention. We were all tense, which none of the Mythics seemed to miss, especially not Hades, who lifted an eyebrow.

Wren, to her credit, didn't waver. "Thank you for coming. I really appreciate it. And I'm not going to patronize you by pretending that we all don't know there's a reason I asked you here." Sucking in a deep breath, she straightened her shoulders. "When I first arrived, on the word of some Oracle in the drive-thru of my barista job, I had no idea what the hell was going on. I unintentionally bonded these guys, tied their souls to mine."

I found I had no anger about that anymore. I hadn't felt this fulfilled in so long; it was hard to remember why I'd been so against it in the first place.

As if she could read my thoughts, she smiled over at me. My heart felt like it was blooming in my chest. "Apollo brought a second prophecy, after the attack with Ekhidna. I can't remember the exact wording—"

*"With the death of the mother, the new weavers will be born into the tapestry and a new age will begin,"* Cy inter-

jected, the somberness of his tone so at odds with his normally bright nature.

Wren tilted her head at him. "That's the one. It was a prophecy from Delphos."

Hades's jaw was tight, and I wasn't sure if it was the mention of Apollo, or Delphos, or just the situation in general. "That seems problematic, but unfortunately, Asclepius can no longer resurrect people from the dead," he said nonchalantly.

Wren just gaped. "Uh, what? No, that wasn't..." Shaking her head at Hades, and then Asclepius, she blinked at them owlishly for a moment. "I didn't even know that was an *option*, and even if it was an option, I'm not sure I'd want to be a zombie?" Her voice rose an octave toward the end, and I almost laughed. Nodding, Hades waved for her to continue. Wren was still shaking her head softly from side to side, but went on. "If the prophecy is true, and I die, it is possible that they will all come with me." She pointed to me and the others around the table, each of us looking so serious, it was like we were already at her wake.

"And then these babies will be alone and nearly defenseless in a world where they're hunted by all the different Pantheons for power. We decided, as a group, that we would ask—if the worst-case scenario happens, and we're no longer around to care for them, would you consider taking them in and caring for them? Protecting them?"

Persephone gasped. Her eyes bounced between Hades and Asclepius, the former staring so intensely at

Wren that I wondered if he was using his magic, and Asclepius, who just looked surprised. Persephone and Asclepius both turned to Hades, because the final decision would end with him.

"You want us to take your infants to the Underworld?"

"Yes, if we all die." Wren sounded resolute.

Hades and Persephone had one of those silent conversations born from being with a person for centuries. Finally, he turned back to Wren. "We agree. We'll care for them and protect them, until they are old enough and well equipped enough to protect themselves, and then we will return them to the living plane."

Persephone reached across the table, gripping Wren's hands. "We'll love them like they're our own flesh and blood." She paused. "In the modern sense. Gods haven't traditionally been great parents."

Letting out a shaky breath, I watched something loosen in Wren's frame. One more worry, gone.

Asclepius laughed. "Well, that was a curveball. I thought you might have called us here because Wren is so close to active labor. I'd give it about an hour?"

As one, the whole table turned and looked at a sheepish Wren. "Oops?"

# CHAPTER 16
## TERON

How could I have missed that she was in labor? She'd come to me yesterday with lower back pain and some irregular contractions, and I'd told her it was Braxton Hicks, which I'd been sure it was. She hadn't said anything at all today, which should have been my first damn clue.

"Stop freaking out, Teron. I'm *fine*. These things are slow. You said so yourself." She was trying to keep *me* calm?

Huffing out a deep sigh, I gave her a reassuring smile. "I know. Still, I'm going to spank your ass red for hiding this from me all day."

Stroking my arm, she lay on the chaise lounge in the clean room we were using as a birthing suite. "This dinner was important, and my contractions were so far apart. If I was truly worried, I wouldn't have hesitated, I promise."

Honestly, I was kind of glad that Asclepius was here

too. The universe had a funny way of providing, especially when it came to Wren. As it was, the Demigod of Medicine was looking over her chart, fiddling with the new-age equipment, genuinely looking like a kid in a candy shop.

Standing over one of the incubators, he shook his head. "Can you imagine if we'd had these back when we walked the earth among the humans? The new lives I could have saved..." It was the lament of medical practitioners everywhere. Especially back in the old days, where sometimes your only cure would've been a Demigod like Asclepius.

Wren winced, letting out a small moan of pain. Her contractions were getting closer together. She was dressed in one of Milo's oversized shirts that hung down to her knees, and a pair of long socks that met the hem.

I patted the mattress of the specialty birthing bed that I'd had shipped in. Honestly, was it necessary? No. But I wasn't taking any chances, and it doubled as a normal hospital bed anyway. Maybe we'd have an entire maternity hospital dedicated to Wren at the end of this.

"I'll give you your epidural. It'll make everything a lot more comfortable." I'd been practicing epidurals on Demke, but the pressure of doing it on Wren was giving me heart palpitations. If she'd left it any longer, though, she wouldn't even get this.

I once again second-guessed myself about whether I should attempt a Cesarean section instead. I had all the equipment necessary, and with Asclepius here, another set of competent hands. Almost all triplet pregnancies ended in a C-section, and I was stupid to believe that this would be the better way.

I reminded myself again why this would be okay. The presenting baby was in a good position. Head down, like he knew his job. The babies all had their own amniotic sacs and placentas, which was much safer. Their positions were fine. If it became a problem, we could adjust then.

Demke was here, and he was a God of fertility and rejuvenation. While that didn't necessarily equate to being helpful during birth, his magic would keep everything calm and help Wren with her exhaustion. And Asclepius could keep everyone stable.

I internally talked myself through the steps of giving an epidural, and when it went smoothly, I breathed a sigh of relief, glad she couldn't see my indecision on my face. I'd made everyone stay outside the room except Demke, and now Asclepius, because the less desterilization of the room, the better. But I knew they were all outside, relying on me not to fuck this up.

As Demke stroked her hand, I busied myself setting up anything we might need for any eventuality. Surgical equipment. Anesthetic. Humidicribs. Suction bulbs. I'd bought everything, but hoped to only use a fraction of it.

Before I knew it, it was time. I'd never felt so unprepared in my life. The Gryphon was flailing around inside me; he was so close to the surface, I could swear I felt the brush of his feathers beneath my skin. But he knew to stay inside. This was a moment for the man, not for the mate. Still, he spent so much time cooing encouragement to Wren, it was crowding my brain.

*I'm going to need you to be silent when it starts. I know it's hard—for both of us. I just need to concentrate. I don't want to make any mistakes.*

I heard the Gryphon's huff. *You will not make a mistake. I trust you with our mate.*

I wasn't sure if his reassurance made me more scared or less.

Watching the clock on the wall as Wren had a long contraction, Demke stroked her hair where it was sticking to her face. "That one went for a full minute," he said softly.

I rolled my shoulders and came to stand beside her bed. "It's time," I murmured, and the fear in her eyes was like a dagger to my heart. Stroking her face, I leaned down and kissed her softly. "Don't be scared. You're a warrior. You've overcome everything life has thrown at you; this is just one more tiny hurdle. And then you'll have three beautiful babies at the end. A family once more."

She nodded, and I looked over at Asclepius, who stood beside the humidicribs. He would take the babies as they were delivered, and ensure they were all right. If they were too soon, or too... Well, he would step in. But they wouldn't be. I had been monitoring them almost religiously for weeks. They were healthy and strong.

It would all be okay.

"Do you need the same pep talk?" Demke asked lightly, though he also looked fearful.

Snapping my gloves on, I shook my head. I had this. I did a brief examination, happy with how the first baby was holding its own. A perfect, textbook birth was what we were aiming for, and he was in the right spot to make that happen.

I just had to keep my shit together.

As another contraction swept over her, Wren moaned loudly. After it passed, I prepared myself. "Next contraction, we're going to push, okay?" I told her softly.

"How are you ever going to look at my vagina the same again?" she whimpered.

A laugh burst out of me. "With reverent awe, sweetheart. In approximately six weeks' time, I'll prove just how beautiful every single inch of you is to me. But right now, we have a few babies to deliver. Are you ready?" She shook her head, but still pushed. The baby crowned, and I breathed slowly. "And again, Wren. Baby number one is paving the way for his brothers. I promise it'll get easier." It was a soothing white lie; it might be easier, but she'd get more exhausted.

She pushed, and his head popped out. I hissed out my first relieved breath, though I doubted I'd feel anything close to relief for another eighteen minutes... or eighteen years.

"I see his head, and he has your beautiful dark hair.

Okay, we need a couple more big pushes to get his shoulders out, then the rest will slip right out."

She bore down once more, like the goddess she was, and then with little help, baby boy number one was in my arms.

Cutting the cord, I passed him to Asclepius, who suctioned his airways, then he let out a long, beautiful wail. It was the most awe-inspiring sound in the world, and Wren burst into fresh tears. Asclepius brought him over, placing the baby on her chest. I looked up, unable to drag my eyes away from the wonder of life happening in front of me. A tear fell from Demke's cheek onto the baby's head, though I didn't think my oldest friend even knew he was crying.

But there was another impatient baby waiting to be born, already crowning. "Wren, Baby Two obviously inherited your impatience, because he's ready. Are you ready? Hand the baby back to Clee so he can get him all wrapped up and warm." Asclepius lifted the baby gently from Wren's chest, and we went back to work. "Okay, Baby One busted down the doors, and this one is ready to enter the party. Ready? Push, sweetheart. Push!"

She screamed as she pushed, and out came a second tiny miracle. He didn't even wait for Asclepius to clean out his airways—he came out wailing, and it was the best sound I'd ever heard. I'd worried their lungs wouldn't be developed enough, but they were proving me wrong. This one went straight onto her chest.

Two out of three. We were over halfway there.

I rolled my tense shoulders and watched a crying, panting Wren clutch the baby on her chest. Despite the odds, despite the dangers, we were almost there. I sent up a small prayer to both my long-gone Goddess and to my own ancestors.

Baby Three seemed to want to give his mom a break, but I knew she was tiring fast. He wasn't yet in the position needed for her to push, so we waited. Asclepius took the second baby, wrapping him and making him warm, and putting him in the crib beside his brother.

Demke was holding Wren's hand tightly, and I smiled up at her reassuringly. I could feel Griff sending all sorts of feel-good vibes down their link, but he stayed blessedly silent. "We are almost there. Baby Three is just taking his time moving down, but he'll be here soon enough. You are doing so well."

Forty-five excruciating minutes later, Wren was exhausted. As Demke whispered something sweetly in her ear, I could feel his magic in the air. Taste it on the back of my tongue.

Her blood pressure was getting high, and if she didn't deliver soon, I was going to have to resort to a C-section. But finally, the baby moved down enough that I could feel the top of his head.

"We are almost done, Wren. So, so close. I need a few more big pushes from you, okay?" She didn't even nod anymore, just breathed and cried. This was so hard, now that she was mine.

A contraction, a push, and then he was crowning.

Another push, and his face was out. One more, and he slipped into my hands. He was still, and I quickly cut the cord, passing him off to Asclepius.

Still nothing.

The world seemed to hold its breath as we waited. A soft cry echoed around the room, and I realized I was crying too. He was placed on the chest of his mother, and I breathed a sigh of relief.

"Baby Three. He's beautiful," I whispered, my voice thick.

We weren't done, and Wren was still in danger. Third stage was coming up, and I knew it was dangerous, especially with multiples. I prayed that I was enough. But when her blood pressure dropped, setting off the alarms, a panic I'd never felt before consumed me.

"She's hemorrhaging," Asclepius said softly beside me. "Deliver the placentas *now*."

*Fuck. Fuck.* Panic zinged along my nervous system, lighting it up, making my brain foggy. I froze, wasting precious seconds.

*Our mate is dying. Get your shit together. You know what you need to make her healthy and whole. Move it.* The snap of the Gryphon shook me from my stunned stupor, and I went to work. I remembered the medical journals I'd read, the textbooks, hell, even the anecdotes. I knew what to do.

The next twenty minutes were officially the scariest of my life. And without Asclepius there, I wasn't sure she would have survived.

When I finally looked up after she was stable, I wasn't surprised to find my brothers all gathered around the edges of the room, pale and shaky. It was a battle none of them could fight, and they all looked as helpless as I'd felt. The steady beep of her monitors was the only thing soothing the anxiety inside me.

She was alive. The babies were alive. We'd all survived. Four hours she'd labored for. Four hours I hadn't taken a deep breath. But now she would heal, and we could progress to the next part of our lives, with her and the babies.

I rocked back on my heels, slumping onto the floor. Asclepius squatted beside me, his hand resting on my shoulder. "I must go. I've used my powers too much, and I don't want to bring the wrath of Zeus down on your head." I shuddered at the very thought. "You are a brilliant mind in the medical field, Teron. Trust your instincts. Call me if you need me, and we will come."

Standing, he looked at the guys. "Congratulations on the birth of your infants and the strength of your lover. They are both untold treasures." He stroked the sleeping faces of the babies, bowing his head. "By thy guidance, I surrender mine fate," he murmured, and it was a pledge. An old one, but still one that had power.

Hades and Persephone stood back by the door. They both bowed their heads respectfully. Then they were gone, and I dragged myself to my feet. I would rest later, when I was sure Wren and the babies were safe and well.

Because if anything happened to them, I knew I would never rest again.

# CHAPTER 17
## WREN

O

They were tiny. How could something be so small and hold such power over my happiness? I sat by their incubators—all three pushed close together because I was worried they'd miss each other— pumping milk, in awe. They were truly amazing.

My whole body felt like it had been in a battle. I'd won, but it had been tough. I still looked pregnant. My vagina felt like I'd stuffed it in the garbage compactor.

But the babies were worth every single moment of uncomfortableness and pain. Teron said they were small, but they were healthy, because even though they were premature, they were still Demigods, delivered by two other Demigods, with the support of an actual God. They were never going to follow normal preemie conventions, and already, they were strong enough to be bottle fed, which was a relief. It would take a lot of pressure off Teron, and it was one more major milestone they'd already conquered.

Once a day, I got to hold them, and today, I'd held all three at once. The sense of rightness wasn't something I would ever forget, even if it was terrifying and I'd been convinced I'd drop at least one.

Griff sat in the corner, constantly here, protecting the babies. Or sometimes he was here as Teron, though he was so exhausted, I was pretty sure he willingly gave up control to Griff.

All the guys took rotations sitting with me, or making me go and rest, or eat. They'd been terrified; that much had been obvious. Nate had looked so shaky, I was worried he was about to have his own medical episode.

With all of us taking turns at sitting in the nursery with the babies through the day, it meant they were never alone. I was never alone. Right now, it was Cy stretched out beside me in his human form, his sweats low on his hips as he pressed as close to me as possible on the chaise lounge.

I no longer saw the threads, and wondered if that power had been transferred to the babies. I was also curious if the threads tying me to the guys had disintegrated upon their birth—or were they still with me? I guess we wouldn't know until the babies were older.

"It's hard to imagine that something so tiny could have such a big responsibility to the world. I almost want to hide them from it, to ensure they live a normal life."

Cy gave me a sad smile. "They were born from apple seeds, Wren. They were never going to have a normal, human life. But we'll do what we can to make sure that they get to be children. That they feel safe and secure, until they're ready to grasp their destiny."

I sighed. He was right. "You never told me why our thread looked the way it did, by the way. I haven't forgotten."

He chuckled. "I didn't think you would forget. It's a really long story, and not particularly interesting."

I raised an eyebrow. "I'll be the judge of that."

"Before…" When he said that, I intrinsically knew he meant the time before the fall of the Minoans. Before the old Goddess had died, and the Minotaurs had perished. "I didn't always live on Crete. My mother was a princess here, and my father liked the lifestyle of the island—so much more relaxed than the mainland— so while I grew up here, and it was my home, I was equally as tied to Greece and their Mythics. So I wandered a little while. I met my siblings, and when I tell you there were a lot of them, I mean it. More came after the great war, and there are some I've never met, but the older ones I made an effort to spend time with."

"Like Clee?"

He nodded. "Yes, Asclepius, and his adopted father, Chiron. He was a centaur." My eyes bugged out of my head, and he let out a soft laugh. "But also, I spent a decade singing songs with Orpheus and his wife Eurydice, before the whole thing with the Underworld. I traveled all over, meeting siblings who either loved or loathed our father. I ended up in Delphi with my oldest brother, Delphos. That's where the course of my life changed forever."

Pulling me closer, he rubbed his cheek against mine reassuringly, but I didn't interrupt. "He told me I needed to return to Crete, that an Oracle had made a prediction, and whether or not the Minoans heeded their own prophecy, my fate would forever be tied to the island. He said that a little bird would fly in on the winds of change. If I wasn't here when that happened, the wheel would veer, the outcome would be terrible, and I would never know true love or happiness. I'm pretty sure that last part was just the universe putting the screws to me to ensure that I stayed. An incentive, of sorts." He smirked.

I raised an eyebrow at him. "You're telling me that our fates were tied long before I existed. Hell, before any of my discernible ancestors existed."

He shrugged, his fingers stroking through the ends of my hair. "Not you-you, exactly. The idea of you, I guess. If the Fates had succeeded in diverting your fate, it would have been someone else like you. Pure and strong. Loving. Steadfast. It could have been in your lifetime, or another thousand years from now. There could have been a thousand you's before this, each one slightly thrown off the course of their fate by some small act. We'll never know." He leaned forward, brushing his lips across mine, and I sat there, too stunned to kiss him back. "I'm very glad it's you, though."

Griff let out a menacing huff from the other side of

the room, right beside the cribs. Pulling back, Cy laughed at the giant Gryphon, who could probably actually eat him in a single bite in dog form. "Sorry, big guy. You're going to have to learn to share, but I'll try and keep it contained to when you're the much more reasonable human version of you."

I had anecdotal evidence that Teron didn't mind sharing at all.

The silence consumed us once more, and it was so comfortable. If it wasn't for the nagging feeling in my chest that it wasn't going to stay this way forever, I might have even been content.

"Have you decided what to name them?"

They'd been in the world two days, and I had still only named Bran. Now that I was able to see them, and hold them, I had more ideas. Everyone had bounced around suggestions, from Shanahan to Gerald to Clitus, which apparently meant splendid and famous, and was the name of some Roman soldier, but was spelled like Clitorous and sounded like Cletus. Tryp got no more suggestion chances after that one.

"Bran, for Baby One. In honor of the woman who took me in, Zelda Byrne. My dad's name was Eric, and it doesn't feel right naming him Eric, like I'm trying to replace him, so I thought Emeric was pretty close. For Baby Two."

Cy smiled. "Both great names," he said, brushing his lips over my shoulder again, like he couldn't help himself. "And Baby Three?"

I shrugged. I really didn't know. "Do you have any suggestions?"

He thought it over, standing to stare at the baby in his incubator, his head covered with a tiny knit cap. "When I was wasting endless years, waiting for you, I lived with a fisherman down by the sea. He was strong, and kind. He once ran into a burning hut to save a litter of kittens that had been living beneath his nets and tarps. Not his equipment, which would have been expensive to replace. Not his ledgers, or any of the hundreds of other things that would have made his life easier. He brought out all those kittens, and the hissing and spitting, terrified mother cat, only slightly singed.

"It was just one example of his goodness. He took me in and fed me when he thought I was just a mangy street dog. His name was Zale. It means the strength of the sea, I think. Seems fitting for a baby born on the most beautiful island in the world."

Zale. It felt right, deep down in my chest. "Zale. I love it." Moving to stand beside Cy, I looked down at all three babies. "Bran, Emeric and Zale. Welcome to the world, little ones."

I reached down to twine my fingers with Cy's, and the babies slept on, peacefully unaware of the upheaval their birth had caused. I'd make it my mission to keep it that way for as long as possible.

THE VALKYRIES HAD BEEN KEEPING everyone away, and for those who seemed to disregard their commands, there was Morrigan, who was more than happy to use bloody force. She only had to send a message once for people to stay in line.

When I asked *who* they were keeping away exactly, everyone had gotten really cagey, except Nate. Watching me nearly die for the gazillionth time was definitely having an effect on his brain chemistry. He'd just held me tight, grumbling about Old fucking Gods and a pilgrimage. From what I could gather, now that the babies had been born and the middle Fate had been thrown back like a shot of tequila, different Pantheons were coming to, I don't know, pledge allegiance? Pretend they hadn't been conspiring to murder me for the last nine months?

But they were being turned away, and for that, I was relieved.

It wasn't until nine days after the babies had arrived, and were out of the incubators and being carefully carried around on a range of shirtless men that Nate appeared beside me, his face folded in a frown. "The Valkyries tell me there's someone at the gates who wants to speak to you. I think you'll want to speak to him too."

I frowned back. "Who is it?"

He laughed, shaking his head. "I don't think you'd believe me if I told you. Might be better to see with your own eyes."

I handed Zale to Milo, who looked comically huge with a tiny baby in his arms. The man—er, Minotaur—had taken to fatherhood like a duck to water. He loved them; it was in every soft look, every murmured word. It just made me love him more. And did something to my out-of-action ovaries.

During the long trek down to the gates, Nate stayed at my back. He didn't seem worried about whoever was at the door. Honestly, the whole thing was a little weird. Hrist stood at the gate, her face easy but still alert. She obviously didn't think this person was a threat either.

Stepping around the open door, my mouth dropped open. Nate had been right. I wouldn't have believed him if he'd told me.

Standing on the dusty forecourt in front of the compound was an old man. An old man I'd met many, many times before. An old man who hadn't been able to reach the bottom shelf at Rossi's, so I was unsure how he'd made it halfway around the world.

"Mr. Lunetta? What are you doing here?"

# CHAPTER 18
## NATE

O

Kon Lunetta had been in Boston for as long as I had been. While we weren't friends, or even acquaintances, we both did our best to just live a normal life, filled with normal things, and stay out of Mythic politics unless they were forced on us.

The Egyptian god Khonsu, he was indeterminately old. Older than I was, for sure. Maybe even as old as the Minoans.

But the way Wren gaped at him, I wasn't sure that she had any idea at all. He just looked like a doddery old man—a good way to be underestimated, even for Mythics. We might be old, but we were still prone to our own prejudices.

"Wren. It's good to see you well, child. I hear congratulations are in order."

Still blinking at him slowly, like she couldn't believe her eyes, her mouth opened and closed a few times, but no words came out.

I gave a respectful bow of my head. "Khonsu," I murmured politely.

He nodded back, waving a hand. "Please, call me Kon."

Shaking herself from her stunned daze, Wren repeated her question. "Mr. Lunetta, what are you doing here?" She paused, her eyes squinting in the brightness. "You're a Mythic?"

He chuckled softly at her disbelief. "It would appear so." He looked at her fondly, and it didn't seem feigned. How had they met and gotten close? "The Egyptian Pantheon wanted to send an emissary to pledge us to the new Fates. To assure you that we'll respect their weaves and hope they look kindly on us. I told my counterparts that I have nothing but faith in the fairness of the future Fates; with you as their mother, and Néit as their father, I know they will be empathetic and unbiased."

Wren chewed her lip. "Do you want to come in?" She was hesitant, but I didn't think it was because she was scared.

Khonsu just shook his head. "Not necessary. You deserve the time and peace to bond with your children. This is a special moment, and as such, I want to give you a gift."

She gave him a watery smile. "I left your last gift back in Boston, at Mrs. Byrne's house. It's probably been destroyed by monsters by now." The hitch in her voice had me reaching out and resting my hand gently against her spine.

Waving a hand, he smiled back at her. "No, I strengthened the wards around Zelda's home. Although she has returned to the wheel, she deserved better than to be caught up in some new Mythic war. No one will be getting into that home except you, Wren, and those of your direct bloodline."

With that, Wren burst into tears. Some of it was probably the wild hormones flowing around her body, but on the other hand, I understood. It was a small act of kindness that needed no repayment. An act of kindness for a woman whose life had been a mere blink to the God in front of us, but it was proof that Zelda Byrne had deserved better. That she was someone special among the mass of humans.

Wiping her face on her sleeve, she nodded solemnly. "Thank you. I appreciate that."

"That's not my gift, though," Khonsu continued. "The presence of the Valkyries would suggest that I am not your first caller."

Hrist snorted. "Not even the fifteenth."

He nodded sagely. "The opening of Crete, combined with the birth of new Fates, would have all the different Mythics coming out of the woodwork, I imagine. Myself included." He gave a self-deprecating smile that looked charming on his elderly face. I had a theory that Khonsu could age himself, then revert back to his younger years, which had allowed him to stay in Boston so long. Like the waxing and waning of the moon he was associated with.

Shrugging, Wren gave him a soft smile. "I'm glad to

see you, Mr. Lunetta. And I honestly understand why people keep coming. We expected it."

Khonsu huffed. "Impatient, these young religions. Always in such a rush. No, my gift to you is to restore your ward around Crete. It will not be permanent, because not even I am strong enough to keep out the hordes of Mythics from different Pantheons for too long. Not without some serious sacrifices, and I don't believe that's something you'd desire?" Wren looked so horrified, he laughed again. "It should hold for six weeks or so. Enough time to bond with your babies and make sure they are strong and hale to weather the coming tides of fate."

The gift of time was one without price. Touched, I bowed my head once more. "We appreciate your gift, Kon."

His gaze suddenly flicked behind us, and his eyes went wide. "Teron?"

I looked over at Teron, whose Gryphon was the last of his kind. I'd forgotten that their territory had dipped right down into Africa, especially Egypt.

"Khonsu?" Teron gasped. "Old friend, it's good to see you! I heard that you still lived, but after so many years, I never put too much hope in the rumors." Dodging around us, he walked straight up to the old man and hugged him tightly.

How tightly had the weavers of fate tied me to this course, when my old life and my new life kept tangling together?

They talked to each other excitedly in Egyptian,

while I stood there dumbly. Like big, dumb, antisocial muscle. I hated that I couldn't pull an ancient, powerful being who owed me some inexplicable debt out of my arse, and use that to keep Wren safe, the way these guys could.

Wren leaned into my side, and I tightened my arm around her. Breathing her in, I pushed my magic inside her so I could hear the very thump of her heart, the whoosh of air exiting her chest. I needed to feel she was alive, because far too many times over the last few weeks, she'd come perilously close to death.

I kissed her head, ignoring Khonsu's raised eyebrow. I didn't care what he thought, what *any* of them thought. This little mortal was mine for the brief flash of her life, and I would defend her with my immortal soul if I had to. I let all that show in my eyes. He could run back to Boston and tell them all that— hell, tell the whole fucking Mythic world that Néit, scorned Celtic God of War, had once again fallen, this time for a mortal woman.

Teron, with his back to me, missed the subtext of our silent conversation. "Are you coming in? Stay and have a drink with us, for old times' sake?"

Khonsu shook his head. "Not this time. You need to bond as a family, and relax into your moment of peace, because I fear this tenuous truce won't last very long at all. Do you have your former ward glass? I will strengthen it the best I can, return your island to the fortress that it once was. None will be able to enter, but if any of the Mythics currently on the island leave, they won't be able to return either. Not for six weeks, at the least. Also, passing through the ward to leave would be… uncomfortable."

Teron nodded. "I'll be right back."

I moved toward Hrist, who was still on guard, despite the obvious familiarity of this God to us. I respected that. "You heard him. If you need to leave, you won't be able to return for six weeks. Would you like to go now?"

She shook her head. "We have our mission. And if necessity means we must leave, we can survive *uncomfortable.*"

I had a lot of respect for these warriors. I had no doubt they could survive much more than being uncomfortable.

I called Clio, but her phone went to voicemail, so I sent her a quick text saying if she wanted to leave the island, she had about fifteen minutes before leaving would feel like getting your gooch waxed by a mountain troll. She couldn't say I didn't warn her.

Teron reemerged, and I wasn't surprised to see Demke with him, as well as Erus. From what I could gather, Erus had cared for the ward for the last however many years. He wasn't inherently magical, and I think his care mostly consisted of making sure it got sunlight and didn't get smashed in a game of racquetball. Still, he was the closest thing to a keeper they had. He held the glass jar, with the thread inside—strung from the top to the bottom like the filament of a lightbulb—now broken, no longer glowing or holding the ward strong.

The way they all cast uneasy looks at the ward glass told me that the way it was previously made sat in the forefront of their minds. The entire Minotaur race had given their lives for that previous ward.

I looked at Khonsu, who I barely knew personally, but knew by reputation all too well, and wondered if we were about to be fucked over in an ironic repetition of fate. However, he took the ward glass carefully, as if he knew the sacrifice that had been used to power it.

He inspected the broken hair inside, and when he unscrewed the jar, the hair turned to dust and floated away on the wind. Someone behind me made a choked noise, and I realized that was probably the last piece of their Goddess they'd possessed after all this time. I looked over at Demke, and there was loss in his eyes once more, but it wasn't the destroyed look that had been so evident when we first arrived. The God of Renewal was finally healing himself.

Khonsu looked up. "I'll need three strands of your hair, dear Wren."

I narrowed my eyes at him, but Wren just shrugged. Plucking out three hairs, she handed them over, like DNA didn't have power amongst some Pantheons— like you couldn't be cursed to become a sea otter forever with just three hairs.

So trusting, *mo stóirín.*

Chanting, Khonsu twirled the hairs between his fingers, twining them together until they threaded into one thin hair rope. Anchoring it inside the jar, he chanted louder and louder until all the flesh on my body was covered in goosebumps, the energy wild and untamed.

Finally, the thread of hair glowed gold, and a rush of magic spread out from this spot. Khonsu screwed the heavy gold cap back on. Smiling, he handed the glass jar back to Erus. "That should give you time to breathe, to plan. To love and live."

Wren launched herself toward the old man and hugged him tightly. "Thank you."

He patted her hair softly. "It is my pleasure, little Wren. You were kind to an old man when it didn't benefit you at all, even when it was harder for you to reach the bottom shelf than I. That unselfish kindness is a rare and beautiful thing, which should be rewarded." He gave her shoulder a few gentle pats. "Now, I should be going. I only gave myself a small window to leave, without the same blowback as others. Wren, it was a delight to see you safe and well." He gave her a soft look. "Zelda would be proud of you."

Wren's lip wobbled, and I tugged her back into my chest. Khonsu gave me the same sparkly-eyed, old-man look, like we weren't roughly the same amount of ancient. After several thousand years, you no longer wondered who was older—you were all the same amount of old. "Zelda would be proud of you too."

It shouldn't matter what an elderly mortal thought of me, but Zelda Byrne had been no ordinary mortal. She was special.

I nodded back. "I hope so. I have no doubt she'll

find a way to come back and haunt me if she isn't, though."

As Wren laughed, the tears dried in her eyes, and we said goodbye to the old Mythic. I had to trust in his power, trust in his word, and while that didn't come naturally, I had to have a little faith.

So, for the first time in almost a year, I let down my guard and relaxed.

# CHAPTER 19

## MILO

"Happy supposed-to-be birthday to you! Happy supposed-to-be birthday to you! Happy supposed-to-be birthday dear Bran, Emeric and Zale, happy birthday to you!"

The babies just blinked at us owlishly, their gazes moving from faces to the small cake covered in candles that they couldn't blow out. Despite the fact that we'd had them with us for five weeks now, they'd only just reached their due date and made it to the size of average newborns.

They were healthy. They were happy. And so was I.

Wren blew out the candles, and we all cheered. I lifted Emeric up against my chest, gently stroking his back, which was still smaller than my hand. They were tiny replicas of their mother, though she didn't see it. I could, though—it was there in the small tilt of their noses, the little rosebud lips. Three little pieces of my Wren.

I loved her even more now. She held Zale in her arms, while Néit was casually holding Bran like he'd done it a million times, like they weren't tiny and breakable. I had no idea how he did that. I always expected them to break. I felt like that old adage of a bull in a china shop—too big, too clumsy.

I watched my family as they ate cake and laughed with each other, the love flowing more freely than the alcohol I used to drown myself in to feel nothing. Now I felt so much that my chest threatened to burst.

Tryp picked up some gift bags, shooing away the animals from beneath the table. I huffed a laugh as he found Von, the battle kitten, curled up in one of the bags. I didn't know how this messy chaos had become our lives, but I wanted to thank whoever put us on this path.

Tryp rolled his eyes, lifting the kitten onto his shoulders as he passed the bag over to Wren. "We got them a gift. It wasn't Von, though she is definitely a gift," he cooed at the small cat. She was definitely enamored with the Genii, and if she wasn't curled up near the babies, she was usually with either Erus or Tryp.

Wren shook her head. "They can barely lift their heads; they don't really need gifts," she chastised gently, but her eyes were dancing.

She pulled out an absolute abundance of the pacifiers that they adored, which they also lost at an alarming rate. I wondered if some of the dogs hadn't been stealing them away. Underneath those were a couple of board books, because Teron insisted reading was important, even at this young age. Lastly, there were three tiny stuffed axes.

Wren looked at Néit, raising an eyebrow. He just grinned back. "Just like Daddy's, hmm?" she teased. "Thank you, guys. We love them. But you all are the best gifts they could have. This life filled with love and happiness is all we need."

I leaned over and nuzzled her hair, breathing her in. These last five weeks had been bliss. The island was blockaded, thanks to some old Egyptian God, and even the Valkyries had taken the opportunity to relax a little. They were out by the pool now, laughing and swimming, though still on alert. I wondered if they'd ever had a day off in their eternal lives.

The village now had time to rebuild, and the residents had time to either leave, or come to terms with the insanity of having Gods in their midst. Some of the younger townspeople had suddenly become believers, and I appreciated the tiny power boost.

But more than that, I was happy to be normal. Slipping Emeric into the baby carrier on my chest, I stood. "We better get ready. Clio and Morrigan will be here soon, and the townspeople will start to gather outside the walls."

We were celebrating. The first village-wide party we'd had in, well, nearly a century. It was a thank you from us—or maybe an apology. Demke was looking excited; years ago, we used to have a huge annual celebration in his honor, as well as one for the Goddess. They'd been some of the best days of our long lives, and although it was different now, that old thrill still buzzed around the group.

Erus stood and stretched. "I'll go check the ward once more, make sure it's strong so we can all relax."

Demke stood as well, his hand reaching down to stroke Zale's head, and then the long mahogany fall of Wren's hair too. He looked at Cy. "We best go talk to the Valkyries and the pack about security for tonight's event."

It had been Cy's suggestion that they pair up the Valkyries and some of the pack into teams. Now, most of the Valkyries had hound offsiders, and those offsiders were looking a little chunkier than the street dog waifishness they'd once had. I had a sneaking suspicion that some of them would find their way back to Asgard when this was all over.

Cy walked over to Wren, rubbing his face over the top of her head. He was touchy-feely, and you didn't need to be one of the Fates to know that their destinies were tightly intertwined. Whatever history they had, they were keeping to themselves for now, and I was okay with that. I wasn't like Teron and Demke, with their insatiable quest for knowledge and the need to know the hows and whys of all of life's little mysteries. Wren knew, and she seemed happy with it, and that was good enough for me.

Emeric was now asleep against my chest, and I reached out for Bran. Néit stood and slipped him into place into the carrier. The sheer width of my chest meant I could babywear all three at once.

Wren slid Zale into the last spot, then leaned forward to kiss me softly. "Have I ever told you how sexy you look strapped with babies?"

I groaned deep in my chest. "Not today, you haven't."

"I'm starting to see the appeal of keeping you barefoot and laden with newborns," she joked. "If only you could have the babies too."

Kissing her hard, I wished I could as well. I loved that this was one small thing I could do for my family. I wasn't just a tool made for war; I could be something soft and nurturing too. "If I could, I would. I'd have a dozen kids running around this place. Tiny little girls with your big eyes. Boys who look like toddlers when they're born. Little siblings for these guys."

However, nearly losing her during childbirth still gave me nightmares. I wasn't sure any of us was in a hurry to do that again.

Bran was snuffling around, hungry, and I knew it was time for their feed and nap, especially if we wanted to stay at the party for a while tonight. Leaning forward, I whispered in Wren's ear, "Why don't you go have a long bath while I feed, change and put our babies down for a nap?"

She groaned and bit her fist. "Milonos, I do believe you have dirty talk down to a fine art," she purred, but her eyes laughed at me.

*So beautiful.*

Dragging myself away, I headed to the kitchen to put bottles in the warmer. Rocking from side to side, I made shushing noises so Bran didn't wake his brothers. I hummed a lullaby that was buried deep in my brain, one that my mother had sung to me and my siblings. The words were lost to time, but the tune was still there on my tongue.

A longing for my family, for my own kind, hit me in the chest. Having Wren and the babies had ripped open a wound that had only healed on the surface. I had this family now—and some of them I'd had for lifetimes more than I'd ever had my blood family—but there was something tragic about being the last of my kind.

Shaking off the hints of melancholy, I grabbed the now-warm bottles and moved toward the nursery. It was beautiful. Tryp had painted a mural of winged horses and clouds floating through an azure sky, and I'd made most of the furniture over the last few weeks, usually at night as I kept watch. The babies were still sleeping in the one crib I'd made, swaddled tightly. They almost seemed incomplete when they were sepa-rated; they'd cry and fuss until they were all together once more.

Moving to the bed, I slowly unstrapped each sleeping baby like they were bombs seconds from deto-nating. Zale and Emeric stayed blissfully asleep, and I shifted them gently to the crib, except for Bran, who was staring up at me with big, unblinking eyes. The color should be impossible this early in their life, but it was a vivid, ensnaring blue. It was one of the few differences between the boys. Each had a different eye color, from Emeric's murky brown to Zale's foggy hazel that lightened to green more and more every day.

Bran's expression seemed older than it could possibly be, and while it had been a little disconcerting at first, I'd grown used to his stoic baby face.

"Let's feed you before your brothers wake up, what do you say?" I whispered to him. Sliding into the reinforced rocking chair, I held him easily in my arms, feeding him the bottle as he continued staring up at me. "You're an old soul, aren't you? You've been here before." He waved tiny hands, like he was trying to grab the bottle for himself. So independent already. "You've got such a big destiny, but I'm always going to be here to stand between you and danger. I promise you that."

Bran just continued to drink and stare into my soul. I chuckled low, enjoying the moment. His brothers would wake soon, because they were like clockwork when it came to feeding. Then it would be a matter of juggling one, so the other didn't think he was going to starve and start crying down the house. As if they knew what I was thinking, one of them let out a tiny whimper of indignation.

Tryp poked his head into the nursery. He'd probably been loitering outside the door, waiting for this moment. Tryp had been a surprise when it came to parenthood. He'd always been the most easygoing of us, all about whatever felt good. But he loved Wren, and I knew he loved these babies as an extension of her. He was the first to offer to do night feeds, he changed diapers, he snuggled fussy babies. He was more helpful than any of us could have predicted.

He seemed to enjoy it too, which was almost as surprising. Smiling into the crib, he looked over at me. "Need a hand?"

Bran still had half a bottle to go, so I nodded. "Yes."

With gentle but greedy hands, he picked up Emeric and cuddled him close. "It feels almost supernatural, the connection I feel to these little guys. I don't need Wren's vision to know that my destiny is wrapped tightly to their happiness," he said softly, and I grunted my assent. "And I don't mind, even a little," he cooed in a high baby voice. "It doesn't hurt that I saw your mama naked a minute ago, all slippery and wet in the bath, and that just makes the whole situation so much sweeter. Who would want to escape this fate?"

Smiling to myself, I looked down into the face of the baby in my arms once more. "Who indeed?"

# CHAPTER 20
## WREN

O

A huge bonfire in the center of town threw off so much heat, it was almost like a Hell pit had reopened. But the laughter and the smell of food on the air gave a far more welcoming atmosphere than a portal to Hell. Someone was playing a guitar, with several people singing along, though I didn't understand any of it. I'd picked up a few Greek words in my time here, but most of the time, the guys spoke to me in English.

I looked over at Milo, who was proudly showing off all three babies strapped to his chest to a long line of admirers. The villagers didn't know they were Mythics, or anything other than the most beautiful babies in the world. I trusted Milo with them, because he would murder this whole town to save them, regardless of his feelings toward the people. He was my marshmallow warrior, and he loved the triplets. It was there in every soft look, every stroke of their heads, the way his forearm banded beneath all three.

Plus, he was huge enough, and strong enough, to carry them all.

It was weird to see my guys among the... well, mortals. Hell, it was weird to be outside the walls of our compound. The Valkyries were around, dressed casually, but I knew their weapons were just enchanted so they couldn't be seen. They were there, just like Nate's ax was strapped across his back.

He was more casual than I'd seen him in so long, laughing and drinking with a bunch of elderly residents, listening to their stories in stilted English. The darkness of the night had settled over the crowd, lit only by hanging lights, and it was comforting rather than terrifying.

*Are you all right, my mate?* Griff's voice in my head was a sweet purr, and when I looked over, I saw Teron walking toward me, food in his hands. He nuzzled his cheek against mine as I took the plate. The smells coming from it made my mouth water. Thick slices of meat and fresh bread were piled up on the rough porcelain, along with a huge range of salad that vied for space.

I smiled up at him, but responded to Griff. *I'm fine. I'm having a really lovely time.*

Teron raised an eyebrow. "But?"

"I have my perfect babies, and my perfect boyfriends—and mate—in this beautiful tiny village filled with people who love and care for them, but I miss home. I miss Mrs. Byrne. I miss Rossi's deli. I miss my life back when it made sense."

"Wren—" Teron started, but I placed my finger against his lips.

"But I have no regrets. And even when this is all over, my home is with you guys now, and while my life might be more... complicated, I wouldn't change anything. Not where we live. Not the babies. *Nothing.*"

He lifted me onto his lap and fed me pieces of my food from his fingers, his eyes hungrily watching my lips as they closed around the food. There was a heat between us, and my body was almost healed from the triplets. God knows, my libido had definitely healed and was raring to go.

However, the birth of the triplets—or more specifically, what had happened afterwards—made one fact undeniable. I was still mortal. I'd almost died. Irrespective of the fact that the babies were Demigods at the very least, that hadn't transferred to me. And why would it? I had no higher purpose, other than as a vessel. A vessel was useless once it had delivered its contents.

I kept reminding myself that I wasn't getting anything more or less than what the average person got. I'd have time to see the boys grow into strong men with a world-altering purpose, hopefully. I didn't deserve to be any greedier than that.

Especially not when I had so many partners who wanted to love me in every way a man could love a woman. Including the one beneath me right now, who was trying to be restrained despite the hard line of his cock beneath my ass.

"Sweet Wren. I'm going to trace every inch of your body with my tongue," he purred in my ear, and I practically vibrated in his lap. "I've been dying slowly, waiting for our moment."

"Teron…" I breathed. "We don't have to wai—"

"Teron! I'm so glad you're here!" One of the local villagers appeared in front of us, the leg of his pants rolled up to expose a festering sore on his calf.

*Ew.* The meat I just ate threatened to make a reappearance, and despite the semi-hard dick beneath my ass cheeks, Teron looked at the villager with nothing but kind compassion. It was why I loved him so much.

A disgruntled huff in my brain almost made me laugh out loud. *I can bite off his leg, and you two can go back to what you were doing. He has so much pent-up sexual tension that it can't possibly be healthy. The other day, he jerked off three times in the shower shouting your—*

*Stop!* Teron shouted in my mind, although his face didn't change as he listened to the villager talking about how he'd scraped his calf on an old screw, which had been poking out from a piece of farm equipment, and then his leg had begun to fester. *Ugh, I better handle this before he gets blood poisoning,* Teron told us telepathically as lifted me gently from his lap and placed me on the bench beside him, his long coat doing its best to hide his erection from the man in front of us.

"Let me grab my medical bag, and I'll irrigate and bandage it before it gets further infected." He stood, turning toward me and kissing my cheek. "Later," he promised, and I didn't think he meant picking up our conversation. He wandered away with the village guy, whose name I didn't catch, and I was alone once more. I looked through the crowd, trying to catch a glimpse of my guys.

Erus and Tryp were running the bar, being quite liberal with the rakí, if the amount of inebriated humans running around was any indication. They looked like they were having a great time, though, laughing and joking, dancing behind the makeshift tent storing the liquor. Erus had explained that celebrations and partying had once been their main profession; they'd been cupbearers, or something along those lines. They were there for the vibes, and right now, they were in their element.

Dogs ran through the crowd, including Cy in his canine form. I didn't know if he was keeping the pack in line, or if the town just expected Cy the dog to be at an event like this. That seemed likely. If I'd learned anything about Cy in the last few weeks, it was that he was loyal to a fault. He cared about every single one of his hounds. He cared about every single villager, even if they treated him like a dog. He even cared about my guys, even though their relationship had been strained for a very long time.

I looked for Demke, expecting him to be in the thick of it, but came up empty. Searching further out from the firelight, I saw him at the edge of the darkness, his face tilted up at the moon. Shifting the plate of food from my lap—my appetite gone in the face of the villager's mangled tetanus leg—I moved toward him.

He was so compelling, and I could understand why he'd been worshiped for so many centuries. Everything about him screamed *more*. More beauty. More power. More everything. He had his own gravitational pull, and I was helpless to resist. Moving around the small clusters of villagers, as well as dancing Valkyries, I stepped into the darkness beside him.

He looked down at me, his eyes reflecting the flickering firelight. "Wren," he greeted softly.

"What are you doing out here by yourself?" I kept my voice low. There was something about being here, on the fringes between the light and the dark, that felt almost seductive. Like the possibilities of what could happen here, just out of sight, were endless.

He tilted his face back up to the sky. "Bathing in the moonlight. Soaking in the life around me." He sighed. "If I'm honest, I don't know who I am anymore. How I'm meant to interact with these humans, who have never known me as a God. Who've never heard of my religion, or any religion except Christianity. I don't know how to be normal."

I couldn't help the laugh that snuck past my lips. "Demke, you're about as far from normal as you can get. They might not all know you're Demke, the Minoan God of Renewal, but they definitely don't think of you as anything as mundane as normal."

He shifted his gaze back to me, and I tried to read his expression. Of all the men in my life, I still found Demke an enigma. He was trying—that much was obvious. He was as fond of the babies as any of the others; he took his turns at feedings, and was already researching baby food combinations for when they could start solids. I caught him regularly sniffing their heads, or talking to them in a soft voice in a language I suspected was ancient Minoan.

However, when he looked at me, there was such a weird tangle of emotions, that it gave me whiplash. Longing, definitely. Guilt, maybe, though that was lessening as time went on. Frustration, though I didn't know what about.

"And you?"

I'd been so lost in my thoughts, I wasn't sure what he meant. "What?"

"Do you think of me as normal?" The soft timbre of his voice brushed over me like a caress.

Shaking my head, I looked up into those eyes that seemed alive with heat. "Someone like you was always destined to be special."

Leaning down closer, his fingers brushed across my hip, and the innocent touch felt like it electrocuted me from the clit outwards. "You were also destined to be special, Wren Mahone. Special to the world. Special to my brothers." Leaning forward, he brushed his lips across mine as he whispered, "Special to me."

I kissed him. Not something soft and delicate, or hesitant. I kissed to consume, to own, to burn. I kissed him like I needed him to survive, and he kissed me back with just as much desperation. He lifted me easily, and I wrapped my legs around his waist, holding him tightly like he was going to change his mind and disappear into the darkness. But as he stepped back further from the bonfire, I realized he was going to take us both into the shadows, and a thrill of pleasure coursed through my body.

I bit his lip, making him groan. "*Wren.*" He said my name the way a dying man might say a prayer. Like I was his last chance at salvation.

I felt the rough scrape of something along my back, but I was too consumed by the man who was twined around me to care what it was.

He dragged his mouth away. "I want you more than I've wanted anyone in so long. This isn't what I planned, however."

Looking around, I realized we were in a rocky outcropping on the edge of town. The moon made his hair look like spilled ink, his face carved by shadows. "This is perfect."

He laughed and dropped me to my feet, though he didn't stop kissing me. I didn't know what he was doing, but I could feel the tingle of something on my skin. Like the moment before a storm. Or when you accidentally—maybe on purpose—touched your phone charger to your tongue. It was like a jolt of feeling across all your nerve endings.

Tearing my mouth from his, I noticed the area around our feet was now blanketed in the softest moss and clover, with small purple flowers poking up between the leaves. I gaped in amazement, kicking off my shoes to rub my toes in the soft blanket of green. "Did you just summon us a bed?"

Picking me up once more, he dropped to his knees and lowered me to my back. "Making love to you, under the moon, on a bed of flowers is the very least you deserve."

*This man. No, this God. He's going to ruin me.*

Hell, who was I kidding? I was already ruined.

# CHAPTER 21
## DEMKE

O

She was a goddess at that moment. I no longer cared if she was mortal, that she was destined to break my still-wounded heart. The only thing that mattered to me right now was the taste of her skin. The soft noises she made as my lips traced hers. The glow of her milk-pale skin in the darkness, a beacon to night creatures like me.

I traced my hands up her thighs, pushing up the soft knit skirt she was wearing along with it. Kneeling between her legs, I slowly unwrapped her from the swaths of fabric hiding her body from me. I wanted more of her skin. More of her noises. I wanted to taste every inch.

"Demke," she breathed, and I shuddered, my skin already too tight across my sinew and bones. I sipped the words from her lips as I ridded her of the last piece of clothing that stood between my hands and her flesh.

It had been so long since I'd laid with a woman, and even longer since I'd laid with a woman I cared about.

Her tiny hands ran up under my shirt, finding her own piece of skin, peeling me out of my clothes too. Soon enough, we were both naked, clothed only in the darkness.

I swept my lips across hers, once, twice, three times. "I'm going to make love to you now, Wren Mahone. The way I want you…" I shivered again, and it had nothing to do with the cold.

"Please, Demke."

Her plea went straight to my already hard cock, making it weep. When my hands dipped down to her stomach, she tensed, nudging my hands further down like she wanted them between her thighs, which she probably did. But more than that, I thought she might have been embarrassed about the soft pouch that sat between her hips, the evidence that she'd created life right before my eyes.

Instead, I lifted her chin so I could stare directly into her eyes. "You are a miracle, Wren. Beautiful in every way, every inch of you is as perfect as the next. A madonna." I cupped the mound of her stomach between my two palms and poured magic into her body, making her gasp. I wasn't sure what it felt like exactly, but I had heard it was pleasant.

Her eyes widened. "What was that?"

"Renewal magic. I was healing your womb. I don't want to hurt you."

"Healing… my womb?" she asked incredulously.

Shrugging, I smiled down at her. It still felt almost foreign on my face after all this time. "God of Renewal. Nothing more sacred than a womb. I could have done it earlier, but it's best not to mess with nature too much. Some things are best done the slow healing way." I gave her a crooked grin. "But a little nudge so I can give you as much pleasure as possible didn't seem too unnatural."

Nodding dazedly, her fingers continued to run up and down my back muscles, and I wanted to purr. "My life is crazy," she murmured to herself. "Kiss me, God of Renewal."

Laughing, I stole her lips once more, before traveling my way down her body. She hadn't said *where* I should kiss her, and everyone knew, you had to be really specific when making requests of Mythics. She didn't seem to mind, though, as I licked and sucked at her sensitive breasts. Milk leaked out onto my tongue, that liquid of life, and I groaned. I wanted to linger, but there was something else I wanted to sip at.

I buried my face in the soft roundness of her stomach, but moved quickly down, until her legs were splayed open wildly, though barely enough to accommodate my shoulders. I gripped her thighs and placed them over my shoulders, so there was nothing but cool air between her core and my lips.

As I dipped down to taste her in one long stroke, we both moaned. I hoped the party was loud enough that no one heard us—not because I was embarrassed, but because I didn't want to share this moment with anyone. Not my brothers. Not the townspeople. No one but the moon and the woman beneath me.

She chanted my name as I swirled my tongue and worshiped her. It had been so, so long. She was sweet on my tongue, and I was immediately addicted. Her thighs tightened around my head, stopping me from shifting away from where she wanted me. As if I would. The Great Hunt would have to appear to chase me from this moment.

"Oh god, oh god," she moaned, and I smiled against her folds. I didn't even care that she was technically calling for a different God. I'd take it.

When she came on my tongue, I groaned against her clit, making her tighten her fingers in my hair. I hadn't even noticed they were there. I was solely focused on the task at hand. Or task at mouth, as it would seem.

My dick was starting to weep, and this was going to be over very quickly if I didn't get my cock under control. Climbing back up her body, I shared with her the taste of her pleasure, before I wrapped her legs around my waist, notching my cock against her warm cunt. Then I rolled us until she was straddling my hips.

I ground my back teeth at the all-consuming pleasure. I could come just to this visage alone. She was *perfect*. She reached down and gripped my cock, sliding it inside her in one smooth move that made my eyes roll back into my head.

Heaven. I'd reached the Elysian fields. Nirvana.

"Wren," I choked out, squeezing my eyes shut to make sure I didn't come with one stroke. I sat up, wrapping my arms around her waist, and she twined her own around my neck. This close, it was like we were breathing each other in, becoming one.

She rolled her hips, making me hiss. I was keeping it together by a single thread. I needed more control, and I cast out my magic until a vine climbed down the rockface and wrapped around her wrists, holding them high above her head.

She gasped, looking up at the vines, then down at me in wonder. How long had it been since anyone had looked at me so reverently? Ensuring the vines tightened until her body was one long line in the moonlight, I smiled like an artist. *Beautiful.*

I felt my climax press back a little. This was better, because if she gripped me with her hands the way she was gripping me with her core, I was going to spill inside her immediately.

I let my hands flow over her skin, trying to memorize every inch, every curve, every soft place. I wanted to bathe in her delicious body forever. Then she clenched down around me, and I mentally cursed. She smirked, and I could see the challenge in her eyes. She didn't need her hands to make me come undone. She was going to kill me slowly, though I'd die with a smile on my face. Pressing my fingers tightly on her hips, I took control of the moment, plunging her up and down.

Deep inside her, I felt her mortality. Felt it wrap around my own immortal spark, barely a glimmer against the glow of my God light. I wanted more than anything to give her some of my immortality, to share it with her so she would stay with me and my brothers forever.

But that wasn't how it worked, and the thought threatened to break my heart and ruin this moment. Shaking away the melancholic idea, I thrust up harder and listened to her whimper my name helplessly. That was better.

I wanted her to scream out her prayers to me as I wrung orgasm after orgasm from her soft, delicious form. I wanted her to chant my name until they could hear it over the sounds of the party. And she performed beautifully.

"Demke!" she screamed as she convulsed around my cock. It was too much for me now. I couldn't hold back as she milked me like this, no matter how badly I wanted to make her come more times before I found my own climax.

When she came, it was like she stole a piece of my soul. My seed released deep inside her, and I clutched her tightly to my chest. We stayed together like that, panting and twisted around each other.

"Wow," she breathed. She was good for my ego, because that had been an absolutely rubbish performance. I would only get better as I became less rusty. Or, as Tryp put it, as I blew the dust and cobwebs off my balls.

"Indeed," I agreed, loosening the vines until we were nose-to-nose and I could feast on her lips. I couldn't get enough of kissing her. Had it ever felt like this? Not since I was first made a God, with my

Goddess, had I ever felt this level of rightness. Of pleasure and happiness. "I think we can do that at least three more times before people realize we are missing," I said softly into her ear, and she let out a sweet giggle.

She tugged at her vine-bound wrists. "This was showing off a little, don't you think?"

I grinned, two more vines sneaking out to wrap around each of her ankles. "I haven't even begun showing you what I'm capable of," I whispered in her ear.

Turns out, I could make her come four more times before we were interrupted by a peeved-looking Gryphon in the darkness. *Whoops.*

# CHAPTER 22
## NATE

Khonsu's ward fell at two forty-five p.m. on a Tuesday. Even though there was no physical evidence of the occurrence, the magic felt like a pop around us. Even the babies seemed to sense the change, becoming fussy and disgruntled.

At six-twelve p.m., we had our first guest. A very polite Demigod from the Kalevalans—the Finnish Mythics, though there weren't many of them left—who arrived without fanfare or escorts. Just a blond guy in a pink polo shirt, with a large, wrapped box in his hands. He looked like he was around twenty-five, with a trendy haircut, and seemed far more mortal than any Mythic I'd ever met.

The Valkyries had looked at him with obvious disdain, though when I'd asked if their Pantheons had beef, apparently I'd been wildly off base. He and Mist had once been in a relationship, and had broken up rather fantastically, so now they all hated his guts in solidarity.

He must've had some massive balls, standing there outside the compound, looking pleasant yet unconcerned by the obvious antagonism of the women around him. Milo appeared with the babies so the guy could pledge his Pantheon's allegiance. He pledged, handed over the gift, and left.

Unfortunately, he'd been the first of many. Every tiny, nearly forgotten Pantheon turned up on our doorstep. Old Gods who no longer had a cohort—just interminable loneliness—turned up, proof of what could happen if you were out of favor with the Fates, or were on your last turn of the wheel. Most of the Slavic Mythics sent representatives, as there was no love lost between them and the Greeks, and even some of the Eastern Mythics turned up. Cy had a long conversation with a Kitsune from the Shintō Mythics, who came on behalf of her God, Inari.

I was fairly sure I saw a little bit of jealousy on Wren's face at that. She and Cy were tight, but I didn't think they'd taken that step yet.

We let none of them even close to the walls of the compound, most of them stopped on the outskirts of town by the Valkyries and the hounds, then escorted to us under heavy guard, if the Valkyries decided that they weren't a threat. I didn't know if they'd turned anyone away yet, but I trusted their judgment. If they had doubts, it was better the Valkyries turn them away than I behead them with my ax. Even though a decapitation of prevention was better than a battle of cure.

Or maybe it would be Demke with the threats of beheading. I wasn't sure what had occurred between him and Wren on the night of the party, but it didn't take a genius to figure out it involved sex. Now, the ancient God was as territorial and protective as a junkyard dog—no offense to any of the junkyard dogs that currently protected the perimeter of the town. He eyeballed every single person at the gate, like they were one wrong word from being shriveled to dust on the wind.

I was happy for them, mostly. With the budding of their relationship, all the remaining tension in our group had disappeared, and we were one cohesive unit. A family.

The golden hog from the Norse was weaving around my feet, and it had doubled in size. I had a feeling that it wasn't going to be normal sized. When had mystical mounts ever been pocket sized? There had been no great heroes who conquered their tasks by pulling out their pocket poodle to defeat a chimera. No, they were always above-average-sized great beasts.

Given that in the last month it had gone from fitting in a lunch sack to being able to headbutt my knee, I didn't think this one was going to be any different. "What do you want, Pig?"

Milo, surprisingly without any of the babies, walked over and laughed. "You should call him by his name, or you'll piss off the Valkyries. He is one step below a God to them."

I reached down and scratched the boar's head, and he made a happy grunting noise. "He likes it, don't you Pig?" He snuffled at my hand, and I gave him the last half of my sandwich. Then the ungrateful pork chop ran off. Huffing, I turned back to Milo. "The almost-Demigod just conned me out of my sandwich."

Laughing, he slumped down next to me. "I caught Trig"—that was the raven chick, though he looked like a fully grown raven now—"nesting in the crib beside the babies, and when I went to shoo him out, he bit my fingers. They are far too comfortable here."

I chuckled. They might be like having three extra responsibilities right now, but they were already grow-ing, and I knew I would eventually be glad the babies had their guardians, especially while they were young and vulnerable.

Hrist appeared in the way the Valkyries could do. It was kind of impressive, but also somewhat annoying. They sped into place so fast, it was like they portaled right in front of you. Great for the element of surprise in battle, annoying as hell when you were about to have a sip of your beer.

However, the look on her face replaced my annoy-ance with concern. "What's wrong?"

Milo stood, prepared to race back toward the nursery and the babies. That was his job, should the worst happen and we were attacked again. He was the last line of defense between Wren and the triplets, and anything that wanted to hurt them.

"We have visitors." Hrist didn't seem overly alarmed, but she was tense. That ruled out the Moirai or any of the monsters.

Milo shook his head, already transforming into his bull-headed form. Guess he wasn't waiting for the big reveal. "Spit it out. Who is it?"

"Apollo. And the Oracle Delphos."

*Well… shit.* I looked at Milo. "Go, just in case." He didn't need to be told twice, and was gone faster than you would think a being of that size could move. I looked back at Hrist. "What do they want?"

She shrugged. "They say what they all want. To pledge to the new Fates. But…"

Nodding, I stood. "Yeah, but."

But they were from the Greek Pantheon.

But Apollo was a powerful Mythic.

But Delphos was THE Oracle.

Hrist fell into step beside me as I headed toward the doors, in case they decided to do something stupid. "Get Demke. And Cy—maybe keeping this a family affair might help. And if you see Teron, tell him it might be a nice time for Griff to come and visit."

Hrist didn't reply; she was just gone. Trepidation crawled along my veins. Neither Apollo nor Delphos had been overtly antagonistic, but if the plight of the Minoans had taught us anything, it was not to trust a single damn thing that came out of their mouth.

I was unsurprised to see Demke and Griff at the

door before I even made it there. Hrist didn't mess around, and these two were definitely "kill first, ask questions later" when it came to the Greek Mythics. Even now, Demke's eyes burned holes in the door, like he could see Apollo just there, on the other side.

Cy sauntered up at a slower pace, and while his body language was calm and easy, his eyes looked concerned. This shit could go bad in so many different ways, but there was no point sitting around worrying about the what-ifs.

Then Wren appeared.

"You should go back to the nursery with Milo and the babies." I was glad Demke had said it and not me, because the withering glare she gave him would have shriveled the balls of a mortal man.

She put her hands on her hips and tilted her head in a way that would be cute, if it didn't spell sudden death. "You should mind your own business. I'm not pregnant anymore, and I have just as much right to be out here as you do. In fact, maybe more. Let's go."

She didn't wait for anyone's permission, and honestly, that's why I loved her. She was so sexy when she gave no fucks. Enough to give an immortal gray hairs, but still sexy.

Griff positioned himself beside her, like a huge Gryphon shadow, and I nodded. If it couldn't be me watching her ass like that, I was glad it was him. Once again, I was kind of grateful that we'd fallen into this weird, giant harem.

Did I enjoy the idea that she was fucking them all?

Fuck no. But in these moments, was I glad to have others at my back to protect her? Abso-fucking-lutely. I'd been in grand battles, but the thought of being the one solely responsible for the safety of Wren and the babies actually gave me nightmares when I fell asleep.

Pushing open the door, we were greeted by a wall of Valkyries. Beyond them, the two Gods in question stood around, looking completely at ease.

"Holy shit, Cy. Your dad is beautiful," Wren whispered, and Cy huffed an amused sound.

"Only on the outside," he murmured back, before moving forward and stepping around the Valkyries.

He went up to the second man, who was definitely younger, though it was more of a feeling than a visual age difference. The weight of Apollo's power was only slightly less than that of Hades. The other guy—who I assumed was Delphos—felt powerful, but not even in the same realm as Apollo, let alone Hades.

Cy hugged Delphos, and it was full of affection. "Brother."

The King of Oracles looked down at his brother fondly. "Cydon. It is good to see you after all these years. You look well. Happy."

"As you knew I would."

He laughed, but it was a sad sound. "As you say." He looked past Cy to Wren. "It worked out as it should in the end, though." He inclined his head at Wren. "Wren Mahone. It is a pleasure to finally meet you."

She stepped forward, and I resisted the urge to snatch her back behind me. Holding out a hand, she shook his lightly. "It's nice to meet Cy's family. And thank you, I guess, for the Oracle in my drive-thru? She saved my butt."

Delphos shook his head. "I can't claim credit for the prophecies of my Oracles. They moved off my mountain a long time ago, venturing into the world as was their right. Any prophecies they hand out are their own." He gave her a lopsided smile. "But I'm glad she was where she needed to be."

"She had terrible taste in coffee."

"Cassie always did." Delphos turned to the other Mythic beside him. "Cydon doesn't seem inclined to introduce our father, so allow me. Wren, this is Apollo, one of the twelve Olympian Gods, and the God of Prophecy, Music, Poetry, Medicine and, uh, the Sun? Did I forget any?"

"Dance, Healing, Light—you know, all the fun stuff," Apollo added. "Much like my son, I am glad to meet you, Wren Mahone."

She nodded. "Nice to meet you too. As Cy's dad, not as the Greek God. No offense." She shrugged, like she hadn't just demoted him to a father-in-law, rather than one of the most powerful Gods in existence. "I've met a few of your children now, and they say nice things about you, so that must mean something."

Apollo frowned, like he was wracking his brain for all his children—which, rumor had it, were quite a lot— before he nodded. "Ah, Asclepius. That really did send Father into a bit of a spin when he came out and saved the life of the Mother of Fate. The God he'd tried to banish from the wheel, saving the woman who was going to unseat his power? It does have the spice of one of the old tales, don't you think?"

*His father? That would be…*

Demke hissed. "Zeus can suck my dick."

Apollo threw back his head and laughed. "You've become delightfully modern, old friend." He patted his stomach. "But indeed, Zeus can deal. Needless to say, I am in the bad books. My children just keep causing drama wherever they go. But who says the children should get all the fun?" He straightened his shoulders, then dropped to his knee.

"I'm here to vow my adherence to the new Fates and their weaving of the fabric of destiny."

*Well… I didn't see that coming.*

# CHAPTER 23
## WREN

O

"You're pledging to the wrong person," was all that came out of my mouth. Given the amount of gaping mouths in our small group, I didn't think I was the only one who was surprised.

Apollo looked up at me, and I realized that he and Cy shared the same eyes. "I wanted you to know that I was serious."

Demke looked incredulous. "A false show of good faith before stabbing someone in the back. That isn't in the Greek playbook at all. Excuse me if I'm less swayed by you dropping to a knee and making a vow that means nothing."

Cy was chewing his lip, though his expression was hard to read. He looked at Delphos, maybe for a hint at his father's real motivations. But Delphos gave nothing away, not that I could discover anyway. Cy, though, must have seen something in his expression. "You've had a prophecy."

Anxiety tightened in my chest. No one prophesied about living a long, mundane life. When Delphos shook his head, relief rushed through me.

Prematurely, it would seem. "No, brother. I had a premonition."

Stiffening, Cy looked between his father and me. He gave a tight nod, apparently deciding that answered all his questions. Well, fuck that, because it didn't answer any of mine.

"Prophecy, premonition—what's the difference?"

It was Apollo who answered, standing back up to his full height. I can imagine he would have looked otherworldly once upon a time, but now he looked like a male Tom Ford model. Tall, but not mystically so. Gorgeous, though. "A prophecy is meant for the listener. It isn't set in stone, but it's meant to guide the person who hears it. A premonition is a vision of the future, and Delphos can say no more unless he wants to alter the outcome."

I frowned, wondering if he was talking to me in circles. "But he can tell *you?* Because I have no doubt that whatever his premonition was, it's the reason you're standing here, making grand oaths."

Apollo's smile was full of blindingly white teeth that seemed to glow in the Cretan sun. "Smart. I can see why the greater powers chose you to carry the new Fates. You're wrong, but it was a solid guess." His gaze bounced around our group. "Delphos wasn't the only one who had the premonition. Oracles and seers all across the world had the same vision. It is why Mythics have been lining up at your door like this is the best little whorehouse on the prairie."

No one spoke. That whole statement was a lot, and not just the prairie reference. Here I'd thought that all these bizarre Mythics had been showing up because they were tired of the status quo, but really, there was something bigger going on. A premonition of a future that was so abhorrent, they were flocking to our door.

Shaking my head, I looked at Delphos. "Your last prophecy was wrong."

"Was it?" he asked lightly, but his eyes were full of forbidden knowledge.

"I didn't die in childbirth, and the babies are all fine." I waved my arms down my body, as if to show them I hadn't kicked the bucket.

Delphos gave a soft smile. "You weren't the mother that had to die. The prophecy was fulfilled before your babies were born, by the jaws of Typhon."

Lachesis? She was the mother? It hit me then. The Moirai's other names: The Maiden, The Mother, and the Crone. Lachesis was The Mother.

I narrowed my eyes at Delphos. "Oh, that's tricky."

He smirked. "I don't create the prophecies, only share them occasionally." Mirth fell from his face, and he was serious once more. "This premonition I can't share, but it affects us all."

I looked at Demke, then around at the rest of the guys. I wanted to be tough and independent, but this shit was way out of my realm of experience. So I asked the one bondmate who could advise me without giving away the fact I had no fucking idea what was going on. Although, that fact was already pretty obvious to everyone in a five-mile radius.

*Do you believe him?* I asked Griff.

He made a low noise in the back of his throat that wasn't even close to human. *I do not believe he has any reason to lie, and it certainly fits with our experience of the amount of Mythics that have arrived. I believe the sheer number has exceeded even Demke's expectations.*

*Do we let him near the babies?*

There was silence for a moment. *I think we must. But if he even looks at our cubs wrong, I will bite off his head, immortal war be damned.*

I swallowed down my laugh. *That's why I love you.*

I looked at Demke and nodded. "One wrong move, and your head will roll across the courtyard." I addressed both Apollo and Delphos, because while Apollo was the bigger, scarier God, that didn't mean Delphos wasn't also a threat. They both nodded their agreement, and I looked over at Cy. "Can you get Milo to bring out the babies?" He kissed my cheek, a very obvious sign of loyalty to me, and disappeared back into the house, past the protective wards.

"You certainly have my son smitten," Apollo commented, watching him go. "And apparently, you're wearing off on the others, because there was a time Demke would have run him through with a sword, rather than let him behind those hallowed walls."

I was saved from responding when Demke himself

did. "Cydon has proven his loyalty to Wren over and over. I trust him."

Delphos smiled slightly, but I thought it was a private smile. What would it be like to be a puppet master like that? Knowing all the pieces of the puzzle and just watching mortals flail around, trying to make sense of the world. It sounded lonely.

I was glad my babies had each other. They wouldn't be lonely Gods on a mountain, hiding from being bombarded by prophecies and premonitions.

Moving my gaze to Apollo, I nodded my agreement. "I'm smitten with him too."

Further mundane small talk stalled when a giant Minotaur appeared. For once, he wasn't holding a baby, as Erus and Tryp followed behind, holding Bran, Emeric and Zale. No, Milo was holding an enormous sword, almost as tall as me.

Apollo just smiled. "Hello, Milonos."

"One wrong move, and I'll cleave your smirking face in two."

Apollo raised an eyebrow. "Fair. I promise, I mean no harm here." His voice dropped low. "I meant no harm then either."

I was obviously missing something in their history, but now wasn't the time for a lesson. I'd sit with Milo and tease out the sordid details later. Right now, I wanted their pledge and then I wanted them gone.

Erus and Tryp stepped forward, each of them eyeing the Greek Mythics suspiciously. The babies in their arms were alert and awake, like they somehow knew this was a monumental moment.

Maybe they did. Were they not sort of Oracles too?

Apollo frowned down at the babies. "They are very small."

Cy stepped up close to them, like he was ready to throw down with his family for them. Man, I was definitely falling for that man. "They were premature. That's what happens when an expectant mother is bombarded with monsters trying to kill her."

Apollo held up his hands, palms out. "I had nothing to do with that. From what I know, the Moirai were acting alone."

Demke snorted, looking like he wanted to rip Apollo's head off too. "They're never acting alone. Zeus knows, at the very least. Let's not pretend they do anything without it being sanctioned by Olympus."

Apollo shrugged. "Like I said, I'm on his shit list. What he does or doesn't want isn't passed on to me."

"I'm not an expert on Olympus, but I don't think you pledging to the new Fates is going to get you off that list," Nate muttered.

He had a point. Would this bring down more war on our heads? Why did everything with Mythics have to have such dire consequences?

As if Delphos saw the look on my face, he shook his head imperceptibly. Could he read my mind, or was it just an obvious question we were all thinking about?

Cy trusted Delphos. It was why he'd spent all these years locked inside the invisible wards of the island waiting for me. His Oracle had saved my life, and those of my babies. I didn't completely trust his motivations, but this was one of those leap-of-faith moments, and I just had to pray that this was the right choice.

Did parenthood ever get any easier?

Milo went through the ward first, then Tryp and Erus. Erus was holding Zale and Bran, while Tryp had Emeric bundled in his arms. I *hated* this. I knew they weren't really vulnerable. They were one stumble backwards away from safety. All of us were here, watching for threats, for one wrong move, but it still felt way too vulnerable.

Not wanting to be out of the wards longer than necessary, I waved a hand at Apollo. "This is the part where you drop to your knees again."

He chuckled. "So impatient." He lowered himself theatrically back to one knee. "I vow my adherence to the new Fates, known as the Kuningilin, born from the seeds of destiny. I will accept my fate." He reached up and touched the foreheads of each of the babies while I held my breath, but then he got to his feet and stepped away.

Delphos quickly took his position. "I vow my adherence to the new Fates, known as the Kuningilin, born from the seeds of destiny and from the womb of the Maker's chosen. I am a faithful servant of the Fates and will undertake their will. I will accept my fate." He stood, stroking a finger down each of their heads, then stepped back. The babies eyed him in that baby way, like they were trying to figure out what he was.

The air around us felt tense, like the universe was holding its breath. Finally, it was like a pop, all the sound rushing back into the courtyard. Emeric gurgled and flailed his arms around, and Tryp shifted him to his shoulder.

Apollo shook his head. "So small. You know, once upon a time, they would have been put in clay urns on a hill and sacrificed in my name. Too small to live."

I narrowed my eyes. "Once upon a time, you would have had a baby with your sister, so I'm not sure the old ways are the best ways." Tension flooded the courtyard, and Erus and Tryp subtly stepped back into the wards. *Whoops.*

But Apollo just laughed, a sweet, loud sound that sounded like music. "That is very true, Wren Mahone. Modern medicine and a choice of fuckable women is definitely a boon of this new age." He stretched, showing off golden abs. Man, he was beautiful, but he was definitely not for me. I could appreciate it, though, right? Like fine art. Literally fine art. There were dozens of statues of this man in museums all over the world.

"Well, speaking of fuckable women, we should be off. Until we meet again, Wren Mahone." He dipped his chin at the infants, like they cared about genuflection at this point in their lives, and then surprised us all by hugging Cy. "Son. It's good to see you again. I missed you."

In that moment, I believed him. He was a manwhore—that much was obvious—but the fact that he'd gone against Zeus for both Cy and Asclepius, the fact that not one of them had anything bad to say about him, meant he was probably a decent father. I mean, when it came to the Greeks, the bar was on the floor, but still.

He slapped Delphos on the back. "Let's go down to one of the bars in Heraklion and get you laid, son. I can't even imagine how long it's been." He waggled his eyebrows at Nate. "I hear that the Morrigan herself is in town, and that she's as beautiful as she is deadly."

I watched Nate's face for jealousy, for any hint that his feelings for Morrigan might still exist, but all I saw was mirth. "She will eat you alive, but try your best."

Tipping an imaginary hat at us, Apollo winked, dragging Delphos away. "Oh, I will."

We watched until they were no more than a speck in the distance. "What are the odds she stabs him?" I asked Nate, and he chuckled.

"I give it seven minutes before she tries to gut him. Badb can take care of herself, and Apollo is a big boy. Let them entertain themselves." Kissing my temple, he led us all back into the compound.

I looked around at the group we made. "What did he call the babies? The Klingon?"

It was one of the Valkyries who answered. "The Kuningilin. It's an old Germanic word for wrens. But it also means kinglet. Wrens were considered the king of the birds. The last three powerful brothers born into mythology ended up ruling the sea, the sky, and the Underworld."

*Well, great. That isn't ominous at all.*

. . .

"Child, wake up. There are spiders in your bed." Mrs. Byrne poked me with the cane she sometimes used, and I grumbled, pushing my head under my pillow. "Wren Eloise Mahone, *wake up*. There are spiders in your bed, and if you don't hurry up, they'll pull you into the web."

*Is Mrs. Byrne having a stroke? Should I call 911?*

"Mrs. B, there are no spiders. We just had the place sprayed for bugs, remember? You flirted with the fumigator guy."

Mrs. B would normally laugh, but this time, she just shoved at me harder. "Get up, child. Your babies *need* you."

Consciousness hit me like a baseball bat to the face. I was awake and out of bed before I even realized that I wasn't home in Boston, in my apartment. I was moving toward the nursery before I remembered that I was in Crete and the murkiness of my dream had fully dissipated. The silence of the house was peaceful, and my heart rate started to calm. It was just a night terror.

Still, I was up, so it wouldn't hurt to just check on the boys. A night light cast the room in a gentle glow, shadows still lurking on the edges.

Except the one in front of the crib. That shadow had a knife in its hand, its golden blade flashing ethereally in the low light of the room.

I screamed even as I leapt toward the shadow.

I screamed even as another shadow detached from

the darkness to join the one in front of the crib, another knife in its hand, though this one was an average silver.

I screamed as I hit them like a linebacker, and we all went down in a heap, a sliver of light revealing their faces. Clotho and Atropos, the remaining Moirai, though they'd become something haggard and ugly since the death of their sister, the weathering of age catching up to them finally.

My scream turned into something filled with rage. White-hot, burning rage boiled in my chest. Incomprehensible words echoed around the room as we wrestled for the knife, spittle flying from Clotho's lips as she cursed me in ancient Greek. I scratched at their faces, legs, arms as I tried to kill them. I kicked and fought for my babies. For their lives and mine.

Nate was suddenly there, his ax flying through the air, beheading Clotho. Her head thumped to the floor beside mine, her eyes wide open and her face in an eternal grimace. He spun quickly and buried his ax in Atropos's back, and she fell beside her sister.

The Moirai were no more.

Nate slumped to his knees beside me. "Wren," he breathed, horror etched across his pale face.

The room was getting foggy at the edges. Were there more shadows? Had they brought reinforcements? I looked down and realized that rage wasn't the only thing burning in my chest.

The golden knife was also there, buried to the hilt.

I tried to speak, but pained gasps and wet sounds were the only thing that bubbled out. Nate was shouting, and I could hear the vibration of feet running, but it was too late. Everything was fading faster now. Then the room was gone, and the only thing left was the light, someone silhouetted there. I *knew* the curve of those shoulders. The cockiness of that stance.

Mrs. Byrne.

"I tried to warn you, child," she chastised gently. "Come now, let's walk. It'll be all better soon." Looking behind me, a small smile curled her lips at the person there. "Well, you're a surprise, but I'm glad you're here too."

Looking over my shoulder, I saw the blocky head of Cy's dog form, and then the darkness was absolute.

# CHAPTER 24
## NATE

I watched the light leave her eyes, and I died right along with her.

Resting my head against her chest, I did something I hadn't done in so, so long. I cried. I prayed to anyone I could think of to guide her back to me. To take me too.

Anything but this pain. This failure.

I didn't hear the others enter the room. Didn't hear their own shock. Their grief. I was only vaguely aware of the mournful call of the Gryphon who'd lost his mate. Until they tried to take her body from me, I wasn't aware of any of them.

Her life was tied to mine. How was I still here?

I looked up at Demke. "You're the God of Renewal—do something!" I yelled. It was unfair, but I didn't give a fuck. She was young and bright, and she'd died for nothing. *That* was unfair. "Bring her back."

Demke's pale face was drawn, pulled down by grief. "My power doesn't work like that."

I shook off the hands trying to grip me. Erus's eyes were wide and watery, but he backed up. I didn't want to be consoled. I'd failed her. I'd failed them.

*The babies.*

Jumping to my feet, I raced toward the crib, and when the Gryphon stepped in my way, I gave a war cry. I didn't care if he'd been Wren's mate; Wren was dead.

Wren was dead.

The only parts of her left were in that crib. *"Move!"*

The Gryphon roared back, making the babies cry harder, and then Milo was there.

*"ENOUGH!"* His anger was a force so great, it was almost a physical blow. Enough to stop me from going fist-to-beak with a monster that could eat me. Milo lowered his voice. "Enough," he repeated, turning to reach into the crib. His big hands spanned three tiny chests, and he hummed a soft lullaby, even though his voice kept cracking. He looked at the Gryphon. "I know you can't change right now, but can you ask Teron if they're okay?"

Another keening noise came from its eagle mouth, but the Gryphon tilted its head further into the crib. The babies didn't seem agitated by his presence, and I realized the Gryphon was as familiar to them as me or the rest of the guys.

Finally, he lifted his head and nodded. I let out a relieved sigh, even though it did so little to mend the hemorrhaging wound in my chest. Turning away from the crib, I realized the others had used my distraction to pick Wren up. Her body was lifeless, hanging limply in Tryp's arms.

It wasn't a dream.

I wanted to break down all over again.

Demke let out a choked noise. "Put her back in the nest. She should lay in state while we prepare her body."

*No. This is bullshit.* "No! She's not dead. This can't be the end. Call Asclepius. Call Hades. Bring her *back.*"

Demke gave me a hard look, but eventually nodded. "I'll try. But pray to whoever your Gods of Death are too, because we will need all the help we can get."

That was when I heard it on the wind—a sound that brought even the strongest warriors to their knees. The call of the *bean-sidhe.* Cliona's cry echoed eerily through the silence of the night, and then the howl of the strays went up and joined in. Hundreds of dogs that had gathered around the town of Amourgeles let out a mournful, chilling sound. There would be no doubt to any person on this island that someone had died here tonight.

Wren was dead.

That's when I realized Cy wasn't anywhere. "Where's Cydon?"

Surely he wouldn't have let the Moirai past the wards. He wouldn't have betrayed Wren like that. But how did the Moirai get so close without alerting the dogs or the Valkyries, or setting off the wards?

Moving from the room, I tried not to look back at Wren. The more I looked at her lifeless form, the harder it was to convince myself she wasn't really dead, just unconscious.

There was thundering on the stairs, and the Valkyries suddenly appeared, one of them with Cy's body in her arms. My heart twisted in my chest.

Erus stepped forward. "Is he…"

Hrist shook her head. "No, but he's unconscious. Nothing we've done has woken him. We've tried everything." She looked past me to Tryp, who was moving down the hallway to Wren's room. She gasped, and the other Valkyries looked shaken.

"Mother of Fate!" Hildr moved forward, but the Gryphon blocked her. "Is she also unconscious?" I could see her staring at the blood-soaked shirt sticking to Wren's body. To the gaping wound in her chest. To the color of her skin that couldn't be replicated by anything alive.

Demke shook his head. "The Moirai attacked the babies. Wren fought them off, but…" Tears filled his eyes. "We were too slow."

The Valkyries lowered their weapons and fell to their knees as one, scary in their synchronization. Mist lifted her face to the ceiling. "We ask that Hel guide the Mother of Fate, Wren Mahone, to the halls of Valhalla so that she may feast with our fallen brethren forevermore."

Hrist stood, handing me her sword. "We have failed in our duty and therefore accept the consequences of our shortcomings. We offer you our lives." Again, she fell to her knees, all of them with their heads bowed, necks outstretched like they were waiting for me to behead them.

*Fucking Dagda's balls.*

I threw the sword back at her feet. "I failed her too. Please stand." I was shaking; I couldn't remember the last time my ax hand had shook. "Your duty is still to the Kuningilin. You are honorbound to protect them. Especially now, while we… while we…" I choked on the next word, but Erus was there.

"While we grieve the loss of our bond."

The Valkyries nodded, moving past us to stand guard in the nursery.

We were a solemn procession, following Tryp as he entered her room, moving toward the huge Gryphon nest where she'd slept. We laid her down on top of the blankets, still warm from our bodies, where we'd been sleeping not forty minutes earlier.

How could this have happened? I was meant to follow her. I wasn't meant to live in this world without her.

Demke appeared with two thick gold coins, carefully placing them over her closed eyelids. "To pay the Ferryman to get her across the river."

Hrist laid Cy down next to her, and I saw that his chest was barely moving. He was alive, but barely. Had the Fates done this? Had Cy found them first?

I had so many unanswered questions, but I wasn't going to let Wren go so easily. Death wasn't going to keep her from me.

I looked up at Demke. "Why didn't we die with her? That's what was supposed to happen, right?"

He shook his head. "I don't know, but I suspect that when the babies were born, our bond threads transferred to them."

I hadn't signed up for that. Though maybe I had. I would protect those babies with my very life, until my dying breath. I just never thought I'd have to do it without Wren. Not for a very long time, at least.

Is that what was wrong with Cy? Had he followed her into death? And if he had, why wasn't he also dead?

Exhausted, I climbed into the bed beside Wren, uncaring that I was sticky with her blood. Uncaring that her body was cooling rapidly. I wanted to lie with her one more time before my immortal life went on without her.

I GROWLED at the person who was trying to wake me. I wanted to stay in this blackness, untouched by pain and grief, where the whole ordeal could've just been a bad dream.

Except that fucker just kept trying to shake me awake.

"Néit, wake up." Badb was on my bed. On Wren's bed.

"Get off!" I shouted, and she showed that she still had a little good sense as she moved away quickly.

Beside me, Wren was still lying prone, coins over her

eyes, though someone had removed her bloody sleep shirt and swathed her in soft white cotton. She looked like a corpse now, no life left in her body, almost like a wax figurine.

I hated it.

Jumping from the nest, I moved as far from the bed as I could get. As far away from that thing in the bed, who *wasn't* the great love of my immortal life.

I looked over at my ex-wife and growled. "She's dead. She's dead, and you did *nothing*." It was like an arrow to the heart. "*I* did nothing. And now she's dead."

Badb's face softened. "I know. I heard Cliona's cry, and the Valkyries filled me in on the rest. Néit, I'm so sorry. I didn't even feel them enter the wards. Didn't feel their bloodlust. They must have portaled directly into the nursery with the last of their power. They could never have restored themselves to being the Fates; this was petty revenge from deranged beings who didn't know when to quit. There's nothing you could have done."

She stroked my arm softly, a touch that had been a regular thing so long ago, but now felt foreign. Would I forget the feel of Wren's skin too?

"I didn't want to wake you, but thought I should tell you that I had a dream."

I frowned. She'd woken me to tell me she had a dream? *What the actual fuck?* I was a fucking mess, and she wanted to tell me about a dream?

"Get that look off your face, God of War. I wouldn't

disturb you if it wasn't important, and you know it." She sucked in a deep breath. "I had a dream about Fea."

Another knife in the heart. Another love I couldn't save.

"Did you just come to rub salt in my wound?" I spat.

She narrowed her eyes at me. "Shut up. I had a dream about Fea, and she was walking in the Underworld with your Wren. I think she was trying to give me a sign. I think Fea's trying to help Wren get back."

# CHAPTER 25
## WREN

I was disoriented when I woke, but I knew with absolute certainty that I wasn't at home, curled up beside one of the guys. It was cold and hot at the same time, like a bad fever. Plus, it smelled a little like an asscrack.

Cy appeared in my vision, but I could barely see him in the shadows.

Shadows.

The Moirai.

The knife.

I sat up with a gasp, my hand going to my chest, but there was no knife there now, not even a wound. I didn't know why that made me feel more anxious, rather than less. I wasn't in my sleep shirt either. Instead, I was in a long white dress that looked somewhere between a slip and a wedding dress.

*What in the actual hell?*

Cy shifted from dog to man, and for some strange

reason, he was wearing pants. Normally when he changed, he came back naked. His stark white hair stood out in the darkness of our surroundings.

I tried to clutch on to those last few memories, but they were fleeting, just out of my grasp. But there was something about Mrs. B?

"Cy, what's going on?" I whispered, my throat feeling raw.

He looked uncharacteristically solemn as he squatted down beside me, his thighs flexing in a way that was both hot as hell and wildly inappropriate in the moment. "I don't know how to tell you this, Wren, but you're, ah…" He scratched his chin and looked uncomfortable. "Not living?"

I blinked at him slowly. "My life to the fullest? Because I'd have to disagree."

"Uh, no, not quite. You're not living *at all*. Like, you're dead. We're on the banks of the River Styx."

"The banks of the River where?" I shook my head, because his words made no sense. It sounded like he'd said I was dead.

I couldn't be dead. We were having a conversation.

"The River Styx. You're dead. I came with you, because we are intrinsically bonded. My soul is yours and always has been," he said softly, which was a wild thought, but I'd come back to it. Because if Cy was here, did that mean the rest of the guys had died right along with me?

My gaze flicked around, looking for them. Were they down here too? Had they been removed from the weave altogether? "The guys? Where are they? Did my death…" It was too horrifying to suggest.

Pulling me to my feet, Cy shrugged. "I don't think so. When you died, I kind of just appeared by your side. I'm hoping that if they aren't here too, they're still topside with the pups."

I wanted that too; really, I did. I would wallow happily in eternal damnation, if it meant my babies got to have a long and happy life with all those protectors.

But a selfish part of me was grief-stricken that I would never see them again.

Looking around with fresh—dead—eyes, what I saw was an expanse of blackness, with huge black cities popping up like the boroughs of New York City. On the wind was the howl of thousands of angry souls, the wail of a million mourning hearts. Nothing was growing; there was no sun, no moon, no stars. Just an endless abyss of darkness and the swirling river right at my feet.

The River Styx.

Looking down into the murky depths, I could see pale, screaming faces flowing with the current. I jumped when a hand wrapped around my arm, but it was just Cy, pulling me back against his chest. "Be careful. If they lure you into the river, they get to take your place on Ferryman's barge. Trust me, you don't want to be in there." Tugging me back from the edge, like he didn't trust me not to take a swan dive into the death pool, he turned me to face him. His eyes ran over my face as if he was trying to read my thoughts. "You seem to be taking this well. More people struggle with the death thing."

Yeah, I was firmly in the denial stage; it just didn't feel real. I didn't *feel* any different. I was still me, but in a new location. Maybe if I hadn't had Cy here, then I'd be more of a mess. But with him, it didn't seem so scary.

As long as I didn't think about the babies.

Or the look on Nate's face as I died.

Or the other guys.

The pain in my chest had nothing to do with a knife wound now. I wasn't ready for that reality just yet. Back to denial for me.

I shrugged at Cy, like I didn't give a fuck that I was no longer living. "I might be dead, but at least I have you, right?"

He gathered me up in his arms, pressing me against a chest that was still warm, with a strong heart beating beneath my cheek. "You'll always have me, Wren. In life and death, this one and the next."

Someone cleared their throat behind us. "Uh, I don't mean to interrupt, but do you know why I was summoned here? Do you need a guide?"

We both turned at the soft, sweet voice. The woman behind us was faded around the edges, like a photo taken on your grandma's smartphone. Just a little smudged and out of focus. She had long blonde hair, and delicate curves. Her pale blue clothes were rough hewn. Whenever she'd died, it had been long before modern times.

Despite her general opacity, she had a soft golden

light that told me she was probably a Goddess of some kind, but one that was long forgotten. I was surprised I could see her glow. When I looked at Cy, I realized I could see his too.

I shrugged. "No idea. We just got here."

She frowned at me. "Just now?"

Nodding, Cy eyed the woman warily. "What's your name?"

The woman tilted her head. "Fea. You're a Demigod too? They don't normally send two soul guides, but I can't be sure. This is my first time." She looked around, like she was searching for another soul. Someone else for her to guide. But there was no one here. She smiled brightly, like me being dead was the greatest thing to ever happen to her. "It must be you. You don't think Arawn thought I was so incompetent that they sent me back-up, do you? Because I might be new to this, but I've been here a long time. There's no way I couldn't walk you from the River Styx back to Annwn."

There was a lot to unpack in that little speech. "Uh, no. I'm sure that, uh, this Arawn has a lot of faith in your abilities. Cy is just my…" I struggled to find a word for what he was. Bondmate didn't sound serious enough for someone who'd followed you to Hell.

Luckily, Cy had no problems filling in the blanks. "Soulmate. Divinely ordained soulmate."

Fea's face softened. "That's so special. I've only seen a few of those in my time, and each one was more beautiful than the next."

A noise behind us had us all turning back to the

waters of the Styx. A soul was writhing on the banks, and Fea's expression turned pitying. She walked over, stroking the soul's face gently, and I watched its translucent features face go slack with bliss. Then with a giant shove, Fea pushed it back into the river.

I watched the whole thing with awe, and more than a little trepidation. Was Fea good or bad? Her name seemed familiar, but I couldn't remember if she was a Goddess someone had mentioned, or if I'd read about her in a book.

Wiping her hands on her dress, she came back to us. "Poor souls. I always feel bad, but they can't leave the Styx. It upsets the balance if there's no one there to take their place, and there's no way I'm losing my first fresh souls to the Styx. I'd never live it down." Straightening, she flicked her skirts around her knees. "I guess I'm a two-for-one guide then. Welcome to the afterlife. What's your name?"

"Wren. This is Cydon."

"Wren, that's a lovely name. It's nice to meet you both. Come, it's a long walk to Annwn. Not a hard walk, but time is odd down here, and it can feel like a lifetime to get anywhere." She stepped past us, like we were good puppies meant to follow, but I guess no one had told her that I didn't go blindly anywhere with anyone. When she realized we weren't following, she turned and frowned. I kind of felt bad; if I'd been alone, I probably would have followed her across the Underworld itself. But I wasn't alone.

Cy gave her a chagrined smile. "Sorry, Fea. But I

have a stop we need to make first. Some old friends that I need to answer a few questions." He pointed to a speck in the distance across the water, and I squinted to try and bring the tiny dot into focus.

"You know the Ferryman?" Fea whispered, partly in trepidation and partly in awe.

Cy snorted. "I once saw him get so drunk that he puked into the river and tried to make out with Cerberus. So I guess you could say, yeah, we're acquainted."

The dot got closer and closer until I realized it was indeed a barge on the river of dead people. There was a guy on it, and he was jacked. I mean, his shoulders were easily as wide as Milo's, but he was super tall too. He looked like a giant. His body was covered in a large robe, a deep hood hiding his face, with long sleeves covering everything but the tips of his fingers.

When the barge made contact with the shore, it gave an otherworldly thud that seemed to echo around the place. Lifting a hand, he flipped back his hood, revealing a pretty attractive guy with a rugged face. "Cy? What the fuck are you doing here?"

"Hey, Charon. Can we get a ride? I need to see the big guy."

The Ferryman looked between us, frowning at me. "Uh, sure. You two are Mythics, but she's a mortal soul. If she wants to ride the barge, she'll need to pay." He gazed at me sympathetically. "It's just how the magic works. Sorry. Do you have payment?"

I blinked. Should I have died with my purse in my

pocket? Did the Ferryman have Venmo? Was I going to be stuck on the side of the River Styx, just because I didn't carry cash anymore?

Squeezing my hand, Cy leaned close. "Check your pockets."

My dress did indeed have pockets. And in a pocket were two coins. "How'd you know?"

Shaking his head sadly, he curled my fist around the coins. "Because no matter how devastated they would be, they wouldn't send you into the afterlife without the proper rituals to honor you, including giving you coins to pay your passage."

What was left of my heart shattered to dust.

# CHAPTER 26
## DEMKE

You didn't summon the God of the Underworld lightly, and I'd basically had him on speed dial over the past year. But for Wren, I'd march into the Underworld itself and snatch her back.

He came once again when I called, and while I was grateful, I was also surprised. I met him in my garden, on a spot where two hawthorn trees met, their branches tangling together. If it went badly, this was where we would bury her.

Hades walked in the shade cast by the branches, though the sun was now setting and barely reaching over the walls of the compound. We stood silently, and I took a few calming, deep breaths.

Finally, I turned and looked at him. His face was impassive, but I knew that he knew. There was nothing that happened in the Underworld that escaped his notice.

"She's dead." The words echoed around the court-yard like a mournful lament.

"I'm sorry, my friend." And his tone suggested he really was sorry, not just paying lip service.

"I want her back."

He was shaking his head before I'd even finished. "I told you before, Asclepius doesn't resurrect anyone anymore, not even people he respects. I won't lose one of mine to bring back one of yours."

Shuddering out a breath that was perilously close to a sob, I nodded. "I understand. But let me go down and get her myself. I can navigate the Underworld. I can get her out." I turned to him, imploring him to understand my pain, my need. "You just have to let me pass."

He was still shaking his head. "We both know it's not that easy, and there's a reason for that. Few beings, Gods or otherwise, have entered the Underworld voluntarily, and even fewer have brought back a mortal soul. There's always a damn trap, and I wish there was a way I could spew her back up to the surface for you without a cost, but *everything* has a cost in the Under-world. You know this, Demke."

It was a hard truth. There were many tales about people going to the Underworld, for glory or for loved ones, and rarely did they ever bring anyone back. But someone had to be the first, and I was determined that I would be that person.

"Tell me how." He might be old and powerful, but so was I.

He sighed, like I was a frustrating child. "Demke…"

I shook my head once more. "What if it was Persephone? Wouldn't you do anything to save her?"

He frowned. "That better not be a threat, Minoan."

I rolled my eyes at him. As if I'd threaten the fucking God of the Underworld. I wanted Wren back on the living plane, not to join her forever in the pits of Hades. "No, of course not. Just tell me what I can do."

Giving an irritated sigh, he walked over to a bench seat. The dusk light cast longer shadows around the courtyard, like they were lured to the Prince of Darkness himself. "The only way of getting out of the Underworld is to get in and out yourself. Or you enlist the help of Zeus, who has ultimate control over this bullshit."

I rebelled at even the thought of asking Zeus. I'd put aside my pride and ask him, if I thought he'd help, but we'd murdered his Fates less than twenty-four hours ago. I doubted he was going to be willing to offer assistance anytime soon.

Slumping down on the bench next to Hades, I dragged my hands down my face. "How can I do this without her? How can I look into the faces of her offspring every day and tell them that they'll never have a mother because I failed?"

Hades screwed up his nose. "I should have brought Sephy. I don't do... whatever this is." Crossing his arms over his chest, he gave another irritated sigh. "Look, the universe has always had a purpose for your Wren. We mightn't have always understood it, and there is little doubt that it has been hard and filled with obstacles, but perhaps this is just part of her journey."

I rejected that completely. She had come to us for a reason. It was our job to protect her so she had a long and happy life, and we'd failed.

We'd almost failed the babies too. They'd been moved into Milo's room, and both he and Néit would sleep down there. The threat to them in the form of the Moirai might be gone, but they wouldn't be the only threat, or the last. No one was ever getting that close again.

Another sigh. "You're going to be stubborn about this, aren't you?"

I shrugged, because yes. I'd already lost one love to the wheel of time; I refused to lose another before it was her turn. "Yes."

"Fine. Have you ever stopped to think she isn't in the Underworld, you bull-headed pain in the ass? She isn't Greek. She isn't a follower. You're the closest thing to a God she's ever believed in, but I don't think sucking your cock counts as worship. Why would she be in the Underworld?"

I pulled back. If she wasn't there, where the hell *would* she be? I tried to think what her faith was, but she'd never given any hint that she preferred one to the others. I'd always thought that was why she'd been chosen by the universe to carry the new Fates, but what did that mean for her after death?

"She's not in the Underworld?"

"Not when I left."

*Fuck.* What should I do? How did I fix this?

I hadn't realized I said it out loud, until a cold hand landed on my shoulder. "As much as it pains me to say it, maybe you should have a little faith in destiny and her plans. Trust that as much as you want to get your girl back, she wants to get back to you. So keep the things she loves as safe as possible, until she returns or you see her in the afterlife."

He wanted me to do nothing? If the options were searching through the endless plains of the afterlife, and letting the universe decide, I was between a rock and a hard place.

With one last pat on the shoulder, Hades disappeared as quickly as he'd arrived, leaving me with more problems than solutions.

I sat out there until the dusk turned into night. Not for the first time, I wished I wasn't the one who had to lead. I didn't want to have the weight of our collective happiness on my shoulders. Néit was barely functioning, just standing sentinel in whatever room the babies were in, not speaking, barely eating.

The Gryphon had totally consumed Teron and disappeared into the mountains with his grief. I had to hope that eventually he'd relinquish control back to Teron, so he could return. I was worried that with the loss of his mate, the Gryphon would take total control, pine away and die, taking my closest friend with him.

Erus and Tryp were solemn ghosts who had picked up the slack of the rest of us. They had been keeping us fed and hydrated, ensuring we slept when they could cajole us to bed. But it was a reflex, them falling back into behavior that made sense to them, much like Néit's protectiveness. They were as devastated as the rest of us, and sometimes I'd find Tryp crying in the kitchen or Erus staring blankly at the wall, tears in his eyes.

We were all failing. And I still had no solution.

Milo appeared in the darkness, and I wasn't surprised to see him rocking a baby against his chest. So small and reliant on us. Of all the responsibilities on my shoulders, they were the real weight. Their protection was our duty, but so was their happiness. I wasn't sure any of us could provide them with the kind of love that Wren had given so easily.

Except maybe the man in front of me.

"Is he okay?"

Milo nodded, rocking gently from side to side. "He's fine. Just unsettled. They all are." He made a soft shushing noise, but the baby continued to grizzle. I couldn't tell which baby it was in the dark, when the color was leached from the world. "I managed to get his brothers down, but Emeric just needed a little more cuddling."

I looked on in amazement at my brother, who'd been so close to fading away less than a year ago, who I'd feared was about to drink himself into oblivion. And now he was the only one of us with his shit together. I eyed him hard. "You're taking this all… better than I expected."

Sadness spread across his face, a devastation so great, it was a mask of torment, and I felt like an asshole for poking at his wounds. "I'm heartbroken. This pain... I couldn't have ever imagined it. I wouldn't wish it on my worst enemy. But Wren trusted these little guys to my care, and I'm not going to let her down. I'm going to meet her again in the afterlife with a smile on my face, knowing I loved and protected these boys with every fiber of my being." When he sat down beside me, I realized Emeric was now asleep. "What did Hades say?"

I shook my head. "He said she isn't in the Underworld, and even if she was, I'd have to ask Zeus to get her out." He snorted angrily, which basically summed up my feelings on the matter too. "Or he suggested we could wait it out. That she would have better luck trying to get back to us, and that we should trust destiny has something good in store for her."

Letting his head slump back, Milo stared at the moon. "I don't trust anything anymore."

And that was the problem. Neither did I.

# CHAPTER 27
## CYDON

O

Charon was looking between me and Wren knowingly, like just his gaze could make me spill my guts about what was going on. Granted, it probably could, if I'd had any fucking idea myself. Finally, he huffed and turned toward Wren. "So you're Cydon's little bird."

She gave him a weak smile. Her death was catching up with her. "So he tells me."

"The mother of the Kuningilin."

She nodded. "Though the title is new."

Charon laughed, using his barge pole to move through the water, souls swirling around it like they could climb it to get on board. "Do you know why, in some parts of Europe, they call wrens kinglets?" He looked between us, but I actually had no idea either.

"I'm sure you're about to enlighten us, old man."

He snorted. "Who are you calling old? I'm not too

old to throw you in the Acheron for a turn around the sun." His words were softened by the laughter in his voice. We were friends, and I was pretty sure that if I fell in, he would pull me out. Like… seventy percent sure.

Rolling his eyes at me, he turned back to Wren. "As I was saying, there is an old fable—I couldn't tell you where it started—about a flight of birds electing a king. They couldn't decide if it should be the wisest, the strongest, the biggest, or the most fearsome. In the end, they decided that the bird that could fly the highest would become king.

"So birds of every kind raced into the sky, and one by one, they all dropped out, until it was just the eagle flying high above the clouds. When he began to tire and could no longer fly higher, a little wren, which had been tucked inside the feathers on his back, burst out and flew even further up than the eagle could manage. Thus becoming king."

Wren tilted her head at him. "Am I the eagle in this story? Or the bird who cheated his way into becoming king?"

Charon shrugged. "You're you. But I don't think he cheated. He was always going to be at a disadvantage; all the smaller birds were. The bigger, stronger birds underestimated them, and in the end, the underdog won with cleverness. That is something to be applauded, in my opinion. Sometimes you can't bull-doze your way out of a problem." He looked over at me, giving me a heavy look. "Sometimes you have to think your way around it. Especially problems where the odds are not in your favor."

We were silent, and I watched the bank on the other side of the River Styx get closer and closer. I wasn't surprised to see Cerberus on the shore. It was his post, after all. But beside him was someone who *was* a surprise, and I stood a little closer to Wren.

The barge bumped up to the bank, and I picked her up, jumping off the ferry and onto the riverbank. I wasn't risking her accidentally tumbling off the boat into the river. Charon helped Fea off the barge too, and if anyone was surprised to see a random person there with us, it didn't show on their faces.

Wren looked up at the hellhound with wide, scared eyes. I guess he was pretty fearsome; he was the size of a house, with three snapping heads and paws that could crush a small car into a pancake. There was a reason he protected the gates of the Underworld, and it wasn't because he was soft and cuddly.

"Holy shit," Wren breathed, her arms around my neck tightening. "He's not going to eat us, right? I know I'm already dead, but I'm not really down with being chewed up and shit out by a monster-sized dog."

I snorted a laugh. At least she still had her sense of humor. "Nah, he's fine. Basically a glorified Pomeranian." I slipped her to her feet. "Wren, meet Cerberus, the fearsome protector of the entry to the Underworld. Never defeated, except by one ditzy girl with a honey cake." I raised an eyebrow at Cerberus. "Twice."

As I knew he would, Cerberus quickly changed

from his hound form back to his human form. "Hey, Sephy said I *had* to let her pass. What was the harm in eating a honey cake for the effort? You know how hard it is to get a good honey cake in the Underworld?" Bounding over, he wrapped me up in a hug. If it had just been me here, I would have shifted into my dog form and we'd have run and played for a while, but I didn't want to freak Wren out any further. Down here, my dog form was easily as big as Cerberus, but without the extra heads.

"It's so good to see you, Cy. You don't visit enough."

I slapped him on the back. "I've been busy. I'm a dad now."

Wren let out a choked noise at the mention of the boys, and I slapped my own head. How insensitive could I be?

Looking over at Wren, Cerberus dipped his chin. "Mother of Fate. It's nice to meet you. Clee and Sephy have nothing but wonderful things to say about you."

"Not Hades?" she asked lightly, and Cerberus laughed.

"Hades doesn't have anything nice to say about anyone, except Sephy. Don't take it personally. I've been his companion since nearly the dawn of the Underworld, and I'm pretty sure he barely tolerates me."

Charon laughed, and so did I. It wasn't true; anyone who'd seen them all together knew that the love between the guys and Persephone was something they would write sonnets about. Epic poems would be penned about their love. But they were very private, and other than Hades, Persephone's relationship with the guys was kept pretty under wraps.

"How's your mom?" I asked, and I watched Wren put the pieces together.

Cerberus was one of the great monsters of the Greek myths, and his parents were... "Holy shit, your mother is Ekhidna. I'm so sorry." Wren looked pale, but Cerberus just waved a hand.

"It's not your fault. She was trying to kill you. Anyway, being down here with me is better than being imprisoned beneath a volcano."

That was true. "Typhon ate Lachesis, by the way."

Letting out a belly laugh, Cerberus doubled over. "Good. Fucking old bitches. Bet she tasted like shit too."

The other person on the bank cleared his throat, clearly tired of being ignored. "Are you not going to introduce me, Cydon?"

Thanatos was a bit of an enigma in the Underworld. Little known, and much more in line with the Christian visage of an angel, he had huge black wings that sucked in the light, and skin that had never seen the kiss of the sun. He looked like death, and that's exactly what he was. But he was also my old friend.

"Depends. If I introduce her, are you going to steal her away from me and into those gates from which she can never emerge?"

Thanatos gave a heavy sigh. "Obviously not, Cy. If I wanted her, she'd already be drinking from the River of Forgetfulness." The River Lethe was just past the gates to the Underworld, and it was Thanatos's job to take you there and make you drink, so you'd forget your life and enjoy your afterlife, I guess.

"In that case, Wren, this is Thanatos, the God of Death. Thanatos, this is my Wren."

He bowed at the waist, his wings shifting behind him to counterbalance the movement. "It is an honor to meet you, Wren. Sephy sends her condolences that she couldn't meet you down here personally, but Hades is away, so she's in charge. She's using the time to redecorate the throne room. A few less skulls and a few more flowers, apparently." His lips twitched, and I could imagine them sneaking around putting out lilies of the valley in place of a giant's skull.

Wren raised an eyebrow. "Maybe there's a middle ground, and she can use the skulls as planters? Good, uh, sustainability?"

Cerberus laughed loudly. "Oh, that's a great idea. Can you imagine pansies growing out the eye sockets of those who tried to usurp him? So disrespectful. I adore it. I can't wait to tell her."

There was a brief tinkle of a bell attached to the side of the cliffs that formed the gates to the Underworld. Charon sighed and picked up his barge pole. "Well, death waits for no man. There was a full moon last night, and I swear, it always results in an influx. Plus, if they have to wait more than ten minutes, they succumb to temptation to lean too close to the river." He rolled his eyes. "Wren, it was lovely to meet you. I hope to see you again on better terms. Cydon, come and visit soon. Bring some of that wine we like."

I waved. "I'll bring a whole case, and we'll try recreating 1460."

Charon shuddered. No matter how long your memory was, you always remembered that one time you drank so much, you nearly re-died.

Wren gasped and patted her pocket. "Oh! I forgot." Grabbing a coin, she held it out to the Ferryman. "For my ride."

Taking the coin, Charon flipped it, and it landed into the river, the souls swirling around it like fish around a pellet of fish food. "Thank you. It's a little known secret that every time I'm paid, I throw it in the river, and that coin pays for another passage. It lets a soul rise from the Styx and climb onto the barge, allowing them to cross into the Underworld finally."

She immediately reached back into her pocket and pulled out the second coin. "Everyone deserves a chance." She tried to hand it to him, but he shook his head, a soft smile on his face.

"Ah, the universe chose well. Keep it; you never know when you might need it. I'll take it from you then." Jumping easily onto the barge, he waved as he pushed off.

I turned back to Thanatos while Wren was distracted. "Where is Hades?"

Thanatos just stared at me. "You know where he is, Cy."

"And did they come up with a solution?"

Thanatos shook his head. "No, old friend. There is no easy, 'get out of jail free' card here." Apparently, they'd been playing the Monopoly game I brought down last time. "But we both know that there's a loophole for everything, even death. You just have to find it."

I wanted to roar in frustration, but Wren needed me to be calm. Composed. We couldn't both break down. "Maybe if I could talk to Hades? Or we could summon Apollo?"

Thanatos curled his lip at my father's name. There was no love lost between my father and just about any God in existence. "The only person you could summon who could solve this problem would be Zeus, and he is not welcome in the Underworld." Yeah, that wasn't going to happen on any plane of existence. "Cy, if she steps foot into our domain, she will never leave. Right now, no one is coming for her. She is a child of no faith. But I find it interesting that her guide is a Celt, don't you?"

I looked at Fea. I hadn't realized she was from the Celtic Pantheon. "Do you know who she is? Have you met her before?"

Thanatos shook his head. "I've never met her, but I can tell where she belongs, if that makes sense. Sometimes it helps when it's a busy day on the other side of the Styx." He looked at Wren. "I'll tell you what Hades will tell you. You have two choices. You can join us in here, where you'll enjoy the Elysian Fields and eventually, be reunited with your Gods."

In one thousand, two thousand, three thousand years. Who knew?

"Or you can trust that the universe doesn't want to fuck you over one more time, and remain open to her guidance. You were her chosen one, and there has to be balance. Have a little faith."

*Fucking Mythics. Always so damn cryptic.*

Stepping away, I wrapped my arm around Wren once more. "Thanks, Thanatos. I'll bring you Candy Land next time I come down for games night. I think you guys will like it. Say hi to Hypnus for me."

He inclined his head. Cerberus changed back into the hound, and slobber landed at my feet. I glared up at him. "Ew, I was in the splash zone."

His middle head chuffed a laugh. "Annwn is that way." He lifted his chin, pointing left. "Good luck."

The realm of the dead for the Celtic believers. I looked over at Fea. "Lead on, soul guide."

Wren gave the guys a little wave, and we followed behind this stranger provided by some mystical force with unknown intentions, trusting that she was leading us toward happiness.

# CHAPTER 28
## WREN

The River Styx was endless. Everything on either side of its banks looked exactly the same, and I felt like we'd been walking for days.

Fea looked over her shoulder at me. "Time works strangely here. Well, to be exact, there is no time. Why would there be time? There is no sun to mark the day. No moon, no tide, nothing but the endlessness of eternity. I guess this is where time comes to die too, don't you think?"

I felt like I was Alice talking to the Mad Hatter. *A very unhappy deathday to me, to me.* "So up top, it's probably been how long?"

Fea shrugged. "An hour? A year? A century? It's impossible to know."

I looked over at Cy, who also shrugged. "Time is weird down here. But I've never been down here and missed a century. Usually works the other way. A year down here is a month up there. That kind of thing."

I didn't know why it mattered how much time I was missing. I was dead. My short life had been full of pain, just because the universe had chosen me as some kind of divine incubator. Then, it didn't let me even have a few moments of peace. No, the universe had to fuck me over one more time and let me be murdered.

How fucking dare it?

How was any of this fair?

The more we walked, the more the anger in my chest built and built. Every little part of my life had been about moving me into this position. The people I'd loved. The choices I'd made. The job I'd gotten. All of this was so the babies could be born. And then fate had the *audacity* to cut my life painfully short.

I stumbled over a rock, but it felt like more than that. It felt like just one more obstacle in my path, ensuring that I couldn't even have a moment's peace. "Argh!" Leaning down, I snatched the rock from the ground and threw it as far as I could into the River Styx—which turned out not to be far, because I was weak and the rock was big. And I didn't even have the satisfaction of a big splash, because the waters weren't even really water. They were souls.

Souls like mine.

I turned and screamed into the darkness around me, already filled with howling souls, and I just became one voice in the symphony of suffering.

I screamed and screamed and screamed. "*Why?!* What fucking *more* do you want from me? I've given you everything. Why couldn't you let me be happy for *even just a second?"* I screeched, though I doubted the force who'd done this to me was here.

Maybe I was just unlucky. Maybe there was no Great Weaver. No power moving us all around like chess pieces. Maybe there was just shitty fucking luck, and I'd gotten the bad end over and over again, because that's what I deserved.

Two big arms wrapped around my waist, and I collapsed into Cy's body. I sobbed furious tears, letting them spill onto the barren ground like acid rain. Let my tears soak into the River Styx, like the tears of so many others before me.

Cy didn't tell me it was all going to be okay. Who could predict that, really? He didn't try to appease me or make me feel better; he just did what he'd promised he'd do back on the banks of the river.

He stayed with me, always.

"It's not fair, Cy. It's just *not fair*."

He stroked his hand down my hair. "I know, baby."

"They're going to grow up without a mother, for what? Petty revenge? The Moirai couldn't have been the Fates again, with only the two of them. What was the point of it all?" My voice was beginning to rise again. "I'm so fucking angry. I want to… I want to tear the fucking *world* down. I want to find whoever decided this was my destiny, our destiny, and fucking punch them in the dick."

He kissed my cheeks, chasing the salty tears from around my eyes. "I'll hold their cosmic, all-powerful arms for you so you can get in a couple of good shots before we're turned to dust."

I laughed, but it was a wet, pathetic sound. Beneath it was bitter anger that I didn't think was ever going to go away.

Fea cleared her throat, and I realized I'd just had a huge, toddler-style meltdown in front of this stranger. My guide. What the hell did that even mean? She seemed about as oblivious to the reason she was with me as we were.

"Saying I'm sorry that you've suffered would be woefully pitiful, so I'll spare my breath." She gave me a sympathetic expression that was likely to make me start crying again, so I dragged my face back to Cy's chest. "Annwn is close, and then you can rest."

Nodding, I wiped my face against his shirt, and to Cy's credit, he let me use him as a human tissue. Because you know what else Hell didn't have, besides my loved ones? Tissues. Or coffee, probably.

Nudging me gently, Cy made me walk some more, and I trudged along behind Fea. After another indeterminable amount of time, the scenery began to change. It seemed lighter, with trees beginning to appear, though they were thick, pale things with strange-looking foliage.

"We've arrived," Fea said softly.

I could almost feel the change. The ground vibrated with magic and power that felt slightly different to that of the gates of the Underworld, and even more different to the dead feeling of the River Styx.

Looking over at Fea, I wondered if we'd stumbled through the gates already. "If I'm in Annwn, won't I get trapped here, the way I would have been stuck in the Underworld?"

Fea smiled at me, like she was so happy I was asking her questions, so she could flex her guide knowledge. She really was sweet. She reminded me of a little fairy. "No, because we aren't truly in Annwn yet. We are nearing Tech Duinn. It's where souls go when they first die, and then they move on to Annwn, the Otherworld. Kind of like a holding area."

I didn't know why I was going to the Celtic holding area, but I was just going with it. Maybe if I held off moving to any afterlife, a solution might just present itself for me to… what? Become a zombie? I was dead. Dead-dead.

*Whatever.* I was going to do what I always did—stick my head in the sand and hope it all worked itself out.

Fea was still talking, and I tuned back in, not wanting to miss anything. "Unlike most Underworlds, the Otherworld—we call it Annwn—is often visited by Mythics. It is a whole society, much like earth, with people and politics and happiness. Occasionally, even grand heroes can visit and return safely to earth, maintaining their mortal soul. Unfortunately, no one who is dead has ever returned." She gave me a soft, comforting look. "Tech Duinn and Annwn are governed by two Gods: Donn, who presides over Tech Duinn, and Arawn, who governs the Otherworld. They bicker a lot, but it's good natured. I think a healthy rivalry keeps them from being bored. You know what they say: a bored God is a dangerous one."

In front of us, a big castle loomed. And I mean, it was *huge*. It towered right into the sky, so high I wasn't sure there was an end. Its large walls ran right around, cutting off the view of the surrounding forest. It was certainly dominating.

"You're a Mythic, right? Does that mean you can come and go from the Otherworld?" Maybe Fea could send a message to Nate, to my guys, and tell them that I was okay. That I wasn't scared, or frightened, or sad. It would be all lies, but at least it might appease them.

Fea's expression turned sad. "Unfortunately, no. I was killed by an immortal weapon, which means that my ability to visit the Isles was snuffed out. I'm a permanent resident of the Otherworld now." She brightened. "But I can leave and travel around the Underworld if I like, which allows me to be your guide."

Cy interrupted. "Your name sounds familiar to me. What flavor of Mythic were you?"

"I was a War Goddess, though I was never much for the actual fight. I enjoyed tactics more than the battle."

Another Celtic Goddess of War. What were the chances of that?

"Did you know Néit?"

Fea smiled so wide, her face lit up like a Christmas tree. "Yes, you could say I knew Néit. Everyone knew him. A fearsome warrior, an expert horseman, a fair lord. He mightn't have been loved by all, but he was certainly loved by Badb." She paused on Morrigan's name, her eyes getting soft. "And me. He was my husband."

My feet stopped instantly. My whole body felt like it had slammed into a forcefield. "You were married to Nate—I mean, Néit? I thought Badb was his wife?" I was choking on the words. How many wives did Nate have?

Fea shrugged. "She was my wife too. She was the Morrigan—the most beautiful, deadly Goddess in our history. How could I not love her too? Besides, it was different back then. You could handfast as many as you liked, as long as you loved and honored them, and Néit did love and honor us. He mightn't have loved us as much as he loved a battle, or maybe even that damn ax, but he certainly loved us, and we loved each other." She sounded wistful, like their relationship had been just a month ago, not several thousands of years in the past.

Cy cleared his throat. "That explains a lot, really. I guess I know now why your name was familiar," he squeaked out.

I was saved from saying anything by our arrival at the gates of the fortress. Fea knocked once, and the gates swung inward, showing a giant dressed all in black.

His voice was like a thunder clap. "I wondered when you'd arrive."

# CHAPTER 29
## TRYP

I tended to her body gently. We should have been giving her burial rites, but none of us were ready to say that final goodbye. Instead, Demke was using his magic to keep her in stasis, her body permanently in the state it was directly after her death, decomposition held at bay by the God of Renewal.

Eventually, we'd have to let her go. It had been four days, and I knew it wasn't healthy to keep her up here, in her Gryphon nest, like Snow White, just waiting for true love's kiss to wake her. Breathing out a rough sigh, I leaned over and kissed her waxy lips, dead and still under mine. Unlike Snow, she didn't wake, but there was no doubt in my mind that she was my true love. My heart felt like it was a cold stone in my chest, one bad day from shattering into a million pieces.

The only part of her body that felt warm was the part touching the still form of Cy. If this went on much longer, I was going to have to try and set up some kind of IV system so he didn't wither away beside her. I couldn't help Wren, but I could keep Cy alive. I didn't know how to place an IV, as that was more Teron's domain, but I could learn from the internet, and we had all the equipment.

Still, I did what I could for them both. Instead of letting go and grieving healthily, I oiled Wren's skin, brushed her hair, and made her look like she was still alive, just asleep. None of us could grieve appropriately, I guess.

Standing, I moved out of the room quietly and shut the door. I was the only one who went in there; not even Erus could stand to see her corpse.

The Gryphon—and by extension, Teron—still hadn't returned, and I was beginning to worry they never would. I thought he'd come back for the babies, but so far, it had been Milo who'd stepped up into that role.

Moving into the courtyard, I looked around at all the melancholy dogs, unsure what to do without their leader. They still did their rounds, guarded the perimeter, and seemed to be reporting to the Valkyries. But without Cy, it was like a convoluted game of charades. I wouldn't be surprised if they started to drift away as more time passed without Cy here as a grounding force.

So far it hadn't mattered, though, because the Valkyries were turning everyone away. I think if they could have built a wall and locked the place down like a fortress, they would have. Unfortunately, the villagers needed to come and go from town, and there was no ward that could stop people from portaling in.

Hearing a ruckus at the front of the compound, I hurried down the stairs, looking for a weapon or one of the other guys. What the fuck was going on now? Couldn't we have a minute to mourn? I could hear shouting, so I picked up the dagger we kept strapped under the table in the entryway.

Surprisingly, it was Milo who was raging, in full bull-headed form, attacking someone at the gate. Whoever it was fended him off easily, however. "*You knew!* When you came here, you already knew what would happen," he roared, and it all clicked into place.

Apollo.

Man, he had some big golden balls to return here. Had he had something to do with Wren's death? Because if he'd set anything into motion, there wasn't a corner of the world remote enough to escape our wrath.

Demke appeared behind me. I assumed he'd try and break it up, but he just leaned against the doorjamb, happy to let Milo do his best to gouge a hole in the enigmatic God.

"I didn't know exactly—"

The snort wasn't even close to human, and it was all the warning Apollo got before Milo charged at him, taking them both to the ground. He hammered his fists at Apollo's face, but was always just a fraction too slow. More likely, Apollo was letting him hold him down, but drew the line at letting him get a hit in.

Apollo huffed, shoving at Milo's chest, sending the Minotaur skidding through the dirt. "Of course I knew what was going to happen. I know what happens next too, and what happens after that. I'm gifted with prophecy, you big, dumb oaf. I also know what happens if I screw with the threads of fate, and that is far worse."

Demke's back was ramrod straight. "Worse than her dying?"

"Yes." Apollo's face was solemn, and I was tempted to believe him.

Milo stood up, brushing dust from his legs. "Worse for her, or worse for you?"

Narrowing his eyes, Apollo sneered, "For the world. Don't forget, she dragged my son down with her. It wasn't a decision I made lightly."

I leaned close to Demke. "Like he doesn't have fifty more to replace him."

The air around us crackled, and you didn't need to be a genius to know that we were beginning to piss Apollo off. He straightened his white shirt and linen pants—somehow he could pull off double linen without looking like an acolyte or a sixty-something divorcée named Gladys.

"Look, I came here because I thought you might need some appeasing when it comes to this situation. Because I still love this Island, and because Cy loves the girl and he means a lot to me, despite being one of fifty." He cut a glare at me. "But if you want to fumble around in the dark, go for it. It will all play out how it's supposed to, regardless of your feelings."

Demke moved toward the scuffle. "Let him go, Milonos."

Backing up but still huffing with rage, Milo glared at

Apollo, who seemed completely unconcerned with the fact he was in the direct path of a raging bull.

"Come, we can go have coffee at the *kafenio*. Milo, go and see if Néit needs help with the infants. Tryp, with me." Erus was sleeping, having gotten up and down with the babies all night, and no one wanted to wake him.

What Demke left unsaid was that there was no way Apollo was making it inside the house anytime soon. However, the God in question didn't seem to be perturbed by the implication he was untrustworthy.

As we walked through town, the villagers stopped and stared. They might have been used to us, but Apollo was a whole other level of inhuman. Beautiful, but disconcertingly so. The power he possessed was the kind that raised the hair on your arms. You didn't know if you wanted to walk toward him in awe or run away screaming.

If I could tell them what to do, it would be to run as far and as fast as possible.

We stepped into the café, where one of Stavros's nieces was manning the counter. I wished I knew all their names, but I'd swear, he had a hundred nieces and daughters and granddaughters. It was hard to keep up.

She eyed our group warily, and Demke indicated we'd like three coffees. We sat in the furthest corner of the patio, tucked away from the sight of the casual passerby.

Sighing, Demke steepled his fingers beneath his chin. "I'd apologize for Milonos's behavior, but it's been a rough week, and he was just doing what we've all wanted to do for quite some time."

Apollo snorted. "I expect little from you Minoans. You're basically a step up from barbarians, even after all this time."

Okay, so we were going with barely veiled barbs. Should get interesting quickly.

The waitress came over with three coffees, and an entire platter of pastries and breads. Demke gave her a polite smile, and she hustled away as fast as her aging knees could carry her.

*Smart woman.*

"Let's not pretend we are old friends. Why are you here?"

Sighing, Apollo took a deep sip of his coffee, then grabbed a pastry. "Mmmm, these mortals still know how to cook." Little flakes of pastry flew from his lips. If only the people who wrote epic poems about him could see him now. "I wanted to say how sorry I am about the loss of Wren. I might have only met her for a moment, but she made an impression."

Nothing was more true than that. I'd wanted her as soon as I saw her, and I'd loved her as soon as I got to know her soul. Her death... I pushed away the pain again. That was for later, when we weren't face-to-face with a potential threat.

"Thank you," Demke said stiffly.

Apollo inclined his head. "I'm not sure if you know this—and I assume you don't, given your jibes—but I love my children. I didn't get to see Cydon for centuries, and now I've lost him before I got to truly reconnect with him."

The stories of the things Apollo would do for his children were whispered about among Mythics. Getting Hades to go against Zeus for Asclepius was only the most commonly known. As a general rule, Gods didn't make good parents, too jealous of someone coming close to them in power, but Apollo broke the mold. Even if he did have a ton of children.

"So if you need a selfish reason to attribute this to, let it be that. I want my son back after a few thousand years. I don't want another child stuck in the Underworld forever. I'm sure you've talked to Hades, and he's told you that without asking Zeus"—his scoff told me what he thought of asking the King of the Gods for anything—"getting anyone out of the Underworld is impossible.

"But, Demke, my friend, we both know that nothing is impossible. We are old Mythics with an abundance of long-standing feuds and favors. I may have whispered in a few ears, suggested a few things, to help *maybe* get your girl back to you. I can't tell you what, in case I change the weave, but I don't want you to lose hope yet. He stood, grabbing another sweet pastry. "And don't bury your dead just yet. A long mourning period would be best for all, if you want my opinion." Smiling, he downed the last of his coffee. "I'll leave you to it. I know you're probably busy, and I have a date with a warrior Goddess who hates my guts."

I tried not to let the hope that fluttered in my chest

take root. Not yet, not until I knew that Apollo wasn't just fucking with us, rubbing salt in our wounds. Demke watched Apollo leave, his face pensive.

"Do you think he's speaking the truth?"

He shrugged. "We both know the word of other Mythics is worse than shit, and the ancient Greeks are the worst of all." My heart sank a little, the hope fleeing as melancholy returned. "But still, what does he have to gain from us not burying Wren? Nothing."

We sat in silence and ate the remaining pastries, lost in thoughts and memories, and clutching tightly to the single thread of hope our mortal enemy had just offered.

# CHAPTER 30
## WREN

O

There was no doubt in my mind that the being in front of me was the God of Death. Well, *a* God of Death. I was learning there was more than one of those.

Fea bowed lightly, and because I wasn't an idiot, I followed her lead. "Sir, this is Wren Mahone, of the human realm. My very first soul to guide. Wren, this is Donn. Welcome to Tech Duinn."

Donn was huge. He stood at least eight feet tall, with shoulders probably as wide as a compact car. His bare chest was covered in runes, which were like big black scars, and his robe hung to the ground, pooling at his feet. He had a short black beard and thick eyebrows.

Looking down at Fea, his face was impassive, but was that warmth in his expression? "And an important first soul at that, Fea."

She looked over at me, like it hadn't occurred to her that I could be anything but some average Joe from the mortal realm.

Donn, however, was already ushering us inside. "Come, stay and rest for a moment. There is a feast in the banquet hall; there's quite an influx of souls at the moment. Full moon."

Fea's eyes lit up, and she moved through the darkened halls. Donn's eyes followed her like she was the single source of light in the darkness of his days, though Fea seemed oblivious.

Shaking his head lightly, the Death God looked back down at me. "Come, Wren Mahone. We have much to talk about."

I shot a quick look at Cy, who shrugged and ushered me along. It was disconcerting when a God of Death knew your name. He wasn't exactly the Grim Reaper, but he was certainly terrifying in his own way.

The hallways were indeed bustling with people and servants. Some were souls, that much was obvious. They looked confused and lost, walking from room to room, asking other souls for directions. But some were Mythics, and the longer I was down here, the easier I saw the difference. Dead people looked like a faded picture exposed to too much light—lots of detail, but somehow less. Dim and chipped, even. But Mythics like Fea and Cy? They still glowed like the day they were painted, a technicolor rainbow.

It felt like we were walking forever, but finally, we followed Fea into a cavernous room filled with long tables of food and wine. A huge fireplace, easily the size of a Manhattan apartment building, took up one whole wall, and there were wiry-looking dogs sleeping in front of it. People were everywhere, some standing and talking, drinking mead and laughing, others staring at nothing, their faces a mask of confusion. Still more sat at the long tables of food, gorging themselves on the platters of meats, vegetables, and breads.

Donn indicated an empty table right at the back of the room that was currently unoccupied. It was obviously a table for important people; they'd be able to see the whole room and have their back against a wall. "This way. Fea, you'll be joining us, of course?"

Fea gave us a bright, happy smile. "Of course, my lord. First, I just want to see Caoimhe in the kitchen and see if she has any of her special sugar cakes for my very first guided soul."

Donn nodded, and I swear, I saw his lip twitch. Did the Celtic God of Death have a crush on the little warrior Goddess? They were like polar opposites, but somehow, they were perfect. Maybe they were already a couple, but she seemed more reverent than lovestruck.

Leading us to the table, Donn took a seat right in the middle chair, which was slightly raised above the others. There would be no doubt to anyone in the room that he was the God here. He indicated the seats on his left. "Please, sit, eat."

Cy gave him a sharp look. "This food is given freely and comes without expectation or agreement of any kind, and won't anchor us to Tech Duinn or Annwn?" Donn glared back at Cy, and I thought maybe he'd pissed off the God of Death.

*Fuck, fuck, fuck.*

But then Donn threw back his head and boomed out a laugh, loud enough to draw the gaze of all the souls inside the room. "I forgot about you Greeks and how you use food as a trap." Shaking his head, he waved at the food and large pitchers of drinks. "This is all freely given. Tech Duinn is a passing place for most. Christians would call it purgatory, I guess. The borders of Tech Duinn are free for all souls and creeds to pass through. It's why we house the Tar Pits on the far edge."

I'd heard of the Tar Pits, but I couldn't remember exactly when or why. "We didn't mean any offense, sir. In my defense, I got knocked up by eating an apple, so I'm wary of accepting food from Gods these days."

He chuckled again. "Yes, I heard of that. The mother of the new Fates. Rough business. Sorry to see you here so soon."

I gritted my back teeth so I didn't cry. "Me too." Shaking off the melancholy, I gave myself an internal pep talk. I hadn't given up yet. "Ah, if you've heard about me, then you'll know I'm bonded to Fea's, uh…" I cleared my throat. "I mean, I'm not just bonded; we're partners. A couple. Married in every way that matters to Néit, Fea's former husband."

His gaze was sharp as he scanned the room. "I've heard whispers of that, of course. The Morrigan is quite a regular visitor to Annwn, and stops here at Tech Duinn frequently on her way. She keeps me up-to-date on what is happening topside. She never sees Fea, though." There was disapproval in his tone.

"Why?"

Donn shrugged. "That is a question for the Crow, and not for me to answer. But I believe that the reason for Fea's ultimate demise was quite gruesome. She was certainly traumatized when she arrived here. I suggest you don't bring it up with her." The *or else* was heavily implied.

That line of questioning was closed as Fea bounced back to the table, four slabs of cake resting on her arms. "It's a dessert first kind of day, I think."

The warm cake smelled of treacle, a malty sweetness that was definitely supported by the stickiness on my fingers. Taking a nibble at the edges, I groaned. I wasn't sure I wouldn't get re-knocked up for an endless supply of these bad boys. "Oh my god," I mumbled around a mouthful of cake.

Fea giggled. Once again, it was hard to imagine her juxtaposed against the deadliness of Morrigan or the hard edges of Nate.

"Caoimhe was once the cook for the household of the High King of Ireland. Donn managed to convince her to stay on at Tech Duinn, instead of traveling on to the Otherworld."

Donn grumbled. "She has me by the bollocks, and she knows it. All the riches and boons she could ask for, just to stay and cook for… all this." He indicated the room.

"So, no one is *stuck* here?" It was weird. Purgatory was definitely a place where you got stuck, if my old

Sunday school teacher was to be believed, and it wasn't pleasant.

Donn shook his head. "Only by their own volition. Sometimes they want to wait for their loved ones here. Sometimes they're confused, or they need to work through some things before starting their next life." A flick of his eyes at Fea made me wonder if that's why she was still here. "This castle is not… What's that human song? Hotel something?"

Cy laughed. "'Hotel California.' You've been keeping up with your pop culture references."

The God of Death grinned, and it was kind of creepy. "Even Death needs a vacation occasionally. I like the movies of this modern age. And the rock-and-roll music." After finishing his cake, he piled his plate high with food, and we did the same. "So, as I said, I've been expecting you."

Fea raised both her eyebrows at him. "I just thought that was just a really good line you wanted to use for theatrics."

Okay, that might have been flirting.

The giant God of Death flushed, his cheekbones going pink. It was both adorable and terrifying. "Unfortunately, no. Besides, when do I do anything for theatrics?"

Fea mimed zipping her lips, smiling smugly around her potatoes.

Was I watching a rom-com right now? The Hellmark Channel?

Shaking his head fondly, Donn turned back to us. "As I was saying, I had a visitor not long before your arrival. From the Greek Mythics. We don't see many of your kind down this way, present company excluded." He lifted his chin at Cy. "And he suggested that the unfortunateness of your death was an error in the weave. A grave injustice to the wheel of time. Then he left." Lifting up a turkey leg, he used it as a scepter of sorts. "I don't particularly like being manipulated by other Gods, especially the Greeks."

My skin was tingling with adrenaline, but I wasn't sure why yet. It was like something important was right there, sitting on the edge of the moment, waiting for me to grasp it. "I can understand the feeling."

"But I am fond of Fea, and given you are her first guided soul, I decided to take an interest."

So the God of Death didn't have a crush on Fea; he was balls-to-the-wall in love. Good to know.

Fea frowned at Donn. "What are you suggesting exactly?"

"I think that this Mythic was right. It was an injustice for Wren to die so young, under the manipulations of forces she knew nothing about. I think you should take her to the Tar Pits."

The Tar Pits again. Why did that sound so familiar? It conjured up some scary imagery, but otherwise, I was drawing a blank.

However, Fea's face said it was something important. "You don't mean…?"

Donn nodded. "I think she should go and see the Innkeeper and summon a Weighing."

Fea gasped, and the whole room turned to look at us. I leaned toward Fea and whispered, "What's a Weighing?"

Fea looked like she was in shock, which seemed terrifying. But Donn hadn't said it like the Weighing was a battle royale, where I'd have to fight sandworms or anything like that. More like it was a secret that they weren't meant to talk about. Like Fight Club. The first rule of the Weighing was you didn't talk about the Weighing.

Shaking herself from her stunned stupor, Fea answered my question. "A Weighing is an assemblage of all the high rulers of the afterlife, and they decide if a mortal should be returned to the living plane as an immortal. It's only been requested a handful of times in remembered history, and the request has only been approved twice." She looked me in the eye, pity in her expression. "No one has ever successfully been returned to the living plane."

Glancing at Cy, I saw my feelings reflected on his face. It was a long shot, but it was hope. I could return home. I could be immortal and be with them forever. Determination flowed through my veins. I would be the first person.

I would get my happy ending.

# CHAPTER 31
## CYDON

I tried to smother the flame of hope that the old Irish God was presenting us, but it flickered in my chest anyway. It was burning bright and strong in Wren's eyes, and that was enough for both of us.

We took Donn's offer to stay for the night, and Fea led us upstairs to an empty room. And I mean *upstairs*. We must have climbed thirty flights before we reached our floor. I hadn't even thought it was structurally possible, but clearly, this wasn't a place that had to adhere to the laws of physics. It was more like the TARDIS than Hotel California.

Finally, we stopped in front of a heavy wooden door, which Fea pushed open to reveal a basic room. "Rest, Wren. The walk to the Tar Pits isn't far, but it is arduous."

Wren reached out and gripped her hand. "Thank you, Fea. I couldn't have done any of this without my guide. I appreciate it."

Smiling back, Fea ushered us into the room. "My honor. Get a good night's rest. We'll leave early for the Tar Pits."

Quietly shutting the door behind us, I joined Wren in looking around at the room. It was basic by modern standards, but I imagined that it would have seemed palatial just a century or two earlier. Worn, thick blankets covered a double bed, and it actually had a proper mattress. Given the rest of the place looked like it had been pulled straight from a history book of medieval England, I'd been a little worried that we'd be sleeping on pallets on the floor, or on straw mattresses.

I wouldn't have cared. In dog form, I'd slept in a lot worse places than a comfortable room in a damn castle. But I wanted only the best for Wren.

"How can I be dead *and* this exhausted?" she groaned, flopping down onto the bed.

It was the general effect of this place. I had my theories that it was how they made the non-denominational souls choose, because exhaustion took hold, so anywhere looked like a good place to eternally rest. I didn't tell her any of that, though. I couldn't stand that sadness on her face again tonight.

"Is it just me, or does the God of Death have the hots for our guide?"

She rocketed up into a sitting position. "Right?! They are adorable, though I'm not sure either of them realizes the other one is flirting. So sweet. Do you think we should tell her that he's interested?"

I laughed at her enthusiasm. Who knew playing

matchmaker would pull her from her melancholy? "Only if you first tell her that you're Néit's partner. When she spoke of him, I wondered if she was holding on for him to pass over."

Visibly shuddering, she grabbed my hand and dragged me down onto the bed with her. "Hard pass on that conversation. I'm hoping that she'll drop us off at the Tar Pits and go on her way, so I can avoid that whole thing."

I didn't know how soul guides worked, but hopefully, that would be enough to satisfy whatever force or magical pull was compelling Fea to accompany us. We wouldn't know until we got there, I guess.

I pulled off my shirt, tossing it down beside the bed. Wren was still in the long white gown, like some bride of death, and she hiked it up so she could put her legs over mine, tangling them together.

"Have I said how glad I am that you're here with me, Cy? Even if it's the most selfish feeling in the world."

I shook my head and kissed the top of her hair. "It's only selfish if there was somewhere else I wanted to be, and there isn't." Honestly, being one of the guys topside, mourning over her dead body, seemed worse than a thousand deaths.

"You think I can do it, right? That I can pass whatever this Weighing thing is? That I can go home?"

"Yes. If anyone deserves it, it's you." I sucked in a deep breath. "If it doesn't happen, we'll regroup then. Figure something out. Find a place to rest."

She didn't really understand how big of a deal it was in itself for all the rulers of the afterlife to get together. It would be everyone from Hades to Hel, in a single room. Just the idea of that amount of power made me want to gag. Hades usually tamped it down when he was around us, but he wouldn't down here, in a place with a bunch of other highly powered Mythics. It was going to be like getting electrified from the inside out.

I wished, for the first time ever, that I could speak to my father. I could ask him what the fuck the Weighing was, what it entailed, and how to prepare. I hated walking into things blind.

"I'm sorry I dragged you along with me, though. You didn't deserve to die just because you're tied to me."

I covered her plush lips with my finger. "Stop apologizing."

She nipped the end of the finger, making me groan softly. She looked up at me, her eyes big and shiny and full of desire. It was an expression I dreamed of every night, and woke up aching for every morning.

"Cy?"

"Mhm?"

"Will you make love to me? Prove that I'm still here, even if I'm not alive?"

My whole body shuddered with need, or relief, or something visceral. "Every day for the rest of my immortal life, if you'll let me."

She gave a watery chuckle. "Do you think it counts as necrophilia?"

The laugh that burst out of me wasn't sexy in any way. This woman could make me laugh in the very pits of Hell. She really was perfect.

"Let's hope not. Come here, Wren."

Tugging her up my body, I kissed her hard. I traced her lips with mine, memorizing them in case we never had this moment again. I dragged the death dress up over her head and threw it across the room. I wondered if I could ask Fea for something different, something that didn't scream *Bride of the Undead*.

Wren's body was beautiful. When she'd died, I wasn't sure if it had reverted back to how it was pre-children, or if it had formed on the banks of the Styx in whatever way she saw herself. There was no trace of the small pouch from her pregnancy, or stretch marks, or any of the other beautiful badges that said she'd given birth recently. Even her breasts weren't tight and filled with milk, as they normally were. They were small, fitting easily in my palms as I ran my hands up her sides to cup them.

"So this is how you get back to your pre-baby body," she joked. "Dying seems a little extreme, though."

I nodded, running my thumbs over her nipples, making them peak at my touch. "Especially when you're gorgeous either way." Leaning up, I took her nipple in my mouth, and she threw her head back with a moan.

Her knees were either side of my thighs, and when I rolled my hips, my cock brushed the wetness between her thighs. At that moment, I thought I might die right along with her. I sucked and nipped at her breasts, reveling in the sweet little sounds she made. I wanted to record those sounds, play them back over and over.

She ground herself against my cock, making me worry I was going to blow way too soon. Ripping my mouth from her nipple with an audible pop, I watched as she reached down and grabbed my cock.

It was this point I realized I was not in control at all. She was using my body for her pleasure, to ground herself in the here and now, and I was helpless to slow her down. Not when I was lying beneath her, staring up into her face filled with pleasure. Not when she was notching me against her entrance, and I was sliding in achingly slowly.

"Wren, fuck…" I breathed, and her gaze burned into mine as each pleasurable inch of my cock sank into her. It felt like home. It felt like my destiny. I was afraid to move and blow it all too quickly, to lose this feeling before I'd even grasped it completely.

Finally, I was seated completely inside her, our bodies pressed so tightly we could be one entity, and I let out a shuddering, happy sigh. We might be in turmoil. We might not know what the future held. But I had my whole universe right here in my arms, and if this was the only moment we ever got, then it would sustain me until I could follow her into eternity.

She was breathing heavily, and as I gripped her hips, making her move, her whimpers became moans. When I didn't come inside her instantly, I got bolder, moving her up and down my cock with my hands pressed to her hips, until her moans became screams that could drown out even the River Styx. My mouth returned to those glorious breasts as I licked and sucked and fucked us both into oblivion.

"Cy," she breathed over and over until she was chanting my name and coming hard around my cock. I gritted my teeth as she milked my cock, but it didn't matter how hard I clung to my control, she stole it completely. I came hard, deep, deep inside her.

With shaky arms, she collapsed on my chest, her face buried in the curve of my shoulder. "Wow," she breathed.

I made a strangled sound. Wow wasn't quite a strong enough word to describe the life-altering joy of being inside her, but it would do.

"Wow, indeed," I chuckled. I gripped her tightly to my body, worried she'd disappear like dust on the wind now.

Pushing up on her hands a little, she looked down at me seriously. My heart was in my throat. Was I terrible? Did she not feel the same soul-rending pleasure that I did?

"We can do it doggy style next time, if you'd like."

A chuckle bubbled up my throat, but it had formed into a full-blown laugh as it left my lips. Pulling her body back against mine, I bathed in the sound of her soft laughter combined with mine. *Cheeky little bird.*

When the laughter finally trailed away, her cheek was on my chest, and her hair spread out across my arm and the pillow, I wondered if this was really the Elysian Fields. Maybe I was the one that was dead, and this was just the happiest place I could think of.

"Who were you before you were stuck on Crete, waiting for me?" she whispered into the darkness, and I chuckled softly.

"I was a shadow of the man I was supposed to be for you."

I could feel her smile against my chest. "You romantic bastard. I mean it. I know what your dick looks and feels like, so I feel like I should know more about you. When did you realize you could turn into a dog?"

"I've been able to shift to my other form for as long as I can remember. My mother told me that she thought I'd been kidnapped by my father and a puppy left in my place the first time it happened. She said that she got none of that newborn reprieve, because I was able to shift and trot around the house within weeks of being born."

She shuddered, and I knew she was imagining if the babies were puppies. Three of them would be… rough. Then I felt the moment she remembered she was dead. Her whole body went stiff, and the scent of her sadness burnt my nose.

"I'll get you back there to see them take their first steps, Wren. I swear it."

She reached up and stroked my cheek. "You can't promise that, but I appreciate it anyway. We should get some sleep."

I didn't care what I had to do, but I was going to keep that promise.

# CHAPTER 32
## GRIFF

My mate was dead.

I felt that loss in my soul. I screeched mournfully into the darkness of the mountain range, an outlet for the rage that I'd waited all this time, yet she'd been ripped needlessly from my claws. I was a failure. I had failed her. I had failed my flight.

*You're not a failure, but you are being a giant pain in the ass. You need to go back. Or give me back control.*

The human's voice in my head was becoming irritating. He couldn't climb down from this height anyway. We'd both failed her; I was angry at him too. And he was angry at me. It was the most at odds we'd ever been, since the beginning.

I wanted to follow her into the afterlife, but he wanted to stay, for the cubs. I wanted to stay for the cubs too, but how could I live with this pain? This gaping wound in my chest where her heartbeat once resided?

I made the most basic nest I could. I didn't deserve to be comfortable, not really. I deserved to sleep on a bed of rocks and sharp sticks, a reminder of my failure to my nestmates. I was deep in the mountains of Crete. I'd wanted to fly further, maybe right to Olympus, and rend the heads from the bodies of those who'd thought to come after my family, but the human had stopped me.

*Teron. Use my name. I'm no more human than you are. We've lived side by side for millennia. Stop being a prick.*

I growled low in my throat. I couldn't separate myself from him. His grief and anger sat there in my chest beside my own. It made it so much worse, because the only person I hated failing more than Wren was him.

Ignoring his words, I curled up on the cliff face and looked up at the moon. With every beat of my heart, a word echoed around my brain, like it was being pushed there by that now-useless organ.

*Failure. Failure. Failure.*

Letting my eyes drift closed, I hoped that something picked me off while I slept. I could hear Teron's heavy sigh, filled with grief and anger. Maybe a harpy would fly down and put us both out of our misery.

I dreamed I was with her in her bed, my head resting on her chest. We were in a castle, not that I'd seen many like this in my lifetime, outside of Teron's movies. It was drafty and cold, made of stone, and looked enough like a prison, I wondered if I was constructing a Hell around us both. There was no warmth here, no light. Just darkness and chill.

Beside her was the dog form of Cydon, which was odd for my dreams, but perhaps I was mourning him too. He'd been a good flight mate. I hoped he was with her, wherever she was.

Despite the cold, she looked content, which soothed something inside me. She wasn't in torment. I nuzzled my cheek against her body, but it wasn't the same. The scent of her was gone, her body cold and dead.

Her eyelids fluttered open. "Griff? What's wrong?"

"You died, my mate. I mourn." This was a dream. I didn't need to mindspeak. I could tell her what I wanted to say, and the whole world could hear it too.

She stroked her hands down my neck feathers, making me purr. I didn't think I'd ever feel that again— if this was in my dreams, I'd sleep forever.

"Don't be sad, Griff. I haven't given up yet. I'm going to come back to you soon."

I shook my head. "I saw your body, mate. Heard your heart stop in your chest."

She chuckled. "When has that ever stopped me?" But I knew she wasn't laughing at my pain. My Wren would never.

"At least I'll have the memories of you. I can see you here, in my dreams."

Frowning down at me, she lifted my beak. "Hang on, I thought *I* was dreaming about *you?*"

What? Why would my dream mate say that?

"Are you… Wren, are you real right now?"

She scooched back on the bed, though Cydon stayed asleep. "Are you actually here? With me?"

I reared back, equally as confused. "I am asleep."

"But are you dreaming about me, here? In Tech Duinn?"

Where in the ancestors was Tech Duinn? Could this be real?

"I am in a castle with you. I don't recognize it, no. I assumed my mind was making up places you could be."

She launched herself at me, hugging me so tightly that if this wasn't a dream, I might have suffocated. "Griff! My god, Griff! I never thought…" She pulled back and stared at me as if I was a mirage. "Is everyone okay? The babies?"

I nodded. "They are okay. Sad." That was an understatement. I didn't tell her that I wouldn't know how they were at this moment, since I'd flown off like a hatchling throwing a tantrum.

Grief flashed across her face. "Me too. Griff…" She rubbed her face against mine again. Her features started to get hazy, the edges of the room fading. Panic flitted across her face, and she gripped my fur. "Tell them I'm trying to come back to them. Back to you. I'm going to try for the Weighing—" She was gone as quickly as she'd appeared.

My brain scrambled around to make sense of my dream. Was it just that? The delirium a Gryphon went through when he lost his mate? I'd seen it with my grandparents. My cousins. My parents. As

Gryphonkind died out, I'd seen that delirium over and over again, and could almost track its progress as my loved ones lost themselves to the madness.

But this? It felt different. *I* felt different. But was there a reason for that? Because she was human and not Gryphon? Or was it because her soul hadn't passed over?

There was a third possibility, but I rejected it immediately. I knew for a fact she was my mate. I knew it in my very soul, half of which belonged to her.

But the fact remained that I wasn't succumbing to the madness. I was wild with grief, but I wasn't going on murderous sprees.

I needed more information. There was only one thing left to do. I had to go back, to ask the others.

*Teron, we need to return home.*

The grumble that reverberated through my brain was expected. *About fucking time.*

I LANDED in the courtyard of the compound and watched dogs scatter away. There wasn't a Valkyrie around, and I was seriously pissed about the lack of security, being able to just land from above without seeing a single interception.

*It's time to hand back the reins. I promise, I'll tell them everything you told me about Wren and the dream. We'll figure this out.*

I made a disgruntled noise, but let myself shrink

away, until I was once again merely a presence in the back of a meat suit.

Teron snorted. "Don't talk about yourself like that. And I'm more than a meat suit."

Erus ran through the courtyard, straight into Teron's arms. He hugged him tightly, and guilt gnawed at me. I'd added to their grief, to their stress, at one of the most difficult times of their long lives. I was a bad flight leader.

"Fuck, you're back. We were worried," Erus said, stepping back, his cheeks flushed.

Teron reached out and patted his shoulder. "I'm sorry we worried you. We just needed to sort out our heads," Teron covered for me. We were one, but sometimes I didn't deserve him. "Is everyone okay? The babies?"

Erus nodded. "They're fine, though I think they miss her too. Even at this young age, they know she isn't here." He turned and led the way back into the house. "Guys, Teron and Griff are back!"

He'd picked up the nickname from Wren, though I wasn't mad. For so long, I'd been the Great Gryph, and then just the Gryphon. When Wren had named me, it was the first time I'd had a name in centuries.

The guys appeared one by one, and they all looked like shit. I could feel Teron's anxiety. He was a healer, and I'd ripped him away when they'd needed him most. I hoped I was bringing them good news, not just more pain.

Demke appeared. An old friend, to both me and

Teron. We respected each other, but the look on his face told me how disappointed he was in me. "It's good to have you back." There was a wealth of things unsaid, and he was more subdued than I would have expected. He kept things close to his chest, but his grief was there written across his face.

Teron just nodded. Néit and Milo appeared with the babies, and Teron moved toward them quickly, his eyes giving them a once-over, searching for any signs of illness or problems. He could probably work out their weight just from their size.

To me, they still looked perfect. Tiny little copies of their mother. My young. And I'd just abandoned them. I was a terrible mate.

*We were both going through it. We're going to be better now, and that's what matters.*

"Griff had a dream about Wren." They all watched him tensely, mainly because Teron didn't refer to me very often.

"Is it the matebond delusions?" Demke asked seriously.

Teron hesitated. "I don't think so." He sucked in a breath. "He talked to her in the dream. She said she was trying to get back to us. She was in a bedroom that looked like a castle, somewhere called Tech Duinn. He didn't know what that meant."

Néit blanched. "She said that? Tech Duinn?"

Teron nodded, and I wanted to crow. It wasn't a delusion; it was a real place. Everyone looked at Néit, who was subconsciously bouncing a baby in his arms. I was ashamed that I didn't know which one it was.

Milo looked at him. "Does that mean something to you?"

Néit looked perturbed. "It's the Underworld for the Celtic people. Kind of a halfway place before they move onto the next place." He looked at Demke. "The Gryphon couldn't have known that. How would his mind have conjured that?"

Demke looked hard at Teron, and I thought he might have been looking for me. "What else did she say?"

I did my best to push my voice to come out of Teron's lips. "That she was looking for a way back to us. That she was going to undertake the Weighing." Something about that term tickled the back of my brain, but it was knowledge caught beneath the avalanche of information and memories I'd gathered over the last thousand years.

Demke's brows drew together. "She said 'the Weighing?'"

Teron nodded. A smile curled the edges of Demke's lips, morphing into a full-blown grin. I'd never seen him smile like that.

"What is it?" Tryp asked impatiently.

"It's a chance. A fucking chance. Damn Apollo. We're going to owe him one."

I'd give him Gryphon rides around the world forever, if he brought my mate back to me.

*There's a chance.*

# CHAPTER 33
## WREN

I still didn't know if my dream of Griff had been just a dream or something more. I mean, he'd been speaking from his beak, so I was leaning more toward dream, but it was so vivid and real, I could swear I'd felt the stiff but soft bristle of his feathers. Was it just my way of processing death, or had he really been here with me?

Cy had no answers as we walked away from Tech Duinn. "I couldn't tell you. The bond between Gryphons and their mates has always been a closely guarded secret. Let it give you comfort either way." He leaned over and kissed me for what must have been the fiftieth time this morning, and I couldn't get enough.

I'd woken this morning with everything seeming a little less bleak. I had Cy. I'd possibly talked to Griff, and everyone at home was okay. There was a way for me to get back, even if the chance was small.

Nothing was hopeless anymore.

I noticed Fea looking pensive in front of us. "Are you okay, Fea?"

"You're married to Néit?"

I tripped over my feet, but managed to stay upright, more due to Cy's assistance than my own coordination. "Yes, kind of. I call him Nate."

Fea chewed her lip. "When Donn told me, I almost didn't believe him. Which is silly—it's been a thousand years. Of course he and Badb have moved on. It's why they never visit."

*Ah, my heart.* "I don't think either of them have entirely moved on. And I know they haven't forgotten you."

"Moved on enough to marry someone else, though," Fea snarked.

I shrugged. "Perhaps. But it took Nate thousands of years to move on, and that should be enough. Love sometimes means moving on and learning to give your heart again." This was so fucking awkward, I wondered if I could die twice—once from a knife, and once from embarrassment. I cleared my throat. "They loved you; that much was obvious. They'd want you to find happiness too, a new love, even. Maybe with a God of Death that looks like he is *built,* if you know what I mean." I winked at her, and she flushed pink.

Casting a quick look over her shoulder, like Donn was about to appear and eavesdrop on our conversation, she turned back to me, one hand on her hip. "I'm sure I don't know what you're talking about."

Cy had been quiet the whole conversation up until this point—the damn traitor—but now he laughed. "I'm a man, and I can tell you when another man's smitten. Donn is one hundred percent crushing on you."

"Crushing?" Her eyes went wide, and I reminded myself we needed to tone down the slang.

"Not like grinding your bones to make his bread, kind of crushing. Er…" *What would Jane Austen say here?* "He's enamored of you and desires your affections."

"Oh." Fea walked faster, and I gave her the space she was so obviously trying to take. Glancing over at Cy, I made a face. I was going to kick Nate's ass when we got back topside. And maybe—if it wouldn't get me sent back down here—Morrigan's too. They both should've visited Fea and let her go, let her enjoy her afterlife instead of pining away while the pair of them fucked their way through humanity.

The grounds of Tech Duinn seemed to go on and on, with the gnarled trees in the darkness and the barren landscape that seemed to be both alive and dead at once. Like the depths of winter, everything seemed to be in hibernation.

Fea finally dropped back. "What makes you think Donn holds affection for me?"

Goddess or mortal, thousands of years old or barely sixteen, love made a mess of us all. "Well, it could be the way he watches you like there's no one else in the room."

"Or the way he hangs on every word you say, and

the way his eyes smile when he looks at you," Cy suggested.

"The way he threatened us not to hurt you in any way. Not that we would!" I added, though perhaps I'd already hurt her feelings.

Fea still didn't seem convinced. "Why has he never said anything?"

I shrugged. "Men are stupid sometimes, especially when it comes to women. No offense, Cy."

He snorted. "You're not wrong." God, I loved him.

I turned back to Fea. "While I can tell you're interested in him, you'd have to be a lot less subtle to let him know. He thinks you're still in love with Nate and Badb. That you're just waiting for them to arrive so you can go back to your happy marriage."

She gave a mirthless laugh. "There was love, but I wouldn't have called my marriage happy. We were battle Gods, after all, and those two were infamous. Still are. They had more enemies than friends. Our marriage was wild and contentious, full of passion and lust, but never happiness outside the battlefield or the bedroom. Sometimes those two places were interchangeable." She sighed deeply. "It's how I died, in the end. Their enemies snuck in while we were making love, and stabbed me through the heart. I was the weakest link. The Achilles heel—if I can borrow some of your history, Cydon—of the two greatest warriors of our time."

Having met Badb and knowing what I did about the old Nate, I could see how that would be true.

Clearing my throat, I nodded. "Well, I'm pretty sure Donn doesn't know it. If you're interested, you'll have to be overt about it. Tell him, because otherwise he's going to be your scary protector forever, but never make a move."

Nodding, Fea fell into silence as we continued along, and I fell back a little to Cy's side. I couldn't tell how long we'd been walking, but it felt like hours. Looking over my shoulder, I realized we couldn't see Tech Duinn anymore, which surely had to be a good sign.

Fea had said the Tar Pits were at the furthest corner of Tech Duinn, where a lot of the different Underworlds converged on the banks of the River Styx. It had been decided that the Celts would host the... I didn't even know what it was. A village? An arena?

Anyway, it had been decided they'd hold it, since they essentially had two Underworlds, and it was in their nature to follow the rules of hosting, meaning they'd never use it to make a power grab.

The silence in Tech Duinn was eerie. As we'd walked along the banks of the River Styx yesterday, the sounds of wails and the rustle of souls in the waters had created a cacophony of noise that I'd been sure would send me mad. But the silence of this place was almost as bad. I was relieved when Fea seemed to come to some internal decision and went back to being a genial host.

"So, tell me about your life with my former husband."

*On second thoughts, maybe we could just go back to deafening silence.*

"He was my neighbor." As the story spilled from my lips, I realized how insane my life had been. Short, filled with pain and heartache, but also real happiness. How much joy this last year had brought me, despite the life-and-death moments, the life-altering changes. I had the guys. I had a home. I had my beautiful babies. Even if I never got back, I'd known true happiness. Gentle and peaceful joy, even if it was fleeting.

"You and Néit have children?" Fea breathed. "That was the one point of contention between us all. I wanted to find somewhere peaceful to raise our children, but they could never be far from the fight."

Now it was my turn to be shocked. "Nate had children?"

"Two sons. They went on to be some of folklore's fiercest warriors, as did their sons, until they changed the face of the Emerald Isles. They were born into a life of battles and bloodshed; they had no chance to be anything else. None of our line ever went on to die peaceful deaths from old age."

Sadness washed across her face, and I reached down to squeeze her hand. What could I even say to that? That destiny was a bitch, and there was probably no other path for them anyway?

"I'm sorry."

Tugging her hand gently from mine, she waved away my empty platitudes. "It was the way of the world back then. There was no unified country. Just warring factions, both Mythics and humans. No one ever lived a long time." She stopped. "We're here."

Looking up, I realized a building had appeared in front of us, almost like a mirage. One second, there'd been endless road, and the next, this small stone building. There was a tiny sign above the door, but I couldn't read it. Whatever the language was, it didn't use any lettering I'd ever seen.

Fea looked at me sadly. "Welcome to the Tar Pits. Unfortunately, this is as far as I can take you. What happens beyond these doors is up to you." She pulled me into a hug. "I wish you the best of luck, Wren Mahone. I hope you get back to your sons, and to Néit. When you see him, tell him that I forgive him, and he should forgive himself. Make it up to me by ensuring you and your sons are safe and happy."

I hugged her back. "I will." Pulling back, I gently pushed her back down the road. "Go back to Tech Duinn and ride your very own Death God right to Nirvana. When I see you again in thousands of years, you better be Queen of Tech Duinn and be leading that giant hunk around on a leash!"

Fea looked aghast at the idea. "I, uh, will take that under advisement."

"You've been the very best soul guide! I'll give you an excellent review on Yelp!"

She just looked at me like I was an alien, but waved as she walked away. Turning back to Cy, I sucked in a deep, fortifying breath. I gripped his hand tightly, and we stepped up to the door. I didn't know what was past this point, but it was the first step to getting me back to my life.

"Ready?"

"I'm with you always," Cy murmured.

Pushing open the door, we came face-to-face with a decapitated head.

# CHAPTER 34
## WREN

The decapitated head turned to look at us.

Let that sink in. The bodiless head turned to look at me, glaring like I was the out-of-place thing in the room.

"Who are you?" he grumbled, and I dragged my eyes from the talking head to look around the rest of the room. There were lots of people here—or more specifically, Mythics. I also realized it was a damn bar. It was loud as everyone spoke at once, questions being lobbed at me from all sides.

Now I remembered where I'd heard of the Tar Pits before. From the Valkyries.

"I was talking to you, mortal. Who are you?" the head grumped again.

I slow-blinked, trying to get my brain to come back online. "Uh, hi. I'm Wren Mahone. I was hoping that you could help me arrange the Weighing."

Silence.

This silence was so loud, it could have been a vacuum, sucking out all the air in the room.

"You better come up to the bar, girl, and start at the beginning. A Weighing isn't something you call haphazardly. No one wants to piss off one God of Death, let alone several. It's not worth my head if they decide you're full of shite." He laughed at his own joke.

Stepping softly, I tried not to shrink under the weight of the room's collective gaze. I sat at a barstool at the heavily shined bar, suddenly realizing that the head was in some kind of bubble of magic. It didn't float around like Glinda the Good Witch in Oz on Halloween, but it definitely let it be far more mobile than a head should be.

I contained my shudder, but barely. The meaty bits of its neck were still showing.

"Unfortunately, you'll be needin' to pour your own drinks. No arms."

Normally, I'd be skeptical about accepting drinks from strangers, but if I was going to have a conversation with a head, I was going to need a shot of whiskey. Reaching behind the bar for the bottle and three glasses, I poured us all a couple of fingers of the amber liquor.

I passed one to Cy, then held the other one awkwardly out to the head. "Uh, do I...?"

"Pssh, girlie. I've never needed assistance drinking my whiskey, and I ain't about to start now. Just grab my straw over there." A set of carved wooden straws sat behind the bar in a tall glass. Grabbing one, I popped it in the glass and hoped for the best.

Then I downed my liquor. And Cy's. I shot him an apologetic look, and his eyes laughed at me.

"Well, at least you can shoot your whiskey. I'm Brân, proprietor of the Tar Pits. We don't get many mortal souls. They don't often make it this far into the lands beyond, before finding their final resting place."

I quirked an eyebrow at him. "I was motivated."

"Ah yes, with the Weighing. We haven't had one of those in… well, I don't know. Sucellus, when was the last time we called a Weighing?"

"Maybe one of those monolithic worshipers. Hmm, a Saint something or other?"

Brân winked. "Ah, so it was. What they don't tell you about these Weighings, girlie, is that if you fail, there's no skipping off to some green field somewhere. You're giving them your soul. If you fail, they keep that little trinket for their efforts, and you get obliterated from existence."

Cy hissed through his teeth. So it was all or nothing. That didn't sway me. "What does it entail?"

Brân shook his head, which was odd, since he barely had any neck. Very disconcerting. "I'm afraid that is the first test. A leap of faith. I can't tell you what it involves —you just have to have faith in yourself, and your worthiness."

Did I think I was worthy? Maybe. But really, there was no other option for me. "I understand. I still want to go ahead."

"Ballsy, girlie. Okay, I'll put out the call. You can start on your worthiness by helping me out here in the bar, to cover room and board for you and the pretty boy. What's ya name, boy?"

"Cydon. Call me Cy."

"Demigod, I see. Quite the pair you made, stumbling into my bar. What Pantheon?"

I'd never seen anyone outright ask Cy what Pantheon he was associated with. I assumed it was some kind of faux pas, but maybe this guy was immune from polite society. "I was born Greek, but I ally with the Minoans."

Both eyebrows climbed up Brân's forehead. He really did have expressive eyebrows. I guess if that was your only form of body language, you made do. "Minoans, you say? Haven't seen many of those around these parts in quite a while. Unusual for Mythics to swap too."

Cy chuckled, but his eyes were flinty. "We are an unusual pair, as you said."

Someone yelled for a refill on the other side of the room, and one side of Brân's lips curled. "So I did. I also said you have to work the bar, and I think you have your first customer."

Sliding from the barstool, Cy kissed my cheek. It was a proprietary move. "I'll get it."

I watched him move into the smoky darkness, while the head looked at me shrewdly. "Boyfriend? Husband?"

"Bondmate," I answered.

"If you fail, you'll be gone for good. That's going to be upsetting for him."

I inclined my head. "You know, I have a son named Bran. He's less than two months old. Too young to lose a mother. He needs me. They all need me."

"Bran, you say? A good strong name, if I do say so. Surely, he has a daddy to take care of him, unless it's the little Demigod over there?"

I shook my head. "He does, of course, but he and his brothers have a big destiny, and I feel like they'll need me. To love them, to protect them."

"Brothers, hmmm? All boys? I loved my boys, but they were wild in a way that definitely needed a firmer hand than mine."

I watched Cy pour beers like he'd been a bartender for decades. "Triplets. Three boys."

Brân stilled. "Triplets, you say? And your name is Wren? They wouldn't be the Kuningilin, would they?" He whistled low. "Well, that changes things, doesn't it? Last I heard, the Moirai had lost their middle sister and their powers along with it, and the new Fates had solidified their position."

Gritting my teeth, I nodded. "The Moirai weren't above some petty revenge." I waved to my now-dead self. "The other two are no more, but now neither am I."

He stared me dead in the eye, and I got the feeling that this head had seen some things. "Go help Lover-boy. I'll get to calling now."

I'D LEARNED three things from working the bar at the Tar Pits.

One: there were no opening and closing times in the afterlife. I worked until I felt tired and then I slept, before waking and working again. I didn't even know how many days I'd been working here at this point.

Two: everyone knew everyone else's business. By the end of the first day, everyone knew who I was, how I came to be at the Tar Pit, and that I was calling a Weighing.

Three: customer service was a little like riding a bike; you fell right back into the old habits as soon as they put you in front of a register. Apparently, regardless of if they were a mortal accountant named Steve, or Ninkasi, who I'd learned was the Sumarian Goddess of Beer, a customer was a customer. Ninkasi was a riot, though. And her beer was amazing.

There were Mythics from every Pantheon here, and they all appeared to get along famously. Brân said that it was because his was the only bar in the afterlife that would serve you alcohol irrespective of whether you were a hero or a villain in the above world. If you got banned from the Tar Pits, enjoy an eternity of cold, hard sobriety.

I could see how that would be a buzzkill.

Everyone and anyone could enjoy a beverage at the Tar Pits, and some Gods were more common than others. Anansi, who Cy informed me was a Trickster God from West Africa, came in regularly and was the life of the party. He could tell a story so good, the whole room would be enthralled.

While there were customers from every pantheon,

given the location we saw significantly more Celtic deities, such Cernunnos, the Horned God, who was so fucking beautiful with his ripped body and huge antlers, I honestly thought about crawling into his lap. However, that seductive allure was merely part of his powers, and Cy quickly took over serving him, just to save me from embarrassing myself.

Then there was Sheela, who was some Fertility Goddess with three vaginas, which she happily flashed to the whole bar every time she drank.

My favorite so far was Veles, another horned God like Cernunnos, though Veles was Slavic. He was my favorite because he and Brân bickered like old maids, and also because he always had at least three bunnies, two foxes, and a baby cow with him. I wanted to petition for a calf in every workplace. It was so freaking cute, I couldn't help but cuddle it.

"Beer for you, sir. And a bowl of milk for my favorite customer, Rova."

The huge God snorted derisively. "She does not need milk, girl. Bring her a beer too. We'll see if she can make Guinness when milked, eh, Brân?"

The fact that Brân was just a head was becoming less confronting, especially when you took into account all the interesting-looking Mythics who came in. The Flying Spaghetti Monster had been an especially interesting one. He'd talked purely in 2005 slang, and after winning a game of cards, he'd told a literal God of War, "In your face, you got pwned." Not going to lie, even I only understood half of his smack talk.

Brân rolled his eyes, and it was easy to see he and Veles were old buddies. "If you manage that, you might have a whole new religion to get behind. In Ireland, at least. So, girl, what are you going to do if you get back up top?"

I petted Rova the cow's big wet nose, and she mooed at me softly. Man, she was so adorable. "Hug my babies. Find homes for all the stray dogs in my care. They've waited long enough. One—no, *two* orgies with the men I love."

The bar laughed. If the people in this room loved anything more than beer, it was animals and orgies. Not together, though… I hoped.

Veles snort-laughed. "A worthy course of action." He looked over at Brân. "She's got my vote." With that, he downed his beer and whistled, causing all the animals around him to come to heel. "See you in a few weeks, Wren Mahone." Then he left.

I looked at Brân. "What does that mean?"

The bodiless Demigod merely grinned. "Means you impressed the first of the rulers of the afterlife. Congrats, girlie. Only a few more to go."

I looked over at Cy. What the hell did that *mean?*

# CHAPTER 35
## CYDON

From what I could tell, the collective Mythic rulers of the afterlife could come to the Tar Pits and judge whether Wren was worthy of even the time it'd take to hold this magical Weighing ceremony.

It wasn't like a fairy godmother who could bibbidi-bobbidi-boo her into immortality. This was a serious thing, though no one could—or would—tell me what it entailed. Only that her mortal soul was the price, and if she failed, she would be gone from the wheel. I couldn't just stay with her in the Underworld and wait for everyone else to arrive. We couldn't stay here at the Tar Pits and hope the guys would come to visit.

She'd be completely gone, and everything in me rebelled against even the concept. I'd tried to broach the subject, but she shut me down immediately. Sure, it had been with kisses, but they'd only softened the blow of her words.

"I don't want to live a thousand years waiting for

the people I love to die, when I could spend a thousand lives with them, and their children, and their children's children. At best, this would be a half-life. You'd make me happy—and you do, so freaking happy—but they're all the pieces of my heart too. What would you do, in my shoes?"

That was the last time I'd mentioned it, because in her shoes, I would also risk it all to get back to her. So as much as my heart ached at the thought I might lose her, I subtly began grilling the bar's patrons about the Weighing. Some were oblivious, others tight-lipped. But if you hit them right as the mead was rushing to their heads, some of them were as chatty as a human on spring break.

I poured more mead for a grizzled old warrior Mythic. I didn't know which Pantheon he was from, or even his name, but he liked to talk when he was drinking. "Yeah, we're just here for the Weighing," I told him casually, topping his glass up all the way to the rim. "They make it sound hard, but my girl is the best. How could it go wrong?"

The Mythic snorted. "Everything. They mightn't even come, and you'll be stuck here slinging beer for that oversized football for eternity. Or they will come and judge your girl, and decide she isn't worthy."

I growled. "She's the most worthy person I know."

He downed half of his drink in one go. "Their version of worthy and yours are different. Those bastards see nothing but the bad. And if they do decide she's worthy of the Weighing, that shit is..." He shuddered. "It isn't good. A soul disappearing is something that makes me shudder. A cold shiver that takes over your whole body. Cold for *weeks* afterwards."

I sat down across from him. "You've seen one? A Weighing?"

He puffed out his chest. "I was here for the Saint. Patrick? Simon? Who cares. He was unworthy, and he was a fucking saint."

Dread was like a stone in my chest. I stood, slowly moving back to the bar. Like the guy said, worthiness was judged differently. Maybe it would be okay.

The problem was, how did we know who she was supposed to be impressing? The big ones were obvious: Hades—I couldn't wait to see him—as well as Lucifer and Hel. But who knew all the lesser known deities, especially from the long-dead Pantheons? I didn't even know if the Minoans had a God of Death. They were all about life.

When I'd said that to Wren, she'd just shrugged. "If I'm kind to everyone, then I should make a good impression on the right ones, I guess?"

*Ugh, I need Google.* For instance, the scowling guy she was serving now grunted more than spoke. He didn't look like he belonged here, but I didn't know if it was because he was a monster who just liked a beer, or because he was a God of Death who didn't want to even be here but was obligated to check out Wren for the Weighing?

Smiling happily, she came back to the bar. "Can I have one of Ninkasi's batch, please? Nergal doesn't like beer. Or people." She smiled as if that was the most endearing thing ever. Grabbing one of the large clay urns of wine from beneath the bar, I poured a large pitcher for the unknown Mythic.

When the doors opened, I almost wept to see a face I knew. Hades strolled in, like he'd been here a million times before, and maybe he had. When he made it to the bar, I resisted the urge to jump it and hug him. "If I didn't think Persephone would punch me, I'd lean over this bar and kiss you."

He grinned. "It probably isn't Sephy you'd have to worry about." He looked around the room, and his eyes snagged on Wren as she emerged from the back with two large flagons of beer. "She's okay?"

I shook my head. "She's grief-stricken. But she's determined to get home, even if it means she might cease to exist." I stared at him. "Hades—"

"Hades!" Wren's voice bounced around the room, drawing everyone's eyes to the enigmatic ruler of the Underworld. She raced over and hugged him like a life buoy in the middle of the North Sea. He patted her back awkwardly. "Thank god you're here. The guys? The babies? Are they okay?" She stepped back, but gripped his sleeve, clearly worried he'd disappear before she got her answers.

"They're okay, Wren. Please, let's sit."

Shaking herself, she stepped away. "Of course. Sorry. Do you want a drink?"

"A whiskey would be great. Brân has some of the best malt whiskey ever distilled down here."

I agreed, and given the distillery Brân kept in the back of the bar, it had been perfected over an endless eternity. I leaned over the bar, grabbing a bottle and a couple of glasses. I figured we'd all need it.

"Brân! We're just taking a short break!" I yelled across the room to the head, who was deep in conversation with a woman in black.

Wren sat across from Hades, and while she'd let his sleeve go, she wasn't taking her eyes from him. "Tell me?" she implored.

"The Minoans are a mess, but they are holding it together for the infants. The Valkyries and the Morrigan have picked up their protection slack, while they all adjust to your death." I winced at the word, and he looked over at me. "The pack have stuck around, but I've never seen so many sad dog faces."

My heart clenched at the idea of my leaderless pack. They relied on me too, and while I wouldn't change anything, I hated that they felt abandoned.

"But since you connected with the Gryphon, there is some renewed hope."

Wren's eyes went wide. "So it *was* real? I did speak to Griff in my dream?" A smile spread across her face, so bright it lit the interior of this dark little bar. "I thought it was just my own grief manifesting him."

"A matebond is a powerful force not even death can break." Hades shook his head. "About the Weighing…"

Shoulders stiff, she stared down Hades, literally one of the most powerful Mythics ever created. "I'm doing it. I'll take the risk to get back to them."

"I expected nothing less. No, the consensus is that you are worthy for The Weighing. It will happen soon. I want you to be prepared, because it isn't an easy task. If you survive it, you will be... different. I cannot interfere once it starts, and I can't alter the outcome, no matter how much I wish I could."

Wren reached across the table and placed her hand over his. "I understand. I accept what has to happen, but you know better than anyone that I *need* to be there, with them, to protect my babies. To ensure they live happy lives, filled with love and not just duty. I trust my guys with the boys, I do. They'll protect them with their lives. But if their hearts are broken because I'm dead, how can they give them the love they need, so they don't end up like the Moirai—warped and twisted creatures, drunk on their own power?"

I resisted the urge to spit on the ground at the name of the old Fates. Hades nodded at her words, like he knew exactly what she meant.

"Have you ever seen a Weighing before?" I asked him.

"Several. None have ever been successful, though."

That was not reassuring.

"Is it physically taxing? Like, should she be doing sit ups in her spare time?"

Wren laughed. "If it involves sit ups, I'm in trouble." I could hear the nerves in her voice. She was worried, and so was I.

Hades downed his whiskey. "It is not an obstacle course. She will not have to be physically strong. But it is painful. Prepare yourself for that." Standing, he reached out and squeezed Wren's hand once more. It was the most I'd ever seen Hades touch anyone who wasn't one of his inner circle. He really did like Wren, which was reassuring in itself. "It will happen tomorrow. I will tell Brân. Prepare yourself, Wren Mahone, because this time tomorrow, you'll either be home or you will cease to exist."

Then he disappeared.

I looked at Wren's wide, fearful eyes. In the next moment, she shook her head, the fear replaced by determination. "It's almost over, Cy. Regardless of what happens, I need something from you. A promise."

I knew what she was about to ask, and I wasn't sure I could fulfill that promise. If she was gone, I didn't know if I would be anything more than dust. "You know I'll do anything for you, Wren. But don't ask this of me."

She shook her head at me sadly. "If I die, I need you to return to Crete. I need you to show the boys how to love with their whole hearts, despite the potential for hurt. I need you to teach them that the weak and beaten-down have the potential to be heroes too. I need you to show them how to be good leaders, good men. I know you can do it, because you're one of the best men I've ever met." She gripped my hands tightly, her knuckles blanching. "*Please*, Cy."

It felt like a deathbed promise, and it was threatening to break my heart.

"I promise."

# CHAPTER 36
## WREN

I'd never seen the Tar Pits so empty. In all the time I'd worked here—which was indeterminable, really —it had always been bustling with bodies. Today, in Brân's words, only the brave or the stupid remained.

"It's a room filled with Death Gods, girl. Some are notoriously easy to offend. No one wants to spend an eternity in Christianity's Hell, being poked in the ass by a demon, just because you pissed off Lucifer."

I felt like I would've recognised the Devil if I'd met him in the bar, so he must have sent an emissary. Who knows who that could've been, though?

Cy paced back and forth, and if I thought I could make him leave, I would. He didn't need to see this. But I knew he wouldn't go. He'd stay for this whole ordeal, because he was loyal and he loved me. It was in every line of his body, in every achingly handsome curve of his face. It was in the way his fingers brushed my hand or arm or thigh every time he walked past, like he was trying to reassure himself that I was still here.

Finally, after such a painfully long time that it almost had to be part of the trial, the doors opened. Hades walked in beside a beautiful woman, her face a skull. Or her skull was a skull, and she had no face flesh. I wasn't sure how I knew she was beautiful, but I did, deep down in my chest. She was in flowing red robes, clad in beautiful roses that looked real, though I didn't know how flowers that red could grow down here. The hood of her robe was elaborately embroidered with gold thread and flowers. She held a scythe in her hands, but even that was intricately engraved. She was a beautiful Death.

Brân murmured softly, "Santa Muerte. Holy Saint of Death. She has a small offshoot of Christianity, I believe." When two men walked in behind her, I wasn't even surprised to see one was blue. I looked at Brân, who rolled his eyes at me. "Yama. He's the blue one. Big guy in many of the East Asian Pantheons. He gets around. And beside him is Mictlantecuhtli, from the Aztecs."

The other man was skeletal, but unlike Santa Muerte, he still had skin pulled tight across his bones, so tight he looked like a drum. Looking at him made my brain ache. They congregated together, solemn and filled with power.

The next figure to walk through the door was one I knew. "Nergal?"

The huge, ill-tempered Mythic grunted at me in

greeting and went to join the rest of the rulers of the afterlife.

I looked at Brân. "You could have told me he was a God I had to impress."

Chuckling, the head raised an eyebrow. "Would your manner have changed? I didn't think so. He runs the Underworld for the Mesopotamians, though there aren't many of them left now."

Next was another face I recognized. Donn from Tech Duinn arrived, a man who looked like a lighter version of him at his side.

"Donn!" I yelled, drawing the gaze of all the Gods and Goddesses in the room. He smiled, ducking to get further into the room.

"Wren Mahone. I see you were successful. This is my counterpart from Annwn, Arawn."

The golden God in question bowed. "I hear I have you to thank for stopping this giant from being as pitiful as a schoolboy with a crush."

I raised my eyebrows. "Fea?"

Donn scowled at us both, but his eyes danced with happiness. He didn't confirm or deny, but he didn't need to. I winked at him, and his lips curled into a smile before he turned and went to stand with the rest of the assembly.

The power in the room was raising the hair on my arms, and Cy had come to stand closer to me.

A booming laugh announced the next Mythics before they'd even pressed through the doors. Two men in suits walked in, though one was smoking and wearing a grin and a top hat. "Brân! Old head, 'tis been too long."

Under his breath, Brân sighed. "Baron Samedi, from the Haitian Crossroads. Big partier. I better get out the bigger jugs of ale," he muttered to himself. "Beside him is—"

The other man was there immediately. "Lucifer. The Devil." He flicked his wings behind him, and until that moment, I hadn't even seen them there. They stretched back behind him in long shadows. He stared down at me in a way that made me feel the size of an ant. "Hmm, I thought they were lying to me, but it's true. You don't seem to fit anywhere, despite your early adherence to Christinianity. I thought Peter was just slacking." He turned to walk toward the rest of the group, but stopped, looking over his shoulder. "Zelda says hello."

I pulled back, like he was reaching for my throat. "Mrs. B is in Hell? That can't be right."

The Devil was instantly back in front of me. "And if she is, would you bargain your soul to take her place, so she could ascend the heavens?"

Would I give all this up for Mrs. B? Would I swap my soul for hers? Guilt still ate at me for her death, and I'd loved her like a mother until the day she died. I owed her so much, and there wasn't a woman who deserved Heaven more than her. Would I give up my immortality for her, though?

Someone called for Lucifer, and he smirked. "Saved by the bell from an eternity in Hell," Lucifer purred.

"Unfortunately, your soul isn't up for grabs right now anyway. Maybe later. Though we both know Zelda is talking shit in Heaven. She asked a favor from me and my Reaper, on your death. Only woman I've met in a while who could make a deal with the devil and still end up behind the pearly gates. Wily old bat." A relieved breath rushed out of me, and his laughter echoed around the room as he joined the others.

The last three people came in all at once. A woman stepped in first, with pale skin and deep black hair that fell to the back of her knees. Behind her was a man with equally dark hair, but skin so green, it reminded me of the jungle. His eyes took me in, but his lips remained pressed closed.

"Hel, from… well, Hel. Norse," Brân muttered. "And beside her is Osiris, from the Egyptian Pantheon."

My eyes had snagged on the last person, though. His power was immense, and his presence filled the room. I knew who he was, the same way I knew who the Greeks were. Possibly one of the most famous Mythics of all time, and I guess it made sense why he was here.

"Anubis," I breathed, and Brân made a noise of agreement. The Weighing made sense now, and honestly, I felt like a bit of an idiot not figuring it out before. "Weighing. He's going to weigh my heart."

Looking at me sadly, Brân merely nodded.

Like they'd all been waiting for Anubis to arrive, the collective rulers of the afterlife all turned to look at me. I felt like just their gaze alone might incinerate me. They were all so different, so varied in not just appearance, but in power and beliefs. The silence was both heavy and deafening all at once. The people at the edges of the room, who'd stayed to watch my weighing, were so quiet, I didn't even think they were breathing.

The jackal-headed God, Anubis, stepped forward. "Wren Mahone. Do you still petition for the Weighing?" It sounded like a question, but there was only one answer. I had a feeling that I'd wish I was dead if I wasted the time of all these powerful Gods.

But I hadn't changed my mind. I bowed low. "I do."

Anubis inclined his head. "Osiris will remove your heart, and I will weigh it against the feather of Ma'at, the Goddess of Truth, Balance and Fairness. If your heart is heavier, I will take your soul and feed it to Ammit, removing your soul from the weave and the wheel permanently. The process is not pleasant. Your soul being torn out is not a gentle caress."

I licked my lips, my throat suddenly dry. "And if I'm found worthy?"

Anubis's eyes told me he didn't see that happening, but not in a condescending way. I think he just believed this whole thing was rigged. "If you are found worthy, your heart light, then you will eat the feather of Ma'at. You will become immortal and be returned to the human plane, until you die in the way of the immortals."

I nodded. My heart was thundering in my chest as I second-guessed every single thing I'd ever done in my life. That time I'd gone out underage drinking—would that be the heaviness that tipped the scales? The way I'd raged after my parents death? The fact I was banging at least seven guys might be bad.

Still, there was no other choice for me.

Osiris stepped forward. So far, he hadn't spoken, but he lifted his hand in question. Was I ready for this? To let this Mythic remove my heart? My knees were shaking, but I held my chin high. I met his eyes, so black they may as well be pits of tar themselves.

Sucking in a breath, I closed my eyes slowly, reaching for the connection I had with Griff. It was quiet and still now, and I'd thought severed, but I hoped as I poured love to the place where it was, he'd feel it. Let them all know that I loved them.

Opening my eyes, I inclined my head respectfully at Osiris. "I'm ready."

There wasn't any pomp or ceremony. His hand shot forward and burst through my ribs, before he dragged my heart back out. I gasped, falling to my knees. I knew I was already dead, my heart no longer beating, but the pain was real.

It felt like hooks were being dragged from my veins, my blood being replaced by acid, and I screamed. I screamed and screamed until the room around us disappeared, and all that was left was a rapidly flashing reel of my life.

Everything was there in a flash. My first steps. My first friend. My first sadness. My grandmother dying. Saving a baby squirrel when I was eight. But more than that, there were inconsequential moments flashing in front of me. Spilling milk on the floor when I was four. Catching the bus at twelve. Random things. On and on it went, until we got closer to the end. That damn watermelon. The apple. Java Llama. Nate. The guys. Dying.

It stopped as suddenly as it had started. I sucked in a breath, like Osiris's hands had been around my lungs and he'd finally let go. I lay on the floor, looking up at the chandelier over the bar. I needed to turn my head. Needed to watch.

I saw Cy fighting against the hold of Hades, who was gripping him tightly, probably to stop him from doing something stupid, like attacking the God of the Egyptian Underworld.

I watched as Anubis placed my heart on a set of scales that appeared from nowhere. On the other side was a golden feather about the length of my pinky finger. It must have weighed basically nothing. They'd been right; I'd been full of hubris to think I could overcome this test. No one who had lived would have a heart light enough. I was about to be swallowed into nothingness.

I looked at Cy, and his eyes caught mine. I hoped he could read all the things I couldn't say out loud. I apologized that I put him through this. I told him how much I loved him.

Someone made a noise, and Cy tore his eyes away from me, back to the scales. They tipped wildly in one direction, my heart heavier, than back the other way. Back and forward they rocked, the whole world moving so slowly that each rock of the scales felt like it took a lifetime. Or a deathtime.

Finally, it evened back out. Someone gasped in the background, and Lucifer glared in their direction. Anubis turned to Osiris. "It's balanced."

"But not lighter?" Hel asked, her voice soft and melodious. "Does that mean the challenge was overcome or not?"

"Surely not good enough to warrant eternal life. Put her heart back, and she can work the Tar Pits forever. Or go on to one of the afterlifes like an average mortal," one of the Gods argued, which started an argument.

The whole time, I lay there, a gaping hole in my chest, waiting for my fate to be decided. Hades let Cy go, and he rushed over to me, his eyes continually dipping to my chest and then back up to my face.

I lifted my hand to his cheek. "It's fine. It doesn't hurt." Just a small lie. My chest didn't hurt, because my whole body was on fire. "I'm sorry you have to see this," I whispered.

"I couldn't have left even if I wanted to," he murmured, kissing my cheeks and the tears I hadn't realized were pooling there.

Osiris finally raised his hands. "The universe is about balance. Good and evil. Villains and heroes. Happiness and tragedy. We all know this. She has achieved the balance sought by the universe, and I believe that she should gain her immortality and be returned to the world. It is the will of the universe. We are not more powerful than the will of the stars themselves."

Yama stuck his hands on his hips. "You aren't the ruler here, Osiris. We vote. Those in favor of just putting her mortal soul back in her body and sending her on her way, raise your hands." I couldn't see who raised their hands. "Those in favor of feeding her soul to Ammit and going home?"

I sucked in a breath between my teeth, and Cy went pale, but let out a quick, relieved breath. "No one raised their hand," he whispered.

Yama grumbled. "Those in favor of gifting her immortality and sending her back to the living world?"

Cy was now crying. Was that a good thing or a bad thing?

A force pushed him away, and Osiris was there above me, my heart in his hand. He pushed it back into my chest, and the pain stopped immediately, making me cry out with relief. Reaching down, he helped me to my feet. His skin felt both cool and hot at once, like there was fire living inside him, barely contained by a physical form.

Anubis was holding the feather from the scales, which he handed to Osiris. "The Assemblage of Death have seen your heart, Wren Mahone, and have agreed to gift you with immortality. Eat the feather of our revered Ma'at and begin your new life."

I opened my mouth, and Osiris placed it on my tongue. Like a wafer, it disappeared into nothing, but I could feel the power flood my body, chasing away the lingering aches, chasing away anything that felt like mortality. It felt like all my cells were vibrating together. It wasn't painful, but it wasn't comfortable either.

I clenched my teeth, praying I wouldn't break them all. Eventually, I collapsed back to my knees, and for an indeterminable amount of time, my body transformed.

Finally, I felt alive in a way that I couldn't even explain to a mortal person. Nothing ached. Nothing felt wrong. It was like a day where you felt your best, but then a hundred times better. Climbing to my feet, I felt like a newborn deer. My knees trembled, until Cy wrapped an arm around my waist, anchoring me to his side.

I looked over at Brân and then Donn. "Thank you two, especially." Donn waved a hand, like it was nothing.

Brân looked so happy. "It was an honor, girlie. Come and visit the Tar Pits next time you're in the neighborhood."

I turned to the rest of the Mythics in the room. "Thank you all. I appreciate the gift you have granted me."

Hel lifted a perfectly arched brow at me. "It's the will of the universe." She turned toward the door. "Oh, when you make it back to the mortal plane, be sure to anchor yourself there."

I looked at her, wide-eyed. "How do I do that?"

It was Hades who answered. "The way all the Old Gods liked to consummate things. An orgy."

Then he snapped his fingers, and I disappeared.

# CHAPTER 37
## ERUS

"**E**RUS!"

I was just putting Zale down to sleep when Tryp's shout echoed through the house. I had a moment of indecision. What did I do? What if we were being attacked?

I looked at the boys' animal companions, and the half-dozen dogs in here. "Guard them with your lives," I commanded as I ran from the room toward Wren's suite, where Tryp had been bathing Wren's body. I couldn't do it. It hurt my heart too badly.

I screeched around the corner and into the room, where a white-faced Tryp stood over the bed. But that wasn't what made me fall to my knees with shock.

It was the fact that Wren was sitting up in bed, smiling at me. "Hello, Erus. I've missed you."

I fell forward, rested my forehead on the cold tiles, and cried with relief.

She was back. She was *back*.

Launching myself to my feet, I was on the bed in seconds, kissing every inch of her warm, alive skin I could reach. "I love you. I love you. I've missed you *so much.*" It was an understatement, but there wasn't a word for how I'd grieved her. "I love you." I continued to kiss her until Tryp pulled me back so he could rub his cheeks and lips over every inch of her skin.

A low chuckle had me looking to the left, at an awake Cy.

"You brought her back to us," I sobbed, and he reached out to squeeze my shoulder.

Shaking his head, he smiled at me. "No, brother. She brought herself back. She wouldn't contemplate an existence without you all. Speaking of which, we need the rest of the guys. We need to anchor her to this plane for a little while."

I wasn't sure how we did that, but I wasn't going to risk being too slow. Leaping off the bed, I raced through the house, calling for everyone as I went. "DEMKE! MILO!"

I ran straight into Griff, whose head was whipping around frantically, like he knew she was here somewhere. I gripped his neck, a gesture I never would have done before, in case the beast bit off my head. But I was too happy to worry about offending him now.

"You can feel her, can't you? She's in the nest. She's back. Go, go!"

The Gryphon raced away faster than even my supernatural sight could track.

"NÉIT!" I shouted, and finally, the others appeared.

I was out of breath as they all stood in front of me. "She's back. *She's back.*"

Néit's eyes went wide. "Wren? She's back?" Milo didn't even wait for my answer, just dodged around me and ran down the hall toward her room.

Grabbing Demke's arm, I dragged him toward the bedroom. "She just woke up. Scared the shit out of Tryp. She's back." Néit was sprinting down the hall too, saying a prayer in Gaelic as he ran. "Cy said she needs us to anchor her to this plane. We have to hurry."

Demke didn't ask any questions as he ran down the hall after me. As we got closer, we heard voices in the nursery. Wren was there, above the crib, crying over her sons. Happy tears—at least, I hoped so.

"They've gotten so big. I was gone for so long."

She'd been gone for three weeks. The longest three weeks of my life.

Cy put his hand on her shoulder. "And you'll be able to watch them grow forever. But you have to cement yourself here, on the mortal plane, before you're dragged back and we have to come back up all over again."

I hissed a pained sound, but Wren just smiled. "I'm immortal now. I'm not going anywhere ever again."

As I felt for her, I realized it was true. She was a Demigod, like me. She'd be with us forever. Happiness I hadn't felt since... I didn't know when, ripped through me.

"Immortal?" someone breathed behind me, like they couldn't quite believe it. How had we gone from having nothing to having everything we could have ever dreamed of in a moment?

Cy pushed her toward us with gentle hands. "Go. The companions and I will watch the boys. Go show your men how much you missed them." He looked at Demke. "She needs to anchor herself here with an orgy."

Sex. The Old Gods had always loved a good orgy.

Not going to lie, me too.

Néit didn't hesitate. Scooping her up in his arms, he strode back to the nest. We all followed, even Griff. I looked at the Gryphon. "I think we're going to need Teron for this one."

Huffing out an annoyed breath, he rubbed his cheek against Wren's head, squawking with disgruntlement at Néit. She just laughed, stroking his head. "I missed you too, Griff. I'm going to hug the shit out of you later."

Making a purring noise, he shifted from the Gryphon to Teron in the blink of an eye. Teron gripped her face and kissed her so hard, there was no doubt in my mind he was going to anchor her to the mortal realm with everything in him.

Placing her down on the Gryphon's nest, Néit kissed her reverently. She pulled back, gasping for air. "I met your wife, by the way. Any more wives I should know about?" she teased, as he kissed all over her face.

"Only you, *mo stóirín*. My treasure. My wife." He kissed her and kissed her, his lips tracing every inch of her face, but Milo was getting impatient. Shoving his huge shoulders in there, he gripped her cheeks and kissed her desperately too. It was a branding kiss. An anchoring one.

"I kept them safe for you. Made sure they knew how much you loved them, every single day." He was talking about the babies, and judging by her renewed tears, she knew.

"I had no doubt you would, my love. There's no one I trust with them as much as you." She looked at Néit. "And you." Then Demke, Teron, Tryp and me. "And you and you and you and you. All of you. I knew they'd be safe and cared for, if I couldn't come back."

The possibility of her not coming back being voiced out loud sent everyone into a frenzy once more, and Tryp came up beside me, his arms wrapping around my waist. We'd let them have this moment, because I'd already used my lips to ensure she was really here. Really back with us. Each of them needed their own moment for this.

I was happy to watch. As Tryp slid his hands down my body, I knew that we'd both be more than happy to watch. She looked tiny in between their big bodies, and as Néit moved down between her thighs, I got a better view. She was different from the Wren I knew. She'd always been either heavily pregnant, or still flush with motherhood, since the moment I met her. This woman, spread out on the bed like a feast for greedy Gods, was younger, curvy but strong, with sweet little breasts and thighs I wanted to bury my head between.

Actually, she'd always had thighs I wanted to bury my head between, but right now, Néit had that privilege. Pushing her thighs to the side, he showed her glistening core to the whole room, and I moaned deep in my chest. I knew how she tasted, but I wanted to jog my memory so badly that my mouth was watering.

Demke was there now, at the head of the bed, and he had his *I'm in control* face on. I briefly wondered how this little power play would turn out, but when he said, "Put her on her hands and knees," no one complained. Not even Néit, who just lifted his face, manhandled her over, and then reburied his face back in her delightful little pussy. Kneeling at the foot of the bed, Demke swooped down and kissed her in a long, steamy kiss that had so many promises attached, it was a wonder they weren't playing in a slideshow above his head.

Milo had taken the opportunity to get naked, and I'd forgotten how beautiful he was. He was all strong, bunching muscles, the tight lines of his body screaming power with every flex. Sliding his body under hers, he took her nipple in his mouth, and judging by the way her back arched, sucked hard.

"Fuck, they make a beautiful scene," Tryp moaned in my ear. His hand slid down inside my sweats, gripping my cock that was so hard, I didn't know if his grip was going to be torment or sweet relief. He stroked achingly slow, not rushing anything as we watched her body undulate between them all.

She was getting close to coming on Néit's tongue. I could see it in the way she gripped at the sheets, and the large scratches on Milo's chest. Finally, she came, and it was the sweetest fucking sound I'd ever heard.

Still, Tryp didn't stroke me any faster, though I could feel the hard press of his own cock against my ass. Neither of us wanted to miss a second of this.

When Teron stepped forward, the others all paused, and I realized that Teron and Wren had never had their moment. Their relationship had been one of love and care, of a bond closer than any of us could imagine, but they'd never physically been with each other.

"Mate," he breathed, and I knew the Gryphon would be riding close to the surface. Grabbing her up into his arms, he plunged her down onto his cock. If she needed to be anchored, his huge dick would do it.

She clung to his shoulders as he whispered words in her ear, which I couldn't hear but knew exactly what he was saying. He was promising her that he'd never let her go again. He was telling her that he loved her. I knew it, because it's how we all felt.

I watched as he manhandled her body up and down his own, like she weighed nothing, and watching him sheathe himself inside her was the dirtiest, most beautiful thing I'd ever seen. When she came around his cock, she looked like a Goddess, and she felt a little more real.

She was really home.

Milo pulled her down from Teron's arms, nuzzling her cheek. "You're not done yet, Little Bird." Putting her back on her hands and knees on the bed, he lined himself up with her cunt, uncaring that she had Teron's release dripping from her.

Honestly, it made it even hotter. I let my head fall

back against Tryp's shoulder as he pumped me faster. Milo slid inside her, and they both groaned. I couldn't blame her; Milo had a fat dick. Demke, who'd watched all this with hungry eyes, wasn't done either, though. "Open your lips for me, Wren. I want you to suck my cock until I'm fucking the back of your throat. Until you can never leave this plane of existence again. I want you to swallow me down until I take seed in your stomach and brand you as part of me forever."

Moaning, she opened those plush lips as Tryp panted with both pain and pleasure. Yeah, any hope we had of lasting until our turn was quickly evaporating.

Demke slipped his dick into her mouth, just as Milo thrust into her core, and it was a carnal fucking vision straight from my fantasies. I had to grip my balls hard so I didn't blow on the spot.

Milo pumped into her, pushing her onto Demke's cock, setting the rhythm, and watching the big bull sweat trying to hold back was its own kind of erotic. The slapping of skin and the wet noises of Wren sucking Demke's cock were the only sounds in the room.

Tryp stroked me faster, harder, rubbing his cock between my ass cheeks. "Tryp," I breathed, both in pleasure and admonishment, but I didn't tell him to stop. I couldn't. He stroked faster, in time with Milo's thrusts, and I could almost imagine it was me there, fucking her into Demke.

My cock strained, and as Wren came, her thighs shaking wildly, I spilled all over Tryp's hand. Milo came with a bellow that probably shook the building, and given the silent, scrunch-face scream on Demke's face, he was coming too.

I felt the rapidly cooling sensation of Tryp's release on my back, and I sighed, pressing back against him, smearing it between us like an unholy butterfly painting.

Climbing over Teron, who was lying content on the side of the bed, I licked the sweat salt from Wren's stomach, then collapsed with my face pressed there. *My Wren.* "Welcome home," I whispered, and she ran her fingers through my hair.

Tilting my chin up so she could meet my eyes, which were more serious than I'd ever seen them, she smiled. "I'm never leaving again."

And she wouldn't. Because she was a Goddess now, for real. She would live forever at our sides, never growing old, untouched by the march of time.

We could be happy for eternity.

# CHAPTER 38
## MILO

It was like a dream, watching Wren so alive—no, more than alive, *immortal*—and back in our home once more. She moved around the room with Emeric in her arms, showering him with love. I was never more than a few feet from them, and it would take a little time to dissipate the panic that she'd be wrenched away again.

Cy was lying out in the courtyard in the sun in his dog form, his pack writhing around him like a wiggly mass. They'd missed him as much as we'd missed Wren. He was their leader. Their protector and guardian. Without him, they'd been lost.

I had Bran and Zale in my arms, rocking them back and forth, and I finally felt that we'd achieved happiness. This was my nirvana. My Elysian Fields.

Tryp and Erus also hovered around her. Eventually, she was probably going to tire of us smothering her. But until she had to stare at our dead bodies hopelessly, she was going to have to give us a little grace.

The Valkyries had all come and gushed, expressing their happiness that she was okay, and laying their heads on the line because of their failures. She'd cut that off quickly. There wasn't anything anyone could have done to prevent the remaining Moirai portaling in. No one could have predicted the spitefulness of them.

Teron appeared, wrapping his arms around her, Emeric cradled between them. He kissed her softly. Actually, it was probably lucky she was immortal now; otherwise, she'd have a permanent case of beard rash from the sheer amount of embraces she'd been getting in the past week.

If she needed to be anchored to the mortal plane, I was pretty sure she couldn't be more anchored without being a ship in the Aegean. We'd fucked her in every position, in every room, in every combination of pairings since she'd arrived back.

If I could sew her to my side so she'd never leave, I would.

Tryp and Erus each plucked a baby from me. "Come on, little ones. It's time for your swimming lessons," Erus cooed. He had recently declared that if the babies were going to live on an island, and have access to the pool, then they needed to learn to swim as soon as possible.

Bran just waved his arms, like he knew what the Genii was talking about. And maybe he did. There was an ancient intelligence in their eyes sometimes.

Wren didn't like to talk about her time in the Afterlife, only to tell us that it wasn't as bad as it could have been. Cy said a little more, enough to know that he never wanted to do it again.

I didn't need to know the nitty-gritty. I just needed her here.

And she would be, always, as an immortal. I begrudgingly thanked the universe, even if I'd cursed it just as often.

We walked outside as the babies splashed in the pool with Tryp and Erus, the Genii never taking their eyes off them as they guided them through their swimming drills. It helped that the babies loved the water. We all sat out on the loungers, watching them swim.

Cy had climbed into the water too, an extra set of hands, which also meant six dogs jumped in as well. They kept a wide berth from the swimming babies—probably at Cy's insistence—but it was such a wholesome, joyful sight.

I wrapped Wren up in my arms, pulling her onto my lap, and Néit lay with his head on her thighs. Maybe we could take her upstairs and…

"You sure they aren't mine? They certainly seem to love the water."

The voice beside me didn't belong. Immediately shifting Wren to the other side, I stood between her and the God on the lounger beside us. Néit had his ax, but water was wrapped around his wrists, holding him still.

"Poseidon? What the fuck are *you* doing here?" Cy called.

"Nephew! Good to see you back, and looking so well. Fatherhood also suits you." He reclined back. "It's been so long since I've been on Crete; I forgot how lovely it was here. Not my favorite of the islands, of course, but still quite nice."

Demke appeared next to us. "Crete is still not open to the Greeks," he growled, and Poseidon raised a brow, glancing at Cy.

"I hate to tell you this, Minoan, but there's one swimming in your pool. And by all accounts, Hades is here more than he's in the Underworld these days."

Someone snorted. "An exaggeration, as always, brother." As if he'd been summoned, Hades strolled into the courtyard. "Why is it so fucking bright today?" He sat under a large umbrella with a scowl.

Demke looked like he was going to have a stroke, but I was glad Hades was here. He'd been good to us, and while you could never trust the Greeks completely, I trusted him enough.

Poseidon chuckled. "It's a beautiful day, Hades. Don't be such a grump." He looked over at Demke. "To answer your unasked question, I was summoned here. I have enough to deal with in the sea, without worrying about your land-lover quarrels. Did you know Typhon has just walked into the ocean? It's caused a damn outcry amongst the sirens."

Frowning, Demke looked at Hades. "I didn't summon you."

"No, I did."

I whipped around, and this time, I did draw my sword. Zeus stood by the pool, wearing nothing but a Speedo that was at least one size too small.

The babies had been whisked away, Erus and Tryp knowing what to do in the face of a threat, and the dogs were also suspiciously absent. Cy had definitely sent them to protect the children.

I hated that these fuckers could just portal in and out of our home.

"What are you doing here?" Demke growled, clearly losing his patience as Teron shifted to the Gryphon. Néit stood on the other side of Wren, who didn't look all that perturbed to be standing in front of three of the most powerful Mythics ever weaved.

Whatever she'd seen down there during her death had changed her. It had made her almost fearless in the face of power. I couldn't decide if I found that terrifying or insanely attractive.

"Always so disrespectful, Demke."

"You were never my God, Zeus. We give the respect we receive, and you always thought we were less."

He shrugged. "You *were* less. It wasn't personal."

I snorted loudly, shifting to the bull. "The death of my entire race was personal *to me*." I was going to splatter this ancient fuck, even if it was the last thing I ever did. I went to step forward, but Wren's small hand around my wrist stopped me.

Hades held up a hand. "I assume we aren't here for you to rub salt in their wounds, Zeus. But if the Minotaur gouges a hole in you because you're an insensitive fuck, I'm not going to stop him."

Poseidon snorted a laugh. "Me either. I might even enjoy the show." He looked to the left, where the ocean could be seen on a clear day. "Let's go. Not all of us sit around all day, fucking nymphs and drinking ambrosia. I have a kingdom to run."

Hades lifted his chin at the God of the Sea. "What he said."

Zeus rolled his eyes. "Fine. Maybe I just wanted to catch up with my brothers?" The deadpan expressions of both Hades and Poseidon called bullshit. "Look, I'm not sure if you know this, but my Moirai are dead, and Hera is pissed."

Néit hefted his sword. "We're quite aware."

Poseidon chuckled. "Me too. There's a monster roaming my ocean with pieces of Lachesis still in his teeth."

Zeus looked at Wren. "I wish to call a truce. The old Fates are dead, and the new Fates have risen. I wish to protect my Pantheon from retaliation as they come fully into their powers."

He wished to protect himself, he meant. *What a snake.*

Demke stepped between the God of the Sky and the woman we loved. She might be immortal now, but Zeus could still strike her down with a thunderbolt. "Your truces mean nothing, Zeus. You break them as easily as you make them," he spat.

Zeus sighed, as if we were being tedious. "I thought

you might feel that way, which is why *they're* here." He nodded at Hades and Poseidon. "Do you know who the last powerful brothers woven into an age were?" he asked Wren.

It didn't take a genius to know the answer, and my girl was as smart as she was suspicious. "I'm going to say you three."

Zeus nodded. "You're correct. We rose up and created an entire belief system around us, grasping at the power handed to us. I am loath to let that power go now." I tensed, ready for a fight, but he just sighed heavily. "But I also acknowledge that the Ouroboros has turned. It's time for a new age and new Fates. As I said, I'd like to call a truce. To do so, I am willing to bind myself to the promise not to raise hand or army against the new Fates, or you all, in return for goodwill."

Hades raised a brow. Yeah, it sounded a little too good to be true to me too. "Nor will you influence, by prophecy or inference, anyone associated with you or your domain, to bring harm to the new Fates, known as the Kuningilin, or their caretakers and loved ones?" He pursed his lips. "And the island of Crete remains the domain of the Minoans, and will become the protected home of the Kuningilin?"

Zeus huffed. "Yes, all that too. Brother, some would say you've switched allegiances."

Shrugging, Hades gave Zeus a predatory smile. "I just like watching you get a little screwed."

Poseidon grinned, and I felt like we were once again just pawns in a disagreement we knew nothing about.

Pulling a golden trident from fuck knows where, he used it to cut the palm of Zeus. "Wren, come here. You will have to stand in the place of the Kuningilin until they are older, as their mother and guardian."

Néit stayed right on her ass the whole walk over to the Sea God, his ax raised, ready to chop heads. She looked over at Hades. "They aren't trying to screw us over, right? I don't hold any ill feelings toward the Greek Pantheon—in fact, I'm quite fond of several of its members—but I swear, Zeus, if you're fucking with me, I'm going to find a way to hold one of your lightning bolts and shove it fair up your—"

Luckily, Poseidon interrupted. "I like you. No wonder Hades has gone to bat for you. I thought Persephone was just making him soft, but you really are entertaining." He sliced her hand on a different prong of his trident, dripping a single drop of Zeus's blood into the wound. She swayed on her feet, and I lifted my sword to Poseidon's throat. "Calm now. It's just the effects of his blood. A single drop is quite potent. But now they are tied, and he is bound by his word."

*It can't be that easy, right?*

Hades was dusting his pants off and standing, suggesting it *was* that easy. "I've got a girl to see and faces to look at that aren't your ugly mugs. Wren excepted, of course. Zeus, it's never a pleasure. Poseidon, you should watch the new *Little Mermaid*. I think you'd like it."

A pit the size of a manhole opened up in the ground,

and he stepped inside it. It snapped shut, leaving just us and the two possibly hostile Gods.

Zeus nodded solemnly. "I hope never to see you again," he said lightly to Wren.

She gave him a pleasant smile back, but it was filled with teeth. "It won't be a moment too soon."

A lightning bolt hit the ground, the sound deafening, and then he was gone too.

Poseidon sighed and sunk back against the sun lounger. "Those two are always so dramatic. They need to relax a little, go with the ebb and flow of the waves. That binding should hold Zeus, and while I don't think you have anything else to worry about from our Pantheon, that doesn't mean there won't be others who will try and take advantage. That's the life of a Mythic, really. Always jockeying for power and prestige. No one wants the ocean, though—I could never understand why."

"Sand in your arse crack?" Néit suggested, and Wren laughed.

Poseidon chuckled as he stood. "It very well could be. I'll enjoy fucking with people from the ocean, thank you very much. So long, Wren Mahone. Minoans. Nephew." He leapt, diving into the pool, and then he too was gone.

"Should we fill in the pool?" Néit demanded. Quite frankly, I was down for the idea.

Demke shook his head. "Unless you want to start flushing toilets with buckets, all roads lead to the ocean."

Sighing, I grabbed Wren back in my arms and relaxed, just a little. The Greek Pantheon had been the boogieman of our lives for so long—well before Wren and the babies—that this felt almost like a dream.

Wren rested her head against my chest. "Is this the part where we live happily ever after, with no snake-headed monsters, bitter old hags, or night sludge? No side quests to Hell?"

I pressed my lips to her forehead. "I sure hope so."

# EPILOGUE
## WREN

I looked at the raven sitting on the sconce at the base of the base of the stairs. She turned her head, giving me an expression that I knew was meant to look innocent, but usually meant anything but.

"Trig, you tell them to come down right now, or I'm going up there to the hovel they call a bedroom and dragging them down by their ears."

She trilled at me and flew up the stairs. I could hear them all up there, music playing loud enough for the Underworld to hear. Von the war cat came down the stairs first, and she butted her head against my knees, weaving around me like a fluffy kitten and not a fifteen-hundred pound big cat that could eat me in a bite.

"Did they send you down first to butter me up? Because they're about to miss their own birthday party, and there are a lot of people here to see them."

The boys had come into their powers at sixteen, and had been slowly growing them over the last couple of years. However, today, their eighteenth birthday, was the day that they would pick up their mantle as the Fates and begin their lives outside of our protection.

I was both proud of the men they'd become and terrified of the world they must navigate, though at least they'd do it together. Nate had trained them, all of them becoming excellent warriors with sword, bow, and firearms. Apollo had visited to help with their skills in prophecy, seeing them as some kind of makeshift grandsons—which was terrifying, really.

Zelda rode in on Galt, the giant boar, who loved the girl as much as he loved her brothers. "Mama, Freddy says that I'm not allowed to bring the dogs to the party, that it's only for people and not animals. But they were important too, and I think they should be allowed to have cake."

Although we tried not to figure out whose child was whose, it was very clear to everyone that Zelda—despite being named by Néit—was very much Cy's child. The day she was born, a great howl went up, and ever since, she'd been collecting strays of all kinds. Dogs, primarily, but cats, birds and most notably, a donkey had all become part of our family in the six years she'd graced the earth. Even now, Von had moved her affections from me to Zelda. She definitely had a way with animals.

Freddy, on the other hand, was a bookworm. All about the rules and histories. I didn't know who he belonged to, but I had my suspicions. He was a careful, thoughtful child, and sometimes I forgot he was twelve and not two hundred. But he was kind and loyal, and he took his role as middle brother very seriously. He was more protective of Zelda and Hurley than even his older brothers. He would be a great support to the triplets one day, if that's what he wanted.

The baby in my arms was also no surprise, though we pretended not to know. However, Hurley's flaming red hair was a bit of a giveaway.

Finally, there was a loud thundering on the stairs, telling me the boys were finally making their way down. When they appeared, I tried to hold in my tears, I really did. But they looked so handsome in their tailored pants and shirts, over shoulders that belonged to men and not to my babies. They towered above me now—well over six feet—and although they looked like me, and like each other, all three looked different. At least to me. It was more than their features; it was their personalities, their mannerisms, that set them apart from each other. They may have shared a womb, but they were unique souls.

I didn't know if they'd ever had a conscious discussion about who would fill which role as they settled into being the Fates. Maybe the universe had created them all with the strengths they'd need to shoulder the burden of their individual tasks: the Spinner, who created life, the Allotter, who decided how someone's life should go, and the Inevitable, the one who cut the thread.

Bran was the leader—that had been obvious from the moment they could toddle around. Wherever Bran would go, the other two would be right behind. He was the brave one, always putting himself between danger and his brothers. It was something that only grew more prominent as they got older. He was the one who would shoulder the burdens of death and decay, and I worried about him the most. It was hard, your whole life being death and destruction. Surprisingly, Hades had been very helpful with that, as well as Thanatos, the God of Death.

Emeric was my fun-loving party boy. I'd caught him sneaking out for human parties more times than I cared to count, but he was sweet and empathetic. He wanted everyone to be happy and have fun, including his brothers. He could sweet talk all the old ladies in the village, and honestly, I'd thought about sending him to stay with Delphos on a mountain somewhere in Greece at sixteen, in case he knocked up some human girl down in Heraklion. He wanted to live, and he wanted everyone else to be right there with him.

It was Emeric who made it down the stairs first. "Mama, you look beautiful. Our fathers will have to beat all the other Mythics off with a stick."

"Papa will beat them up using a stick, more like it," Zale said, stopping on the bottom step to hug me. My baby boy. My youngest triplet. He was sweet, kind, full of hope and wonder. It made sense that he'd been given the task of creation. He didn't give me trouble like Emeric, and he wasn't full of bravado like Bran. He was sweet, gentle, and while I didn't worry about his emotional health the way I did with Bran, it was Zale I worried about the most out there in the world. He just wanted to see the best in everyone.

Sure, he was an expert marksman, and in hand-to-hand combat, he could take down everyone but Bran and Nate. Still, I was his mother—it was my job to worry.

I waved them toward the door. "Stop it, you three. Come on, we're running late."

Trig sat on Bran's shoulder, still looking innocent, which just made me more suspicious. Zale reached out and took Hurley from my arms. He threw him up into the air, catching him easily, making the baby laugh. They loved their siblings as much as their siblings loved them.

Zale looked over at me. "Want another one? Hurley's getting big."

"I swear, Zale Mahone, if you bring another baby into our bloodline anytime soon, I will send you to your room for a century. Hurley is enough for now. With you boys out of the house, I might actually get some peace and quiet." I ushered them out of the hallway and into the courtyard. The gates had been thrown open, and tonight, villagers and Mythics would come together to celebrate my boys.

I met Milo in the courtyard, and he kissed each of the boys on the forehead, like they were toddlers and not men. "Look at you three!" He grabbed Hurley from Zale. "You look like grown-ups, not like you were shitting your pants the blink of an eye ago." He held up Hurley and kissed his ruddy little cheeks.

"Come on, handsome. Let's go make some old ladies coo."

I walked my boys out into the courtyard, where they smiled and spoke to the villagers, and their friends, who had no idea they weren't humans. At least, I didn't think they did.

Beyond them, standing apart from the humans, were small groupings of Mythics. Persephone and her harem—with the exception of Cerberus and Charon, who needed to be in the Underworld to run the place in Hades's absence—were talking to Morrigan, who'd flown in from Ireland last night, plus three of the Valkyries. Apollo was standing around, getting more than a little attention from the female population, who had more horniness than sense, but who was I to cast stones?

My guys were also dotted around, some with the locals, others with the Mythics, making sure everyone was having a good time. Nate was chatting with Clio, as well as Donn, who'd come up to binge watch classic eighties movies, and I reminded myself to ensure I sent down some cakes for Fea.

Erus and Tryp were once again in their element, ensuring that the drinks were flowing and the party was happening. Teron was talking to Delphos, who'd come down from his mountain and seemed to actually be enjoying himself. I'd even invited Mr. Lunetta—I mean, Khonsu—who'd been so integral in getting my bonding time with the babies when they'd been newborns. For the first time since the Dark Ages, humans and Mythics from all different Pantheons inter-mingled happily.

Demke came up behind me, wrapping an arm around my waist. My sweet, solemn God. He was hiding it well, but he was nervous about the boys going out into the world too. Though as Griff had told me, all fledglings had to leave the nest.

"Did you expect all this when I turned up on your doorstep eighteen years ago?"

Laughing, he nuzzled his nose into the mass of my hair. The humidity had made it wild, and there was no taming it tonight. "I don't think anyone could have foreseen you, my love. You were like a whirlwind. A gift. But no, I would never have prophesied this in a million years." Leaning in, he nipped at my earlobe. "I love you."

"I love you too."

Zelda ran past, a chicken in her arms and a parade of dogs at her heels, her laughter loud and contagious. Demke reached out and snatched her up into his arms. "What are you doing, my little wildling?"

"Freddy said that they eat the chickens. They can't eat Henrietta. She's special. She's the… She's the…" I watched her try and grasp for an important job for the chickens. "She's the Queen of the Chickens."

Demke lifted her higher, eyeing the confused Queen of the Chickens. "Well, we definitely can't eat the Queen, can we, Your Majesty?"

Zelda shook her head. "No, you can't eat any of them." Her lip jutted out, and I saw Demke waver. We were about to have a stint as a vegetarian household; I could see it now.

"I'll talk to the town. Maybe, uh, the chickens can just be used for egg production from now on."

Snuggling her head under his chin, she smiled. "Thank you, Dede." She wiggled until he was forced to put her, along with the flapping chicken, back on the ground. Cy whistled low, and I noticed two of the bigger dogs join along behind her; they'd watch over the group and guide them from danger.

The triplets stepped up in front of the assembled party, whistling loud. Bran shouted, "Listen up!" As the crowd quietened down, the boys bunched together. When they were shoulder to shoulder like that, you couldn't help but see that they were something special. "We wanted to thank you all for coming. We appreciate the friendship and love that each one of you has shown us over the past eighteen years. We wouldn't be here if it wasn't for the actions of you all. So again, thank you. To our fathers: we are the men we are because of you. We love you all. To our siblings... you know what to do."

Well, that didn't sound ominous at all. I looked at their companions, the boar pressed close to them, and Von, in her tabby size, wrapped around Zale's shoulders. Even Trig sat on Bran's shoulders. Those little shits were up to something.

"Mom, we love you so much. We promise to call you tomorrow."

There was a smoke bomb, a pop of magic, and when

the smoke cleared, they were gone. Those little bastards could *portal*, and they'd just portaled right out of their birthday party.

"I'm going to murder them," I hissed, as the crowd oohed and aahed, like it was some parlor trick.

Demke made a choking noise, which I realized was a laugh. I gave him the stink-eye, and he straightened his face. "We knew they could make a dramatic entrance, but apparently, their dramatic exits are just as impressive."

My lips twitched, and then I was laughing too. My little babies, my apple seeds, were adults now, out there deciding the fates of the world. Nate liked to argue that I'd been the first fate they'd orchestrated, and they'd done a damn good job.

I lifted my glass. "To the turning of the wheel!"

When the cheers echoed back to me, I relished in the dawn of a new age, one filled with love, peace and empathy.

And probably a few gray hairs.

# About the Author

Grace McGinty is eclectic. She has worked as a chocolatier, a librarian, a forensic accountant, and finally, a writer. Like her professional career, the genres she writes are chaotic and out of control. From contemporary new adult to smutty reverse harem novels of every sub-genre, if you like it, she's probably written it.

Except dark romance. She's a marshmallow, and somehow the mean guys always end up cinnamon rolls.

Grace lives in rural Australia with her crazy family, an entire menagerie of pets, and will one day be crushed by the giant piles of books that litter every room.

**Head over to www.gracemcginty.com and join the mailing list for sneak previews into what she is working on and to stay up-to-date with new releases and giveaways!**

**New to Grace McGinty?**

**Like your main characters with a lot of spunk? Check out Tryst In The Dark, available now!**

# TRYST IN THE DARK
## TRYST

I hadn't felt this much rage since Topher Johnstone told me my boobs were small and he'd rather eat sand than be my boyfriend when we were in the second grade. Granted, I'd caught him eating sand more than once, so to this very day, I wasn't sure if that was a yes or no.

I'd still punched him in the gut, though. I'd been a hot-tempered kid.

As I stared at the trashed room around me now, it occured to me that while I'd grown boobs, I hadn't outgrown my temper.

I sat on a bed that was made for luxury. Thousand thread count sheets that cost more than an average month's wages, a comforter probably stuffed with thousands of baby geese, and pillows that were the very definition of fluffy clouds. But I'd never felt more uneasy in my life.

I alternated between anxiety and rage, and it was

definitely one of those emotional roller coasters that made you want to throw up.

The door to my room was firmly locked and bolted from the outside, yet they still insisted that I was a guest, and not a prisoner. I snorted. I was sitting in a gilded cage, waiting to be kicked off my perch.

My mother had said I was just unlucky. I preferred to think that I was Fate's bitch, and she was just edging me until she finally released me from this goddamn torment.

An unlucky quirk of my DNA meant that when I'd turned sixteen, I'd revealed as an Omega.

No one knew why it occurred in some women and not others, even between siblings. Some suggested it was some kind of genetic glitch resulting from the nuclear fallout of the Last World War, while others thought it was evolution. It didn't matter, not really. The results were the same. I was special, and I was a prisoner.

I guess it was the same for Alphas, except no one thought they were incapable of caring for themselves. Alphas were bigger, stronger, and more compelling than the non-designated humans we called Betas.

No, Alphas became CEOs and politicians with far too much sway. Instead of taking away their rights, the government and private corporations plied them with money and responsibility. Instead of telling them who they could see, what they could study, what jobs they could have—like they did Omegas—the government let Alphas roam around, amassing fortunes and females.

Other countries put limits on Alphas, like Canada, who said Alphas weren't able to become cops or lawyers, or hold any role where they could have undue pheromonal influence on a jury.

The US just left them completely unchecked.

What everyone conveniently seemed to forget—or purposefully ignored—was that if Alphas were truly left unchecked, they sometimes became cult leaders and despots, powerful and cruel. They led mass suicides and oversaw pyramid schemes.

Yet it was the Omegas whose lives were monitored and controlled by the government, right up to the year of their first heat. They insisted we were slaves to our baser instincts, that we were a danger to ourselves and others if we went into heat around the general population, like a ticking sex bomb waiting to explode and cover everyone in various bodily fluids.

I wasn't stupid. They kept up this 'Omegas are mentally deficient' ruse for a very specific reason, and everyone knew it.

The general reproductive health of humans had gotten all fucked up at some point. Beta women couldn't really have babies anymore, not at the olden day rates anyway. Don't get me wrong, there were still plenty of women in the country, and some normal old Betas who could still have a baby. But those children were rarely girls, so population rates were slowly declining.

And so they invented the Allotment. Originally, it was just for Alphas, but when there were riots and shouts of eugenics and genocide, they'd expanded it to all male citizens of the US. It was a lottery system, and every unmarried man went into the draw. Alphas and Betas alike, almost like conscription.

It was bullshit. I snarled, standing up to pace.

Today, there'd be a televised lottery. One unlucky man would get his social security number flashed up on the screen, and his life would change forever. Next week, the same deal. And the week after. It would continue until the Department of Designation Associations decided that I had enough.

A knock on the door had me spinning toward the only entrance to the room. It opened, and a younger guy in a nice suit entered. "Sorry, Omega. The Allotment is about to begin. Would you like to watch the draw?"

It didn't help that these things were a massive damn event. Somewhere between a public execution and the old school lottery. Luckily, I wasn't paraded about like a prize mare at auction.

"No."

The DoDA Official's face tightened, maybe with pity or maybe with annoyance, but he nodded respectfully.

I'd give them that, at least. They gave us more reverence in these Allotment houses than we got in the outside world. People were naturally drawn to Alphas, almost against their will, but Omegas were weaker, easier targets. Somehow, we got blamed for every small societal problem, from the fertility crisis to the economic crash that almost put us back to the Dark Ages.

It made no fucking sense, but whatever.

I shifted my focus back to the suit in my doorway, who was still speaking to me softly, like I was a spooked wild animal. "I'll bring up your dinner. The draw will be held in five minutes, and we'll be along with more detail for you as soon as we've verified the number. He should arrive by tomorrow evening, or earlier, depending on his location."

They could guarantee this because someone would be there immediately to collect the lucky guy. Or unlucky, depending on his feelings. I mightn't have a choice in this charade, but neither did they. If you were picked, you had to come when directed. But at least they had a chance at a normal life. Omegas were never even given a glimmer of that hope.

I'd already tried to run once—hence the locked door —so they'd make us bond immediately. Give me the old ball and chain, both figuratively and literally, because once an Omega was bonded to a mate, any large distance between them was physically painful.

I cleared my throat and tried not to eye the open door like a caged tiger waiting for its freedom. "Thanks." He gave me another tight smile and left.

Less than twenty minutes later, the same guy returned with a tray of food and a paper file tucked under his arm. It was done. There was nothing I could do now but deal with the fallout. There was no longer an escape.

He laid down the tray on the small table beside the window, but I didn't care about the food. His eyes were soft as he handed me the file. Paperclipped to the front was a driver's license photo with some basic details scrawled below it.

I looked at my soon-to-be bondmate. He was... attractive. Not that it mattered; he could look like a mountain troll with a voice like he'd eaten Mike Tyson and was trying to gag him back up again, and I'd still have to bond with him.

This guy had brown hair, and a shadowy beard with a ginger tinge to it. He was tall-ish, around six feet, and had laugh lines around his eyes, but also two small wrinkles on his forehead like he'd frowned a lot.

He was a Beta. He looked blissfully average.

I'd take it.

I looked at the rest of his details. He was from the Midwest, a mechanic by trade. He was raised by a single mom and had a tiny nest egg in his bank account. I already knew he didn't have a wife and kids, or a criminal record, because both of those things exempted you from the Allotment proceedings.

Grady Davis. He even had an average kind of name. I didn't get my hopes up, because maybe he was a prick. Or a psychopath who liked to kill kittens. There was only one way I'd find out.

The Official excused himself, and I began to pick at my food as I opened the rest of the file and devoured everything I could about Grady Davis.

www.ingramcontent.com/pod-product-compliance
Lightning Source LLC
Chambersburg PA
CBHW030518120726

47904CB00005B/1521